Gordon C. Allan
（加）戈登·C.艾伦 ◎ 著

EDWIN
and the Quest for
DROW
埃德温历险记

（汉英对照）

新 华 出 版 社

图书在版编目（CIP）数据

埃德温历险记：汉英对照 /（加）艾伦著. —北京：
新华出版社，2015. 6

　ISBN 978-7-5166-1764-9

　Ⅰ. ①埃… Ⅱ. ①艾… Ⅲ. ①科学幻想小说—加拿大—现代—
汉、英 Ⅳ. ①I711.45

　中国版本图书馆CIP数据核字（2015）第126943号

埃德温历险记：汉英对照

作　　者：（加）戈登·C. 艾伦

出 版 人：张百新	责任编辑：徐　光
责任印制：廖成华	装帧设计：李尘工作室

出版发行：新华出版社

地　　址：北京市石景山区京原路 8 号	邮　　编：100040
网　　址：http://www.xinhuapub.com	http://press.xinhuanet.com
经　　销：新华书店	
购书热线：010-63077122	中国新闻书店购书热线：010-63072012

照　　排：李尘工作室
印　　刷：北京文林印务有限公司

成品尺寸：170mm×240mm　1/16	
印　　张：15.75	字　　数：199千字
版　　次：2015年6月第一版	印　　次：2015年9月第二次印刷

书　　号：ISBN 978-7-5166-1764-9
定　　价：45.00元

图书如有印装问题，请与出版社联系调换：010-63077101

This book is dedicated to my wife Yully.

谨以此书献给我的太太Yully（优莉）。

TABLE OF CONTENTS

目　录

EDWIN
and The Quest for
DROW

埃德温历险记

1

THE FAVOUR

The long black limousine weaved its way through the country lanes of Verbum County. The rain was now pelting down against the car and the whistling wind rocked the vehicle back and forth. Edwin tried to peer out from the back seat but all he could see was the blackness of the tinted windows.

Unable to take in the sights, he had time to reflect on how curious this day had become.

It had started off well enough, with a huge breakfast, the prospect of spending the day riding his bike, and the joy of knowing this was the very first day of the summer holidays. But when his mother suddenly called him into the living room and closed the door behind her, it wasn't long before he realized the day would not be going as planned.

Edwin's mother stood beside the large picture window that looked out onto the front garden, clutching one of the drapes for security. Edwin could tell she was agitated.

"What is it, Mom?" he had asked hesitantly.

There was a pause and then she started to talk in a voice he could barely recognize.

"Darling," she said, sounding as if she was about to cry. "Since . . . since your father passed, it has become very difficult for me. There are things you just don't understand . . ." She stopped talking, to catch herself from saying more about that. "That is to say, there are important things you will know in time when you are ready," she continued. "But right now, I need to get

1

蒙恩

一辆黑色长型豪华轿车在维尔本县的乡间大道上穿梭前行。急促的雨点重重地拍打着车窗，车身在呼啸的寒风中剧烈震颤。埃德温透过隔热车窗向外张望，却只看到漆黑一片。他完全辨不清方向，百无聊赖中回想起今天发生的一切，觉得颇为古怪。

早起后一切都挺正常。暑假的第一天让他心情格外轻松，他一边享用着丰盛的早餐，一边盘算着待会儿骑单车打发时光。但是，当母亲突然把他叫到起居室，还随手掩上了门时，他很快就意识到，今天绝不会像他设想的那样简单。

埃德温的母亲在正对着前花园的景观窗旁坐定，手里紧抓着窗帘，好似抓着一根救命的稻草。埃德温看得出来她的情绪很激动。

"怎么了，妈妈？"他迟疑着问道。

她犹豫了一下，但是一开口，那语气却令他感到如此陌生。

"亲爱的，"她的声音听上去仿佛带着哭腔，"自从……自从你的父亲过世后，咱们家一直举步维艰。有些事情，你还不懂……"她再次停顿，似乎想稳定一下情绪，"我的意思是说，有一些重要的事，等你准备好了，总有一天你会知道的。"她继续说道，"但是现在，为了先处理你父亲的身后事，我不得不四处奔波。"

some of your father's affairs in order and to do that, I will have to do a lot of travelling."

"I'll come with you, Mom. Don't worry. I can help. It's my holidays. I don't have to go to school, remember?"

"No!" she replied, abruptly. "I need you to help me by agreeing to something else."

"Okay . . . whatever you want," said Edwin, not sounding very convincing.

After a long moment of silence, his mother dropped the bomb.

"I need you to go stay with Cedric Bellamy for a while . . . just until I finish what I have to do here. Two, maybe three weeks tops. That's all. I promise."

She swirled around with a strained grin on her face that pleaded with Edwin to agree to her proposition.

Edwin stared at his mother with a look of shock. Of course he had heard of the infamous Cedric Bellamy. How could he have not. His father would announce every Friday that he was heading off to continue his work with Cedric on some big project. But whenever Edwin asked his father about the big project or why he had never met Cedric himself, his father would nervously laugh off his questioning, then talk about how talented Cedric was and how much he admired him.

"Don't worry. You'll meet him some day," his father would say. "When the time is right. But now is not the time. He is a very busy man and he has no patience for distractions."

His father would then pass an anxious glance to his mother, as if to say "Help me with this." On cue, his mother would change the subject and start asking Edwin if he had finished his homework or cleaned his room or washed out his ears.

"我跟您一起去，妈妈。别担心，我可以帮您。现在正在放假，我不用去上学了，对吧？"

"不行！"她断然拒绝道，"我有别的事需要你帮忙。"

"好吧……我愿意为您做任何事。"埃德温话语间带着几分犹豫。

两人各自沉默了一会儿，然后她说出了一番令他难以置信的话。

"我想送你去塞德里克·贝拉米家借住一段时间……这边的事情忙完后我就去接你。估计两个星期，最多不超过三个星期，我保证。"

她转过身来，脸上带着牵强的微笑，似乎在哀求着埃德温同意她的决定。

埃德温目瞪口呆地看着母亲。他早就听说过塞德里克·贝拉米这个名字，现在想起来言犹在耳。父亲在世时，每逢周五就说要去找塞德里克做大计划。但每当埃德温追问父亲究竟是什么计划，或者为什么他从来没见过塞德里克时，父亲总是神色紧张地一笑了之，然后就把话题扯开，说起塞德里克如何才华横溢，而他又是多么崇拜他。

"放心吧。总有一天你会见到他的，"父亲总是这样说，"等时机成熟了，我自然会带你去见他。但现在还不是时候，他是个大忙人，没有闲工夫浪费在这些琐屑的小事上。"

父亲总是面露难色地望向母亲，似乎在暗示她"帮他一把"，接着母亲就会伺机岔开话题，询问埃德温是否完成了作业、打扫了房间或者清洗了耳朵。

Edwin realized that the last time he had tried to ask his father about the big project and the great Cedric Bellamy was the day before his father had died.

His father died on a Saturday in May, a day that had started out not unlike this one, with his mother calling him into the living room.

"Your father is gone," she had wailed. "The gas . . . the gas. It's that damn gas that did it," she screamed.

Edwin figured his father must have died in some sort of gas explosion, but he knew enough not to pursue the details with his mother, she was so upset. He would bide his time and wait for her to tell him the truth. He loved her too much to force the issue.

While he missed his father terribly, he felt for his mother even more. She seemed abandoned and so lonely. He wanted to help but something was troubling her, something other than the death of her husband. And now here she was asking him to stay with Cedric Bellamy. But why? He wondered if her desire to get his father's things in order meant suing the gas company.

"Edwin, will you do it?" asked his mother in a pathetic voice.

Edwin looked up again and saw that his mother was waiting for his answer.

"Of course, Mom. If you want me to stay with Mr. Bellamy, then I will. I'm sure he is a nice person," he said halfheartedly.

"He is a very good person, Edwin, and Henry . . . your father, loved him dearly. It's important that you meet him now," she said, almost as an afterthought. He will be sending a car to pick you up later this afternoon. I'll pack your clothes. You won't need much. It's only a few weeks," she said, again trying to reassure him.

"But what do I call him, Mom? Uncle Bellamy?"

"Just call him Sir Cedric, dear." Her voice had come back and she was clearly relieved Edwin had agreed to the plan.

When his mother said goodbye to him later that day, she was inconsolable.

"You are such a good boy, Edwin," she said, squeezing him as she sobbed.

埃德温突然回想起来，最后一次向父亲打听他们的计划和那位了不起的塞德里克·贝拉米，正是父亲去世的前一天，父亲是在五月份的一个星期六去世的。当时，母亲把他叫到了起居室，与今天如出一辙。

"你父亲去世了，"当时母亲号啕大哭，"瓦斯……瓦斯，就是该死的瓦斯把他害死的。"她尖叫起来。

埃德温猜测父亲很可能是死于瓦斯爆炸事故，但他不想追问任何细节，因为母亲已经够心烦了。他会耐心等待真相大白的那一天。他太爱母亲，不愿意逼她说出真相。虽然埃德温非常怀念父亲，但他能体谅母亲的难处。她似乎被抛进了痛苦的深渊，形单影只，无依无靠。埃德温希望能帮母亲减轻痛苦，但除了父亲的死，好像还有别的烦心事在困扰着她。而此时此刻，她居然央求他去塞德里克·贝拉米家暂住数日。到底发生了什么事？他想知道，母亲所谓的"处理你父亲的身后事"是不是打算起诉瓦斯公司。

"埃德温，你愿意吗？"母亲凄声问道。

埃德温再次抬起头，发现母亲还在等他的回答。

"当然愿意了，妈妈。如果您要我去塞德里克家，那我就去，我想他一定是个好人。"他敷衍道。

"他的确是个好人，埃德温，而且亨利……我是说你爸爸，非常敬重他。你现在就得去他家，"她说出了似乎盘算已久的决定，"今天傍晚前他会派车来接你，我会帮你打包好衣服，带几件就够了，只是几个礼拜而已。"她说着宽心的话，试图再次安慰他。

"我该怎么称呼他呢，妈妈？贝拉米叔叔？"

"叫他塞德里克爵士就行了，亲爱的。"母亲答道。她的语气又恢复了平静，埃德温的同意显然使她松了一口气。

随后告别时，母亲显得伤心欲绝。

"你是个乖孩子，埃德温，"母亲一边紧抱着他，一边低声抽泣说

"I hate to send you away during a time like this. But please understand that it is for the best. You'll see."

"Come on, Mom. Don't worry about me. As you said, it's only a few weeks."

While the words flowed easily from Edwin's mouth, his stomach was churning as he tried to anticipate what it would be like to live with *the* Sir Cedric Bellamy, a man he had never met.

道，"我真不想在这种时候与你分开。不过，希望你能理解，对你来说这是最好的，总有一天你会明白的。"

"别这样，妈妈。您不用担心我，您不是说过了嘛，只是几个星期而已。"

虽然埃德温嘴上说得轻巧，但内心却极不平静，他略显紧张地猜想着与那位素昧平生、"大名鼎鼎"的塞德里克·贝拉米的相处该是怎样一番情景。

2

CEDRIC BELLAMY

At last, the limousine started to slow. The darkened electric window between the front and the back seats suddenly lowered and the limo driver looked over his shoulder at Edwin.

"We have arrived at Bellamy Manor, Master Edwin," he said.

The car was turning onto a driveway that appeared to wind its way toward a castle-like structure in the distance.

"That's Sir Cedric's house up on the hill," said the driver, pointing. "It's an old manor house that goes back to feudal times. It has twenty-two rooms, ten fireplaces, and five floors, including an observatory where you can see for miles."

Edwin strained to get a better look through the front window. As the car barrelled down the gravel road, he could see the imposing mansion emerge through sculptured grounds spotted with hedges, grazing sheep, and blankets of purple heather.

At last, the car eased its way under a giant portico and stopped in front of two huge wooden doors. The driver rushed round to open the car door and Edwin stepped out. A sweet-smelling breeze swept over his body; he could feel the sun trying to warm the damp air.

"This way, Master Edwin," ushered the driver, carrying Edwin's luggage.

Edwin was directed through the front doors into a great entrance hall with large walls, a gigantic fireplace, and a narrow staircase that circled its way up to the floors above.

2

塞德里克·贝拉米

豪华轿车终于放慢了车速，这时，埃德温发现天气已经转晴，太阳也露出了笑脸。他面前的黑色电动车窗降了下来，司机回过头来。

"我们已经抵达贝拉米庄园了，埃德温少爷。"他说道。

埃德温摇下身侧的车窗，迫不及待想看看车外的景象。轿车转入一条私家车道，远处隐隐约约矗立着一座城堡。

"山上那座城堡就是塞德里克爵士的家，"司机指着远处说道，"这幢庄园别墅始建于中世纪时期，历史相当悠久。这里一共有五层，有二十二间客房和十个壁炉，从观景台可以俯瞰方圆数英里的美景。"

埃德温费力地眯着眼，想看得更清楚些。轿车从砾石路上飞驰而过，一栋金碧辉煌的豪宅从起伏的地面上赫然耸现，映入眼帘的还有零星散落的篱笆、成群觅食的绵羊以及如紫色绒毯般的帚石楠。最后，车子缓缓驶入一个高耸的门廊，停在两面巨大的木门前。司机急急赶过来打开车门，埃德温走下车来。一阵诱人的清香扑鼻而来，和煦的晨阳穿过湿漉漉的空气，带来几分暖意。

"请随我这边走，埃德温少爷。"司机扛着埃德温的行李，在前面引路。

他带领着埃德温走过贝拉米庄园的前门，进入一条走廊，两侧的石壁夹道耸立，侧壁建有巨大的壁炉，一段狭长的楼梯盘旋而上直通其他楼层。

"Please have a seat," said the driver, directing Edwin to an oversized wooden chair. "I need to head off now. Someone will help you shortly."

Edwin perched on the chair and waited. He could hear the car heading back down the driveway. He sat, staring around the room. Then it hit him: This was the place where his father used to work. His eyes teared as he thought of never seeing his father again. While he had not been as close to his father as he was to his mother, he loved and admired him and now wished he had spent more time with him. But his father was always heading off to work on some new project. He'd promise to take Edwin to a football game or a movie the next time he was home, but he rarely honoured his promises.

"You must be Master Bellamay," said a stern voice. Edwin was jolted from his thoughts by a thin, pale man sporting a tweed coat and a white shirt and tie.

"I am Sir Cedric's assistant Dr. Phonic," said the man, remaining motionless. His deep-set eyes scanned Edwin disapprovingly.

Edwin stood and extended his hand but the man turned away. "Follow me. The driver will take your luggage to your room later."

Edwin followed Dr. Phonic up the staircase to the next floor into a lovely bedroom with a canopy bed.

"This is your room," said Dr. Phonic in a monotone. "Dinner is at 7. Sir Cedric will see you then. Back down the stairs and to the right is the dining room," he gestured. "Dress accordingly," he ordered as he hastened down the stairs.

Edwin didn't quite know what "accordingly" meant, but he had brought some grey flannels and a white shirt that he hoped would do the trick. He looked at his watch. It was almost 6:30. He had half an hour to check things out.

His room had a series of old wardrobes, a fireplace, and an adjoining washroom with a big old iron bathtub on legs.

Two doors opened onto a balcony where he could see the grounds. As he

"请您在此稍做休息，"司机将埃德温领至一张高大的木椅旁说道，"请容我先行告退，待会儿会有人接待您。"

埃德温只好坐下等待。他听到来时的那辆轿车驶出了车道，埃德温坐在椅子上四处打量，突然想到：这里曾是父亲工作过的地方。一想到与父亲的永别，他不禁热泪盈眶。虽然父子俩的感情并不像他跟母亲那么亲密，但他仍然十分崇敬和爱戴自己的父亲，此时此刻，埃德温多么希望以前能花更多时间陪伴父亲。但是父亲总有忙不完的新计划。父亲曾承诺陪埃德温看足球赛，也曾许诺下一次回家一定会带他去看电影，但他很少兑现自己的诺言。

"您一定是贝拉米少爷吧。"不知从何处传来一个严肃的声音。

埃德温从思绪中猛地回过神来，只见一个身着斜纹软呢外套和白色衬衫、扎着领带的男人站在面前，看上去身形瘦弱、面色苍白。

"我是塞德里克爵士的助理，弗尼克博士。"这名男子面无表情地说道。他深陷的双眼不以为然地上下打量着埃德温。

埃德温站起身来，向他友好地伸出手，但他却转过身去，说道："请随我来，一会儿让司机过来取您的行李。"

埃德温跟在弗尼克博士身后，顺着狭长的楼梯来到楼上一间典雅的卧室内，房间内放置着一张四柱床。

"这是您的房间，"弗尼克博士不动声色地说道，"晚餐安排在7点，您可以与塞德里克爵士共进晚餐，您刚才经过的楼梯右侧就是餐厅，"他比画着方向。"请穿着得体的正装就餐。"他嘱咐完这句话，便匆匆回到了楼下。

埃德温其实不太明白何谓"得体"，但他想着随身带来的几条灰色法兰绒长裤和一件白衬衫应该不至于失了体面。他看了看手表，现在快6点半了，他只有半小时收拾打点。

房间里有一排旧式衣柜和一个壁炉，相连的盥洗室内放着一个古典四脚浴缸。另有两扇门直通顶楼阳台，可以俯瞰周边的景致。他站在阳台上盯着

stared out at his new surroundings, Edwin wondered what he was going to do for the next few weeks. There didn't appear to be any other children around and Dr. Phonic didn't seem like a particularly fun guy.

Suddenly, he heard the sound of a car. The black limousine was returning. It soared up the driveway in a cloud of dust, then disappeared under the portico. A few moments later, he could hear car doors opening and closing and then voices.

"Are you sure everything is secure? I don't want him to gain access to that room," bellowed a voice Edwin did not recognize.

"I have re-coded the lift," said another voice that Edwin knew was Dr. Phonic.

He retreated back into his room. He had a pit in his stomach. He knew that whatever was being protected by the man and Dr. Phonic was also being protected from him.

By 6:45, Edwin had unpacked and dressed in his white shirt and grey flannel trousers. As he looked in the mirror, he still wondered if he was dressed accordingly and whether he really was welcome at this place. Ah, who cares, he thought to himself. If Cedric was a good friend of his father, everything will be fine.

Edwin headed back downstairs, following Dr. Phonic's directions to the dining room, a room as grand as the entrance hall. It had huge stone walls, a massive fireplace and roaring fire, a rich Persian carpet, and long wooden dining table so well polished he could see his reflection in it. A series of large oil paintings hung on the walls; they looked like famous people from the past. Edwin tried to read a brass nameplate under one of the paintings.

"Those are yer relatives!" called a booming voice. Edwin whipped around to see a tall, rather overweight man with a round, balding head and pink cheeks. He sported a bright plaid kilt and a short jacket.

风景出神，对未来几周的生活感到一片茫然。附近看不到与他同龄的孩子，而弗尼克博士看上去又不像是一个谈吐风趣的人。

突然，他听到汽车的声音，那辆黑色轿车驶入他的眼帘，它在尘土飞扬中急速开过车道，最后消失在门廊下。过了一会儿，他听到车门开关声，还伴着零星的交谈声。

"你都安排妥当了吗？不能让他进入那个房间。"一个陌生人高声说道。

"我已经重新设置了电梯的密码。"埃德温立刻听出这是弗尼克博士的声音。

埃德温回到了自己的房间，他心里忐忑不安。他非常清楚，这两人正极力隐瞒一个秘密，阻止他了解事情的真相。

6点20分时，埃德温已经安顿好行李，换上了白衬衫和灰色法兰绒长裤，他注视着镜中的自己，不确定着装是否得体，也不知道自己在这里能否被真心接纳。"嘿，我才不在乎呢，"他自言自语道，"如果塞德里克真是父亲的好友，那么一切都会好起来的。"

埃德温回到楼下，按照弗尼克博士所指的方向来到开阔的餐厅。餐厅大小与门厅相差无几，四周石壁高高耸立，高大的壁炉内炉火熊熊，精美华贵的波斯地毯将长方形实木餐桌映衬得愈加光可鉴人。墙壁上悬挂着多张巨幅肖像油画，想必都是些声名显赫的历史名人。埃德温走到一幅画作前，仔细端详起下方的铜制铭牌来。

"他们都是你的亲戚。"不知从哪儿传来一个洪亮的声音。埃德温忙转过身来，看见一位面色红润、圆顶秃头的男子立在眼前，此人身形高壮、大腹便便，身着鲜艳的格纹短裙，外搭一件特制外套。

"That is Dorian Bellamy, yer great-great-grandfather," said the man, pointing to the painting of a distinguished man sitting beside a hunting dog, "and that one is yer great-uncle George who died in the Boer War." Edwin stared at the painting of the younger man wearing a dark military suit and a Pith helmet.

He couldn't see too much family resemblance in the two men but he suddenly felt an incredible sense of history in seeing his own flesh and blood immortalized on the walls. He turned back toward the tall man.

"Are you . . . Sir Cedric?" asked Edwin hesitantly.

The man slapped the boy playfully on the back. "That I am, wee lad. That I am," said he, in a Scottish drawl. "And you are the spitting image of yer father. Please, do have a seat."

Cedric lead Edwin to the table and Cedric sat down at the head. A few moments later, waiters dressed in white paraded into the room carrying an assortment of delicacies: A platter of sliced roast beef, a bowl of Yorkshire pudding and roast potatoes, a basket of hot rolls and creamy butter, and another bowl containing peas, carrots, and corn. Two vessels were placed in the centre of the table. One contained red wine and the other milk. Cedric grabbed the wine carafe and poured himself a glass. Edwin followed by pouring himself some milk.

"This house was built in 1320, Edwin," said Cedric, savoring his wine. "It was acquired by yer great-great-grandfather Dorian Bellamy in 1742. No one knows how or why it came to him, particularly as he was by no means a wealthy man. But for some reason, one day Dorian was poor and the next day he owned this," said Cedric, opening his arms and gesturing around the room. "No one can figure out why. Very curious, indeed."

The waiters started to serve the roast beef and vegetables and Edwin ladled on some rich gravy. He looked over at Cedric who was wolfing his dinner and washing it down with a steady flow of wine.

"那是你的高祖父道林·贝拉米，"他指着一位牵着猎犬的风度翩翩的男子说道，"那是你的叔爷爷乔治，他不幸在布尔战争中牺牲了。"埃德温看到他又指向一名身着深色军装、头戴遮阳帽的年轻男子。

虽然在这一张张脸上看不到太多相似之处，但看着墙上这些家族先辈的画像，埃德温的心中突然涌出一股说不清道不明的沧桑感。看了一会儿，他转过身面向那名高大的男子。

"您是……塞德里克爵士吗？"埃德温迟疑着问。

男子爱抚地拍拍他的后背。"正是本人，小伙子。正是本人，"他带着拖长的苏格兰口音说道，"你跟令尊还真是一个模子里刻出来的啊。来，咱们坐着聊。"

塞德里克领着埃德温来到餐桌边，然后自己在桌首就座。未几，一列身着白色制服的侍者手捧佳肴美馔鱼贯而入：一盘烤牛肉片、一碗约克夏布丁和烤土豆、一篮新鲜出炉的面包卷配上奶香扑鼻的黄油，外加一碗豌豆、胡萝卜和玉米。餐桌中央的锡制水罐内分别装有牛奶和红酒，塞德里克抢先给自己倒上了一杯，埃德温也自倒了一杯牛奶。

"这栋宅子始建于1320年，埃德温，"塞德里克小啜了一口酒，说道，"1742年，你的高祖父道林·贝拉米把它买了下来。没人知道他为什么要买下这栋宅子，更没人知道他靠什么法子把它弄到手的，他可绝对算不上什么有钱人。反正不知怎么的，道林好像一夕之间就成了这里的主人。"塞德里克摊开双臂，两手指着房间绕了一圈，"个中原因不得而知，说起来还真是有几分诡异。"

侍者端上了蔬菜烤牛肉，埃德温为自己舀上几勺香浓的肉汁。埃德温隔着餐桌看了塞德里克一眼，只见他正狼吞虎咽地吃着晚餐，不时倒上一杯红酒自斟自饮。

Edwin liked Cedric. He was quite approachable and laid back, so much so that Edwin decided to pursue a line of questioning he hoped might shed some light on his father's work with Cedric.

"Excuse me, Sir Cedric, but what is your job? I mean what do you do for a living?"

Cedric looked up from his plate and flushed. At that moment, Dr. Phonic entered the room, looking his usual sour self.

"Ah, there you are, Preston. Please do join us," Cedric said.

Dr. Phonic grunted and seated himself opposite Edwin, avoiding eye contact. The waiters hurried back in again and prepared Dr. Phonic's plate.

"Edwin here was just asking me what I do for a living," said Cedric, exaggerating his intonation.

Dr. Phonic looked up quickly, then stared at Edwin with piercing eyes.

"Well, Edwin, if you must know," said Cedric with a forced smile, "I am a bibliophile. I collect books. Twenty-two-thousand to be exact. Isn't that right, Preston?"

Dr. Phonic grunted in agreement.

"Wow!" said Edwin.

"Of course that wasn't my job when I was younger. In my early days, I worked as an etymologist at the local university. Do you know what an etymologist is, Edwin?"

Edwin shook his head.

"An etymologist is a person who studies the history of words and how their form and meaning change over time. And Dr. Phonic here is a professor of linguistics, an expert on languages. He and I have done a lot of work together."

Edwin wondered what on earth could possibly interest those two men in such boring topics. He really hated subjects like reading and anything that required him to write.

埃德温很喜欢塞德里克。他看起来亲切而随和，因此埃德温决定向他打听有关父亲的情况。

"抱歉，塞德里克爵士，不知您在哪里高就呢？我的意思是，不知您从事的是哪一行呢？"

塞德里克抬起头来，一瞬间涨红了脸。此时，弗尼克博士走进房来，脸上还是那副闷闷不乐的表情。

"啊，普雷斯顿，你来啦。来和我们一道用餐吧。"塞德里克说道。

弗尼克博士哼了一声表示回答，随后在埃德温对面坐下，但他似乎刻意回避着埃德温的目光。侍者急忙走进来，为弗尼克博士端上餐具。

"埃德温刚还在打听我做什么营生呢。"塞德里克故意拿腔拿调地说道。

弗尼克博士迅速抬起头来，直直地盯着埃德温的眼睛，仿佛要看穿他的心思。

"好吧，埃德温，如果你非要问的话，"塞德里克面带苦笑地说，"我是一个藏书家，我收藏各类古册珍籍。确切地说，已经有两万两千本了。没错吧，普雷斯顿？"

弗尼克博士哼了一声表示同意。

"哇！"埃德温不禁发出惊叹。

"当然啦，我年轻那会儿，可不是靠做这个谋生的。年轻的时候，我曾在本地一所大学里从事词源研究工作。埃德温，你知道什么是词源学吗？"

埃德温摇了摇头。

"词源学家是专门研究词汇的起源、构词特点及语言的演变规律。弗尼克博士也是一位语言学教授，他可是语言学领域的专家，我俩曾在多个研究计划中合作过。"

埃德温很想知道为什么这两位先生会对如此无聊的课题有浓厚的兴趣。他对阅读和任何与写作有关的科目都厌烦透顶。

"Why do I need to write when I can just pick up the phone?" he would argue with his parents. But Edwin's father had told him that unless he learned how to write and read, he would end up turning to crime and would be in jail by the time he reached the age of seventeen.

Despite not being interested in bibliophiles and the study of linguistics, Edwin wanted to pursue the subject further, to see if it somehow tied into his father's work but something told him he had better not discuss the topic while Dr. Phonic was in the room. That guy was really starting to give him the creeps.

The discussion at the table moved from books to more history about Bellamy Manor and a promise from Cedric to take Edwin into the local village on Market Day, an event supposedly not to be missed.

At last, dessert was served. Large pieces of rich chocolate cake and dollops of fresh vanilla ice cream were quickly dispensed around the table and the waiters served coffee to Cedric and Dr. Phonic. Edwin was presented with a steaming cup of hot cocoa.

At last, the meal came to a close and Cedric beckoned Edwin into an adjoining room. Dr. Phonic gave Cedric a strange look and exited.

"This is my pride and joy," said Cedric, turning on the lights in the room. "This is my collection."

Gradually big pot-lights began to glow to reveal a room the size of a small gymnasium with floor-to-ceiling metal bookshelves stuffed with books of every imaginable size and shape. The smell of leather filled the air and Edwin felt he was in some sort of museum.

"Let's have a look, shall we?" said Cedric excitedly. He put his hand on the tall ladder affixed to a ceiling track. "Hop on, Edwin," he said, climbing the ladder and pulling Edwin up with him. He took a remote control from his pocket and pressed a button. The ladder started to move. As it circled the room, Cedric proudly pointed out each section of his book collection.

"如果打个电话就能解决问题，我干吗还要写信呢？"他总是这样跟父母争辩。但是埃德温的父亲曾告诉过他，不重视阅读和写作的人迟早会沦为街头混混，不到17岁就会被送到监狱里，浑浑噩噩了此残生。

埃德温对藏书和语言学不感兴趣，他想打探更多信息，希望借此了解有关父亲的消息。可是，直觉告诉他，只要弗尼克博士在场，他就最好对这个话题三缄其口。对弗尼克博士的畏惧感让他如坐针毡。

他们继续边吃边谈，从书本聊到贝拉米庄园的历史，塞德里克还答应在赶集日带埃德温去附近的村子参观，本地的集市可是不容错过的重要活动。

最后，侍者端来了甜点。浓郁可口的大块巧克力蛋糕和冰爽的香草冰激凌诱人垂涎，侍者还为塞德里克和弗尼克博士奉上了咖啡，而埃德温面前则摆上了一杯热气腾腾的可可。

酒足饭饱后，塞德里克招手叫埃德温跟自己去隔壁的房间，这时，弗尼克博士给了塞德里克一种异样的眼光后就退席了。

"这是我最引以为傲的珍品，"塞德里克打开灯说道，"是我收藏的传世之作。"

大射灯渐次亮起，将这间小型健身房大小的房间照得通明透亮，与天花板平齐的金属书架上摆满了尺寸不一、外形各异的古籍善本。皮革的气味弥漫在空气中，埃德温感觉仿佛置身于博物馆当中。

"咱们边走边看，好吗？"塞德里克的声音听上去有些激动。他迅速抓紧一架紧靠着墙壁的梯子。"上来吧，埃德温。"他拉着埃德温一同踩上梯子。随后，他从自己的口袋里取出遥控器，按了一下按钮。阶梯开始围绕着房间转动起来，塞德里克自豪地指出每个部分向埃德温介绍着自己的藏品。

"These are my books on ancient history . . . those are my famous novels . . . and these, yes, these," he said, stopping the ladder at a section encased in glass, "these are books that have been here ever since yer great-great-grandfather Dorian Bellamy owned the place."

Edwin stared at the books in the glass cabinet and imagined his great-great-grandfather sitting in front of a fireplace, reading one of the beautifully embossed volumes. He noticed that the middle shelf was completely empty.

"Now, Edwin. You are free to come in here whenever you want. There are only two rules: First, please don't remove any of the books from this room. The temperature and moisture level are carefully monitored to ensure the books do not deteriorate. The second rule is please do not touch any of Dorian Bellamy's books that are in the cabinet. They need to be handled with care and special gloves.

Edwin looked around the room and realized this was going to be the sum total of his entertainment for the next three weeks. Maybe some ancient comic books were buried somewhere in the stacks, he thought hopefully.

"Excuse me," said Edwin, getting up the courage to ask about his father, "but did my father collect books, as well? Is that what he was working on with you?"

Cedric did not flinch and pondered the question thoughtfully. "Henry and I were involved in very special projects. It is a bit complicated but maybe in the next few days you and I will have a good chat and I'll try to explain everything," he said, winking at Edwin. "But, listen, it's getting late and I do want to show you one last thing before you head off to bed." He climbed down off the ladder, pulling Edwin with him. "Please, follow me."

They headed back into the dining room and stopped in front of a wooden wall. Cedric flipped a light switch and two doors opened to reveal an elevator.

"这些是古代史籍……那些都是我最喜爱的小说……对了，还有这些书。"他按停了梯子，指着玻璃柜门后的书说道，"在你高祖父道林·贝拉米买下这栋宅子那会儿，就有这些书了。"

埃德温打量着玻璃书柜上那些看起来颇有些年代的书籍，他想象着自己的高祖父坐在壁炉前阅读这些装帧精美的古籍的情景。他注意到中间的书柜被腾空了。

"好了，埃德温。你随时可以到这里来。只要记住两点：其一，不要把书从这儿带出去。这里的温度和湿度都是经过精心调节的，可以避免纸张变质。其二，不要触摸这个书柜内任何道林·贝拉米老先生的书。这些书都必须戴着特制手套小心处理。"

埃德温环顾四周，意识到在接下来的三周里，这里将是他唯一的消遣之处了。"这一堆书里面说不定藏着几本古代漫画书呢。"他抱着一丝幻想。

"很抱歉，"埃德温终于鼓起勇气提起了父亲，他问道，"我想知道，我父亲在这儿是不是也有藏书呢？他是因为这个原因跟您合作的吗？"

塞德里克并未回避他的问题，而是若有所思地沉默了一会儿。"亨利和我合作了一些非常特别的计划。说起来有点复杂，不过改天我们可以抽个机会好好聊聊，到时候我会跟你解释这一切的。"他冲埃德温眨了眨眼，"对了，时候不早了，在你上床睡觉前，我再带你去一个地方。"他一边说，一边拉着埃德温从梯子上走下来，"请随我来。"

他们回到餐厅，走到一面木墙前。塞德里克按了一下开关，两扇门突然打开，露出了一架电梯。

"A few years ago, I had this elevator installed. I'm just too old to handle all the stairs in this place. Now, to use this elevator, you must have a specially programmed swipe-card," he said, pulling out a large flat plastic card. He flashed the card over a sensor, pressed a floor number, and the elevator started to move.

"We are going to the very top of the house: The observatory," said Cedric, as the elevator began to ascend.

At last it slowed to a stop and the two doors opened again, revealing an octagonal room with floor-to-ceiling windows that looked out over the countryside.

There was something familiar about the design of the room. The tops of the windows leaned forward at an angle and each was divided into smaller panes. Edwin saw a big wooden wheel at the other side of the room. Rum barrels were scattered on the wooden floorboards and hammocks hung from the walls.

"This looks like the inside of a ship," said Edwin.

"Exactly," said Cedric. "Another strange artifact left by yer great-great-grandfather. A few years after he acquired this place, he suddenly started to develop a fascination for pirates and ships. He commissioned a famous local architect to completely redesign the top floor of this house to look like the interior of a ship. We call this the Ship's Observatory Deck."

It was now nighttime. Edwin could see the twinkling lights of the village and a few random lights from houses scattered throughout the countryside.

"Edwin, you must come up here during the day to truly appreciate the view. Tomorrow, ask Dr. Phonic for a swipe card. You will get one programmed to take you directly to this floor. You will not be able to access the other floors; they are out of bounds."

"What's on the other floors?" asked Edwin boldly.

Cedric's expression became serious for a moment, then he placed his hand on Edwin's shoulder.

"几年前，我让人装了这架电梯，我年纪大了，爬不动楼梯了。现在，只有拿着这种特别设计的感应卡才能使用这部电梯。"他掏出一张大而薄的塑料卡，他将感应卡在感应器上刷了一下，按下了楼层号，启动了电梯。

"我们现在去顶楼的观景台看看。"电梯伴随着塞德里克的话音一路上升。

电梯减速并停下后，两扇门再次打开，他们来到了一间八边形房间，透过巨大的落地窗俯瞰幽丽秀美的田园风光。

前倾式窗户和每扇窗户上的小窗格设计让埃德温似曾相识，房间对面的一个巨大木轮吸引了埃德温的注意。木地板上七零八落地堆着朗姆酒酒桶，墙上还挂着吊床。

"看起来好像是一艘船的里面呢。"埃德温自言自语道。

"没错，"塞德里克说道，"这也是你高祖父留下的一个古怪玩意儿。他买下这栋宅子几年后，突然开始疯狂地迷恋上了海盗传说和船只设计。他委托本地一位著名建筑师对整个顶楼进行重新设计，这里的内部结构都是仿造船只设计的。我们把这里称为甲板观景台。"

现在正是晚上，埃德温只能看到远处村庄里隐约闪烁的灯光，透过玻璃窗向外眺望，还有本地农户家中透出的几点微光。

"这里的景色十分优美，埃德温，你在白天一定要抽空看看。明天，你可以向弗尼克博士拿一张直达顶楼的感应卡。但是别的楼层你去不了，因为其他楼层外人一律禁入。"

"其他楼层里都有些什么？"埃德温壮着胆子追问。

塞德里克的表情立刻变得严肃起来，但他旋即恢复了平静，轻轻抚摸着埃德温的肩膀。

"This is an old house, young Edwin. It is constantly under renovation as we try to restore it to its glory days. There are loose floorboards, rickety old walls, and workers on some of those other floors. It's best that you stay away from them."

"I understand," said Edwin who now recalled the conversation under the portico: "I don't want him to gain access to that room." Edwin figured there was something more than simple renovation going on, but he played along with Cedric.

"Right you are," said Cedric, taking Edwin back into the elevator and swiping his card. "Now, it's off to bed for the both of us. Breakfast will be served in the dining room at 8," he said as the elevator started to move, "but I'm afraid I won't be able to join you. I have some business to attend to in the village."

Great! thought Edwin. I'll be stuck here with Dr. Phonic!

When Edwin had finally settled into his big bed for the night, he thought of what Cedric had said when he asked about his father: "It is a bit complicated, but maybe in the next few days you and I will have a good chat and I'll try to explain everything."

How can collecting books be so complicated? thought Edwin.

"这栋宅子年代久远，孩子。为了重现它最辉煌的面貌，我们必须定期修缮。其他楼层里总会有松动脱胶的地板和摇摇欲坠的老墙，还不断有工人来来往往，所以你离这些地方越远越好。"

"我知道了。"埃德温答道，塞德里克在门廊下的那句话仍历历在耳："我不能让他进入那个房间。"埃德温猜测所谓的老宅修缮不过是个幌子，但他佯装不知地应和着塞德里克。

"这就对了，"塞德里克说道，一边领着埃德温走回电梯，刷了一下感应卡，"现在，咱俩都得去睡觉了，明早8点准时开饭。"在电梯启动的瞬间，塞德里克说道："不过恐怕我没法陪你用餐了，村里有点儿事需要我亲自去处理。"

埃德温心下暗想：倒霉！那我会被困在这里和弗尼克博士俩人干瞪眼了！

当晚，埃德温躺在自己宽敞的大床上，再次回想起提到父亲时塞德里克的回答："说起来有点复杂，不过改天我们可以抽个机会好好聊聊，到时候我会跟你解释这一切的。"

"跟藏书有关的事，能有多复杂？"埃德温喃喃自语道。

3

THE SIXTH FLOOR

The next day, Edwin was awakened by the steady stream of sunlight flowing through his bedroom window. He looked at his watch; it was 7:30. After a quick wash, he dressed and headed down for breakfast. As he reached the main floor, he was greeted by none other than Dr. Phonic himself, looking particularly grumpy.

"Sir Cedric asked me to give you a swipe card so you can access the observatory," said Dr. Phonic. It was clear that he did not agree with the idea. "Please take care of this card I give you. It is expensive to replace." He reached into his pocket and pulled out a pack of swipe cards. Just as he was about to hand one to Edwin, his cell phone started to ring and he dropped the cards on the floor.

"Yes?" he said rudely into the receiver. "What? What are you talking about? That's not possible."

Edwin could see that Dr. Phonic was not happy with the person on the other end of the line.

"Just a minute," Dr. Phonic snapped, balancing his phone between his chin and shoulder. He reached down and picked up the swipe cards, pausing for a second as he decided which one to select. He handed it to Edwin, waiving him off in a dismissive fashion, then turned his back and continued talking forcefully into his cell phone.

Edwin headed to the dining room where he found a place setting for one. No sooner had he sat down, a waiter appeared carrying a tray with bacon and eggs, toast, and apple juice.

3

六楼

第二天，晨阳透过卧室的窗口倾泻而下，丝丝暖意唤醒了睡梦中的埃德温。他看了看表：7点30分。匆忙洗漱后，他穿好衣服，下楼去吃早餐。但是当埃德温来到主层后，迎接他的不是别人，正是弗尼克博士，他看上去显得格外阴郁。

"塞德里克爵士让我给你一张感应卡，方便你进出观景台，"弗尼克博士说道，口气里似乎隐含着不满，"请妥善保管好这张卡。若是弄丢了，要重做一张可不便宜。"弗尼克博士伸手从口袋里拿出一沓卡片，正要递给埃德温时，他的手机响了，卡片全掉落到地上。

"什么事？"他粗声粗气地对着话筒叫道，"什么？你说什么？这不可能。"

埃德温看得出来，弗尼克博士接电话的表情很不高兴。

"等一下。"弗尼克博士厉声说道，用下巴和肩膀夹住手机。他俯下身捡起卡片，停顿了几秒想了想，最后选出其中一张递给埃德温。然后，他不耐烦地冲埃德温摆了摆手，埃德温只好先行回避。弗尼克博士立刻转过身去，继续冲着电话嘶吼。

埃德温来到餐厅，发现桌上已经摆上了单人的餐具。他刚刚坐定，一名侍者即端着放有培根炒蛋、吐司和苹果汁的托盘走进来。

I could get used to this royal treatment, he chuckled to himself.

Edwin ate at a leisurely pace; he realized there was very little to look forward to in the day ahead. He thought of his mother and hoped she was coping with whatever she was doing. He wished he could be with her but knew she wanted him here. *If this is what she wants, I will make the best of it,* he thought.

He stared out the large window at the grounds. It was certainly a magnificent estate. Later, he would check out the view from the observatory and maybe walk around the property, but he was now beginning to realize that Sir Cedric's library was probably the only real source of entertainment around.

When he had downed his third glass of apple juice and second helping of bacon and eggs, he headed to the elevator doors and flicked the switch on the wall. A hum signalled the elevator car was descending. At last the doors opened and Edwin stepped inside, pulled out his swipe card, and flashed it over the sensor. He pressed "O" for observatory. The doors closed and the elevator car started to climb.

That's strange, thought Edwin, as he looked at the panel of floor buttons. There were six buttons plus a button for the observatory but he remembered the limo driver had mentioned only five floors including the observatory. He noticed the button to the sixth floor had a blue hue. Was it an emergency button of some sort? Edwin pressed it, knowing nothing would happen because his card had been programmed to stop only at the observatory.

The elevator started to speed up and turn, like a ride at an amusement park. *What have I done?* he worried.

The elevator came to a stop. A door panel in the elevator car opened and a chair emerged.

"Please be seated," announced a mechanical voice.

"这么奢华的待遇，我都快要被宠坏了。"他心中暗笑道。

埃德温一边悠闲地吃着早餐，一边忖度着今天余下的时光想必是百无聊赖。他想起了母亲，暗自祈祷一切都能进展顺利。他多么希望能和母亲在一起，但他知道母亲希望他留在这里。他心想："如果这是她想要的，那我一定乖乖听她的话。"

他透过硕大的窗户凝视着窗外的风景，贝拉米庄园确实气派非凡。他打算晚些时候去观景台浏览一下周边的风光，或许还可以四处走走。此时，他觉得塞德里克爵士的书斋也许是他唯一的乐趣所在。

三杯苹果汁和两份培根炒蛋下肚之后，埃德温直走向电梯门，按下了墙壁上的开关，旋即传来电梯下降的嗡嗡声。电梯门打开后，埃德温走了进去，掏出感应卡在感应器前刷了一下。然后，他按下"0"是前往观景台，电梯门关闭，轿厢开始往上升。

他抬头看了看按钮控制面板，真奇怪，他凑近一看，内心顿生疑惑。面板上有六个按钮，外加一个通往观景台的按钮。但他依稀记得轿车司机说过，包括观景台在内这里一共只有五层。埃德温同时留意到通往六楼的按钮是蓝色的，它看上去像是个紧急按钮？埃德温很清楚自己的感应卡已被重新编程，因此漫不经心地按下通往六楼的按钮。

但他刚按下按钮时，电梯便好似游乐场中的木马一般开始加速晃动。"我做了些什么呀？"埃德温忧虑地说。

电梯猛地停了下来，突然，轿厢内的一扇门打开了，出现了一把椅子。

"请坐。"响起一个机械音。

Edwin hesitated, then cautiously sat on the chair, staring around the elevator to see what would happen next. Another door panel opened in front of him. He could vaguely make out what looked like train tracks. The chair started to move. Sure enough, it began to roll along the tracks until it stopped in front of another door. As the door slid open, a vivid cobalt-blue light came on.

"Please exit the chair and proceed through the archway," said the mechanical voice.

Edwin stood up and moved toward the source of the light. When he stepped through the archway, the door closed behind him, the blue light began to fade, and white ceiling lights started to illuminate the room. As the lights got brighter, Edwin realized he was in a library of some sort, but not the one Cedric had showed him.

It was a magnificent room, panelled in deep, rich oak. There were large leather armchairs around long tables with ornate reading lights and leather blotters. Floor-to-ceiling oak bookshelves stuffed with gilded books soared three levels high around the perimeter of the room. In the middle was a very old desk. On it were computer terminals and files and a stack of books.

Edwin knew he should exit the room as soon as possible; it clearly was a place he was not supposed to be, but something told him to keep exploring. He looked more closely at the desk and files. One file read "Notes on Etymological Transfiguration". What the heck is that? thought Edwin.

On one of the shelves he noticed a school textbook, *A Student's Guide to the Great Adventure Story*. He picked it up and flipped through its pages.

All at once, the ceiling lights started to dim and the blue hue shone once more.

"What's going on?!" said Edwin out loud, dropping the book on the desk. He was becoming scared.

Just as he was about to make his way back to the archway, he heard a sound. He was not alone!

埃德温迟疑了几秒，然后小心翼翼地坐到椅子上，他盯着电梯上下打量，好奇到底会发生什么事。另一扇门在他面前打开，他依稀能够辨识出好像是一条类似铁路的轨道。随后，椅子沿着轨道移动起来，过了几分钟，停在了另一扇门前。这扇门缓缓滑动，透出一道刺目的蓝光。

"请离开椅子，穿过拱门。"机械音再次响起。

埃德温站起身来，向着那道蓝光的光源走去。当他穿过拱门后，身后的大门缓缓关闭，那道蓝光则渐渐隐去，而白色的顶灯照亮了整个房间。在越来越清晰的灯光下，埃德温渐渐看清了周围的环境，原来他来到了另一间书房，只不过这里与之前去过的塞德里克的书斋截然不同。

深色的橡木护墙板将这间宽敞的书房衬托得富丽堂皇。长方形书桌四周环绕着高大的真皮扶手椅，桌上摆着华丽的台灯和皮面笔记本。放眼望去，全是直抵天花板的三层橡木书架，不计其数的镀金边精装书把每一层都填得满满当当。房间中央摆放着一张古色古香的超大号书桌，桌上堆满了电脑、文件还有一堆书。

埃德温很清楚自己应该赶快离开，这里显然不是他该来的地方。但强烈的好奇心却诱使着他留下一探究竟。他走近那张书桌，仔细研究起桌上的文件，其中一份写有"单词变形的词源解析"的字样。"这到底是么东西啊？"他喃喃自语。

他遥望到书桌后的书架上摆着一本教科书，上书：《〈伟大的探险〉学生导读本》。他把书拿下来，随手翻了几页。

突然间，白色的灯光全部熄灭，那道蓝光再次出现。

"发生了什么事？"埃德温把书往桌上一丢，大声说道。他的心猛然一紧，一丝恐惧感袭上心头。

正当他准备沿着来路回到拱门那边时，却听到了异样的动静。这里除了他，还有其他人！

"Pssst."

Edwin looked around but now the room had gone completely dark.

"Pssssssssst," came the sound again, this time longer and more forceful.

Edwin realized someone was trying to speak to him.

"Excuse me, sir," said the voice, "but could you possibly help us?"

Edwin liked the idea of being called sir, but he was still very nervous. He took a deep breath.

"B . . . b . . . but who are you?" he asked.

"My name is Thomas The," said the voice.

"And my name is Beatrice Beautiful," said another voice.

Beautiful? The? Those are funny names, thought Edwin. "They're . . . just REGULAR words."

Unfortunately, Edwin was not very good at thinking to himself. Thomas had heard him.

"That's right, little boy," said Thomas. "We ARE words."

Edwin took another deep breath. "Excuse me, Mr. Mrs. . . . Words, but I never knew that words, I mean you . . ."

"Can talk?" said Beatrice.

"Yes," said Edwin.

"My dear boy," continued Beatrice, "of course we can talk. It's just that we are a shy lot. We take so much abuse when people misuse us or misspell us that we feel, well . . . neglected!"

Edwin thought about the most recent mark he had received on his composition about the History of Rock Music. The teacher had written "Misuse of words! Watch your spelling!"

He began to feel a bit guilty.

"I'm sorry if I hurt your feelings," said Edwin, "but I . . . I just, well . . . I've never met words before, especially in person."

"Don't worry, little boy," said Thomas. "We understand. Here, let me shed some light on this situation."

"嘘。"传来一个声音。

埃德温四下环顾，但此刻房间内一片漆黑，几乎伸手不见五指。

"嘘嘘嘘——"还是那个声音，只是这一次又长又响。

埃德温猛然意识到，对方似乎有什么话要对他说。

"打扰了，先生，"不知从哪儿冒出一个声音，"不知道您愿不愿意帮我们一个忙？"

听见有人叫他"先生"，埃德温心里美滋滋的，但他还是很紧张，他深吸了一口气。

"呃……呃……请问您尊姓大名？"他问道。

"我叫托马斯·这个。"那个声音答道。

"我叫碧翠丝·美丽。"另一个声音说道。

"美丽？这个？他们的名字也太滑稽了。"埃德温暗想，"这些不是……**常见的**单词嘛。"

不巧，埃德温喃喃自语的话被托马斯听了个正着。

"说得没错，孩子。"托马斯说道，"我们的确**是**单词。"

埃德温又深吸了一口气。"很抱歉，这位先生和女士……你说你们是单词，但是我从来不知道单词，我的意思是你们居然会……"

"会说话？"碧翠丝代他补充道。

"是的。"埃德温说道。

"亲爱的孩子，"碧翠丝继续说道，"我们当然会说话了，只不过我们比较害羞而已。当人类滥用单词或拼写错误时，我们难过极了，甚至觉得，嗯……我们被忽视了！"

埃德温不由得想起他最近的一篇作文《摇滚乐的历史》那点可怜巴巴的分数。老师给他的评语是"滥用单词！注意拼写！"

他一下子觉得有点内疚。

"如果我伤害了你们的感情，请你们原谅。"埃德温说道，"但是我……我只是，嗯……我从来没有见到过单词，尤其是像现在这样面对面的说话。"

"别担心，孩子，"托马斯说道，"我们懂你的意思。好吧，让我来给你解释解释。"

The blue light began to fade and the room became bright again. Edwin began blinking and rubbing his eyes. Out of the corner of his eye, he caught sight of two little things that were moving.

"Hello there!" said one of the things.

Edwin lunged backward and landed on a large paperback book titled *How to Cope with Strange Situations*.

"Don't be scared, young boy. We just want to have a word with you." And with that, two very little figures jumped down from the front cover of *A Student's Guide to the Great Adventure Story*.

They bounced along until they landed smack on Edwin's chest. He was literally pinned by two people no bigger than his left hand.

"Hi there!"

Edwin looked down. The voice had come from a lady dressed in the most beautiful clothes he had ever seen. She was wearing a long golden dress with tiny sparkles. Over her dress, she wore a silky black fur stole that contrasted with a set of shiny egg-coloured pearls that hung gracefully around her neck. Edwin could not see her hair because her head was covered with a matching fur hat. He wondered if she was a queen.

"I'm Beautiful," she said, smiling at Edwin.

"You certainly are," he said.

"No, no," said the other little person. "She means her name is Beautiful— Beatrice Beautiful."

Edwin moved his eyes to focus on the second person. He appeared to be a young man. His clothes were very ordinary. He wore a pair of striped railway overalls and matching workingman's cap. He carried a lantern that seemed to be providing all the light in the room.

"Thomas The is the name," he called out. "Nice to meet you, young boy. We are so glad you have come. We've been trying to get help for years."

"Years?!" exclaimed Edwin.

这时，明亮的灯光再次照亮了整个房间，蓝光也渐渐淡去。埃德温揉了揉眼睛，又使劲眨了眨眼睛。突然，他看到眼皮底下有两个小小的身影在移动。

"你好啊！"一个小不点跟他打了个招呼。

埃德温惊得向后一退，撞到了一本大开本平装书《怪事应急指南》。

"别害怕，孩子。我们只想跟你聊聊天。"话音刚落，就见两个小小的人儿从《〈伟大的探险〉学生导读本》上一跃而下。

他们一路跳跃，最后啪嗒一声落在埃德温的胸口上。埃德温被这两个如同巴掌般大小的小人儿完全惊呆了。

"嗨，你好！"

埃德温低头看着他们。说话的是一位女士，她的裙子漂亮极了，让埃德温大开眼界。长长的金色连衣裙闪烁着迷人的光芒，她的脖颈之间优雅地悬挂着一串莹润夺目的蛋青色珍珠项链，与连衣裙外那件柔软的黑色皮草披肩相映生辉。埃德温看不到她的头发，因为配套的皮帽把她的头发都遮住了。他想知道她是不是这里的女王。

"我是美丽。"她笑着对埃德温说。

"您确实很美。"埃德温说道。

"不，不，"另一个小人儿解释道，"她的意思是，她的名字叫美丽，碧翠丝·美丽。"

埃德温转眼打量起第二个小人儿来，他看起来还很年轻，身着一套带条纹的铁路工作服，头戴配套的安全帽，衣着非常朴素。他手里的灯笼似乎照亮了整个房间。

"我叫托马斯·这个，"他大声说，"很高兴能认识你，孩子，我们很高兴你能来。多年来，我们一直希望能找到帮手。"

"多年来？"埃德温惊叫了一声。

"Yes. You see, once we were very popular. People used to visit us all the time. We always had lots of work to do. Then disaster struck."

"What do you mean people used to visit you?" Edwin asked.

"Our book. They used to read our book every week," said Beatrice.

Using a small hand-mirror with which she had been admiring herself, she pointed to *A Student's Guide to the Great Adventure Story*.

"That's the book there," she said, noticing in the corner of the mirror that one of her hairs was an eighth of a millimetre out of place.

"Yes, yes," said Thomas impatiently. "But one day an obnoxious young boy decided to throw—not drop, I might add, but throw our poor book into a trash can. Luckily, somebody retrieved it and ever since, we have been sitting on a shelf, completely neglected. You're the first person to come near us in years."

Edwin looked at *A Student's Guide to the Great Adventure Story*, then back at his miniature friends. He wondered whether he was just having a strange dream. He looked down at the copy of *How to Cope with Strange Situations*.

"Look, young boy. I think that if you come and meet some of our friends, you'll realize we're not a bad lot."

"Friends? You mean there are more of you in here?" asked Edwin, turning his eyes in circles waiting to have more little people land on his chest.

"Not here, silly, in our book!"

By now Beatrice was beginning to find Edwin rather cute and she began chuckling at his funny way of thinking.

"But how do I get into a book?" asked Edwin, not believing he was actually asking such a ridiculous question.

Thomas jumped on Edwin's nose, causing Edwin to go quite cross-eyed.

"Now listen," said Thomas. "Repeat after me: 'Can I have a word with you?' Then hold your breath while sticking your finger in your right ear."

Edwin did as Thomas requested.

"是的！我们一度非常受人欢迎，人类经常来拜访我们，我们总是有很多工作要做。不幸的是，一场灾难发生了。"

"您说的'人类经常来拜访我们'是什么意思？"埃德温问道。

"我们的书——我是说，他们以前每周都会来读我们的书。"碧翠丝解释道。

她用整理妆容的迷你化妆镜指向《〈伟大的探险〉学生导读本》。

"就是那本书里。"她正说着，突然在镜子的一角瞟到一根发丝比标准位置偏离了八分之一毫米。

"对的，对的，"托马斯不耐烦地说，"有一天，一个讨厌的小男孩就把我们这本可怜的书扔到了垃圾桶里，但我觉得他压根是故意的。幸运的是，有人把书捡了回来，打那时起，我们就一直被放在这个架子上，从此无人问津。你是多年来第一个拜访我们的人。"

埃德温看看《〈伟大的探险〉学生导读本》，又看看眼前的两个小人儿，他觉得自己仿佛置身于荒诞的梦境。他低头看了一眼那本《怪事应急指南》。

"听着，孩子，我觉得如果你愿意与我们的朋友见上一面，你就会知道，我们绝不是坏人。"

"朋友？您的意思是，这里还有更多像您这样的人吗？"埃德温问道，双眼滴溜溜转了个圈，想看看会不会有更多的小人儿降落到他的胸口上。

"不是这里，傻孩子，是在我们的书里！"

碧翠丝觉得埃德温煞是可爱，他滑稽的念头让她不禁哑然失笑。

"但是，我怎么能进入到一本书里去呢？"埃德温问道，他简直难以相信自己其实问了这种无聊又可笑的问题。托马斯立即跳上了埃德温的鼻头，埃德温瞧着自己的鼻尖，成了个斗鸡眼。

"听好了，"托马斯说道，"现在请你跟着我重复说：'我能跟你说几句话吗？'然后屏住呼吸，把你的手指插到右边的耳朵里。"

埃德温按照托马斯的要求做了。

Suddenly, there was a swooshing sound.

Then the sound of turning of pages.

Then a large boom!

突然地，只听得嗖的一声。

紧接着是一阵窸窸窣窣的翻书声。

最后是一声震耳欲聋的轰隆声！

4

THE TABLE OF CONTENTS ROOM

Edwin felt a little dizzy. He looked around. Beautiful pictures adorned the walls of the large room and glittering chandeliers hung from the ceiling. In the middle of the room was an unusually large table. Seated at the head of the table was a distinguished little man in a dark suit that bulged because of his rather rotund stomach. Perched in front of his left eye was a monocle.

"Ah, Beatrice, you ARE looking beautiful today," said the man with the monocle.

He immediately walked up to her, took her hand, and began kissing it like a prince kissing the hand of a princess.

"Oh, thank you, Peter," Beatrice said casually, brushing her hair back. "I do feel particularly beautiful today."

"You're also acting particularly vain today," said Thomas, who by now had had quite enough of Beatrice's self-serving attitude.

"Thomas THE! Remember your place! Your family members are just common Articles—no class." With that, she set about adjusting her hand-mirror and attending to hairs not in their proper places.

"Well, at least we're not all full of ourselves like some Adjectives I know," said Thomas, glaring at Beatrice in a disgusted manner.

Meanwhile, Edwin had noticed something else rather peculiar. Either he had shrunk or Thomas and Beatrice had grown, for now he was exactly the same size as both of them.

"Oh, my!" said Thomas, who had shrugged off Beatrice's remarks, "Peter, let me introduce to you our new friend.

Ah . . . What did you say your name was?"

4

目录室

埃德温感到一阵头晕目眩。他环顾四周，发现来到了一个宽敞的房间内。漂亮的图画装饰着墙壁，天花板上悬挂着闪闪发光的水晶吊灯。房间中央摆放着一张巨大的桌子，坐在桌首的是一位个子不高、大腹便便的男士，他身着深色的西服，很有贵族气派。他的左眼戴着单片眼镜。

"啊，碧翠丝，你今天**看上去**真美！"他开口说道。

随后，他走到碧翠丝面前，像王子接待公主一样抬起她的手吻了一下。

"哦，谢谢你，彼得，"碧翠丝一边说，一边把发丝向后轻轻地一甩，"我也觉得自己今天特别漂亮。"

"你今天还特别虚荣呢。"托马斯受够了碧翠丝的自以为是，不屑一顾地说道。

"托马斯·**这个**！别忘了你的身份！你不过是个出身平庸的冠词——连个贵族身份都没有。"

说完这些，碧翠丝便取出化妆镜，开始整理那几根散乱的头发。

"好吧，至少我不会像某些我所认识的形容词那样自高自大。"托马斯说道，满脸挑衅地直视着碧翠丝。

这时，埃德温才注意到一个奇妙的变化。不知道是他自己变小了，还是托马斯和碧翠丝变大了，他的身高现在跟他们已经完全相同的大小了。

托马斯把碧翠丝丢到一边，突然说道："噢，天啊！"

"彼得，我来跟你介绍一下我们的新朋友，呃……你刚才说你叫什么来着？"

Edwin, a bit startled, mumbled, sputtered, and finally remembered his name was Edwin.

"E . . . d Ed . . . win, sir."

He couldn't believe how stupid he sounded. It was as though his mouth was full of jellybeans. Unfortunately, his nerves were getting the better of him.

"Ah, yes, Peter. This is Edwin. He has come to save our book."

"REALLY?" replied Peter. His monocle dropped off his face. "Well, then. Welcome! Welcome! I'm a specialist at introductions. Allow me to introduce myself. My name is Peter Preface."

Edwin extended his hand and Peter grabbed it and proceeded to shake it about a hundred and seventeen times, saying "Welcome" after every tenth time. Edwin finally got his hand back but it had fallen asleep. He decided to start shaking it to get rid of the tingling feeling. Unfortunately, Peter interpreted that as a sign Edwin wanted to continue shaking his hand so shaking and Welcomes continued for another hundred and seventeen times.

"Excuse me," said Edwin, quite exhausted and cowering with his hands pressed tightly in his pockets. "Where am I?"

"Ah, my dear boy! Welcome, welcome!" cried Peter.

Edwin cringed, checking to make sure both hands were concealed.

"Welcome to the Contents Room," continued Peter. "And, if you look over there, you will find the Table of Contents."

Edwin looked at the long mahogany table that snaked its way around the room. Seated at the table were people of every description, each holding a different sign. They looked like salespeople at a giant flea market.

"What goes on there?" asked Edwin, more out of politeness than interest.

"That is where a visitor can get travel information about particular places in our book."

埃德温怔了一下，好半天才回过神来，结结巴巴嗫嚅着说出了"埃德温"三个字。

"埃……埃德……埃德温，先生。"

埃德温简直难以相信自己的声音听起来有多傻气，就好像他的嘴里塞满了果冻豆似的。不幸的是，他的脑子仿佛也不大好使了。

"哦，对了，彼得，这位是埃德温。他是来拯救我们的书。"

"**真的吗**？"彼得问道，他的单片眼镜惊得从脸上掉了下来，"哎呀，那么，欢迎！欢迎！我可是最善于引荐的专家啊。请允许我自我介绍一下。我的名字叫彼得·前言。"

彼得一把抓住了埃德温伸过来的手，摇了大约一百一十七下，每摇十下，他就会加上一句"欢迎。"埃德温终于抽回了手，但是他的手早已经麻了。他本想甩甩胳膊，减轻手上的刺麻感，但不幸的是，彼得以为埃德温想再握一次手。于是，他又抓住埃德温的手使劲摇了一百一十七下，还忙不迭地说着"欢迎。"

"抱歉，"埃德温问道，"不过谁能告诉我，这是什么地方呀？"他可是累坏了，只得小心翼翼地把双手都缩回口袋里。

"啊，亲爱的孩子！欢迎，欢迎！"彼得大声说道。

埃德温向后退了一步，双手紧紧地攥在口袋里，一下也不敢拿出来。

"欢迎来到目录室。"彼得继续说道，"你要是朝这边看，就能看见目录表的内容。"

埃德温看着那张长方形桃花心木桌子，绕着房间内一路蜿蜒。桌子旁坐着形形色色的人，每个人手中都拿着不同的标志。他们看上去就像在一个巨大的跳蚤市场内的销售员。

"这是怎么回事？"埃德温的问题明显是出于礼貌性，丝毫不感兴趣。

"游客们在参观这本书里的景点时，可以从这儿获得旅游信息。"

Peter ushered Edwin to the table along with Thomas who was busily trying to drag Beatrice away from her mirror.

"You see," said Peter, pointing to a particular area of the table, "that is where you can find out what happens in Chapter 7."

Peter was pointing at a rather suspicious-looking man holding up a sign that read "Chapter 7: The Adventure of a Lifetime" . The man winked and Edwin felt a sudden urge to walk toward the table. Peter yanked Edwin's arm and positioned himself between Edwin and the table.

"Be warned, Edwin!" whispered Peter. "The signs those people are holding can be very inviting. But they can also be very misleading. You never know exactly what those guys have in mind or where they will be taking you. Be very wary of holding them to their word."

Edwin looked back at the table and the strange characters trying to flog their wares. One sign read, "Chapter 1: The Adventure Begins". Another sign boasted, "Travel the World in Chapter 4: Only a hundred and twenty pages away".

Edwin became mesmerized with the buzz of activity and the lure of the great table. Finally he looked back to where Peter was standing and Peter smiled.

For a moment, Edwin didn't know what to make of the bizarre scene. At last, he regained his composure.

"Excuse me, Mr. Preface, but how am I to help you? I mean, what AM I doing here?"

"Ah, a good question, young Edwin," said Peter. "You are in what grade at the present time?"

"The sixth grade . . . I mean, I've just finished the fifth grade."

"I see," said Peter, "And what are you learning in your English class?"

"Well, we are reading a few books, and of course we learn how to write and . . ."

彼得将埃德温和托马斯领至桌前，此刻托马斯正忙着说服碧翠丝放下手里的镜子。

"你瞧，"彼得指着桌旁的一个人说道，"在他那里你可以了解到有关第7章的内容。"

埃德温顺着彼得指的方向看去。一名怪模怪样的男子手里正举着一块标志牌，上书："第七章：一生的探险"。他冲埃德温眨了眨眼睛，埃德温真想立刻就冲过去一探究竟。彼得赶紧拉了埃德温一把，却拦在了他和桌子之间。

"小心点，埃德温！"彼得低声说道，"这些人手里的标志看起来可能很引诱人，但也极具迷惑性。你永远不知道他们心里究竟打的什么鬼主意，也不知道他们会带你去向什么地方，对他们要小心提防才是。"

埃德温回头看了看桌前那些表情怪异的人，他们都在摆弄着自己的标志牌，渴望引起他的注意。一块标志牌上写着："第一章：探险启程"，而另一块则写着："第四章：环游世界——距此地仅120页之遥"。

闹哄哄的场面让埃德温都看呆了，他迫不及待地想走过去弄个明白。但他终于回过神来，回过头看看彼得站在那里冲他笑一笑。

一时间，埃德温竟然不敢相信自己的眼睛。他好不容易才定下神来。

"抱歉，前言先生，我要怎样才能帮到您呢？我是说，我在这儿到底能做什么呢？"

"嗯，问得好，年轻人，"彼得赞道，"你现在上几年级了呀？"

"六年级……我的意思是，我刚刚读完小学五年级。"埃德温答道。

"我知道了，"彼得说，"那你们在英语课程都学些什么呢？"

"嗯，我们学习了几本名著，当然还学了如何写作和……"

"AH HA!!!" bellowed Peter, almost knocking Edwin head over heels. "Then you MUST help us—you WILL help us!"

"But how?" asked Edwin, becoming quite annoyed with the whole situation.

"Don't you see?" said Peter impatiently. "This book has been stuck here for such a long time, the words in here think they are no longer important. When they find out you are a young boy who is learning how to read, they won't want to work for HIM."

Edwin, now very tired and still very much confused, turned to everyone and said, "Are you guys joshing me?"

Everyone in the room froze.

"**啊哈**！！！"彼得大叫了一声，吓得埃德温差点跌倒在地。

"那你**必须**得帮我们——你可**一定**要帮我们！"

"怎么帮呀？"埃德温问道，他被这整个事况折腾得有点恼火了。

"你难道还不明白吗？"彼得不耐烦地说，"这本书被困在这儿实在太久了，以至于大家都认为自己不再重要了。但是如果大家知道还有像你这样的孩子正在学习阅读，那么就不会愿意为**他**工作了。"

疲惫不堪的埃德温心里满是疑惑，他转身对其他人说道："你们是在拿我寻开心吗？"

房间里静得出奇，空气仿佛凝固了一般。

5

DROW

The members of the group stared into each other's eyes. They had a look of panic on their faces. Even Edwin felt scared.

What have I done? he thought to himself. Then he heard some whispering.

"Maybe he's a spy for HIM," said Thomas under his breath.

"No, not that CUTE little boy," said Beatrice in Edwin's defence.

Edwin finally got up the courage to talk.

"What's the matter?" he asked.

"We . . . w . . . we were wondering whether you are on HIS side?" said Peter.

"Who is HE?" asked Edwin.

"Oh, thank heavens. We thought you worked for Drow."

"Drow?!" exclaimed Edwin.

"Yes, Drow!" repeated Peter.

"You see, many years ago we were a peaceful group of words. We lived happily together in sentences."

"You mean families," said Edwin.

"No, sentences. In the world of books, we have different names for things," said Peter.

"But I don't understand," said Edwin. "Didn't somebody already write this book? I mean, whoever was the author of this book wrote all the sentences."

"My dear boy, those are quite different sorts of sentences. Look!

5

卓尔

房间里的其他人你盯着我，我看着你，互视了好一会儿。他们的脸上露出恐慌的神色，这令埃德温不寒而栗。

他心下暗想：我做了些什么呀？接着，他听到一阵窃窃低语声。

"说不准这个人是**他**派来的奸细呢。"托马斯压低嗓门儿说道。

"不会的，怎么可能是这么**可爱的**小男孩呢。"碧翠丝忍不住帮埃德温辩护。

埃德温终于鼓足勇气开了口。

"这到底是怎么回事？"他问道。

"我们……我……我们想知道你是不是**他**的人？"彼得说道。

"**他**是谁？"埃德温满腹疑惑。

"哦，谢天谢地——我们还以为你是卓尔的人呢。"

"卓尔？"埃德温大声问道。

"没错，卓尔！"彼得重复道。

"话说，很多年前，我们都只是一群爱好和平的单词。我们快乐地生活在句子里。"

"您是指单词家族吧？"埃德温说道。

"不，句子。在书的世界里，我们使用的是另一套不同的名称。"彼得解释道。

"那我就不懂了，"埃德温说道，"这本书难道不是某一位作家写的吗？我是说，到底是谁写出了书里的所有句子呢？"

"亲爱的孩子，那些都是非常不同的排序句子。瞧！想象一下人类工

What happens when somebody goes to work? They go to a factory or an office and they work with other people. Sometimes, you refer to them as 'one big happy family'. But really, they're only a family when they're doing their job. And so you see, when someone picks up this book, we must go to our jobs."

"You mean, all the sentences in this book are like little factories or businesses," said Edwin, beginning to understand.

"That's right!" said Peter approvingly, "They exist only when somebody opens the book. At all other times, most words are carrying on their own lives."

"But, other books have words like 'beautiful' and 'the'. Are you in those books, too?" asked Edwin.

"Do you know what cloning is?" asked Peter.

"Yes, it's when something is made to be exactly the same."

"Yes, sort of like that. Anyway, we have all been cloned so we can be used in thousands of books. What people don't know is that we can also move between books."

"I don't understand," said Edwin.

"If our book is within six feet of another book, we can exchange roles: Thomas The, for example, can enter any book that is within six feet of ours and assume the role of Thomas The in that book, the Thomas The in the other book can enter our book and assume his role here. It's great because it allows us to travel and experience different adventures. The only rule is that to move between books, the word that is moving has to exist in both books."

"But what does this Drow guy have to do with anything?" asked Edwin.

"Since our book has been stuck in here for such a long time, everyone has become very lazy. Sentence life is falling to bits and now Drow is beginning to control our lives."

"Who is this Drow?" asked Edwin.

作的情景吧！人们得去一家工厂，或者去一栋办公楼，然后与其他人一起工作。有时候，人类将工作单位称为'快乐的大家庭'。但实际上，当他们都在做自己的工作时，他们才是一个家庭。同理，只有当人类在阅读这本书时，我们才必须去做我们的工作。"

"你的意思是，这本书里所有的句子就好比一家工厂或公司。"埃德温说道，他渐渐理出了一点头绪。

"没错！"彼得点头说道，"如果没有人读书，句子就不存在了。在那些时间里，大部分单词都忙着各过各的生活。"

"但是，其他书里也有'美丽'和'这个'这些单词呀。那你们也同时住在其他书里吗？"埃德温问道。

"你听过复制翻版吗？"彼得问道。

"知道，就是原样复制的意思。"

"是的，差不多就这意思。所有的单词都是复制的，这样我们就可以同时出现在成千上万本书之中。但人类有所不知的是，我们还可以在书籍之间移动并肆意穿行。"

"这我就不懂了。"埃德温说道。

"如果两本书之间的距离不超过6英尺，我们就可以互换角色：比方说，当我们的书与其他书的距离在6英尺之内时，咱们的托马斯·这个跟另一本书里的托马斯·这个就可以随意穿梭并互换角色。这其实挺有意思，因为我们可以到处旅行，体验不同生活带来的惊喜。唯一的规则就是，单词必须脱离书本，才能在两本书之间穿梭。"

"但是，那个叫卓尔的家伙跟这个又有什么关系啊？"埃德温问道。

"咱们的书被困在这儿太久了，所以大家都变得懒洋洋的。句子也变得分崩离析，而卓尔一直想要控制我们的生活。"

"但是，卓尔到底是谁呀？"埃德温问道。

Peter sighed. "Drow is an Active Verb who appeared one day on the inner sleeve of our book's cover. I think some kid doodled the word 'Drow' during his English class. Anyway, somehow Drow penetrated our book. He then formed a secret organization known as Alphabet Soup. His band of cronies and misfits recruits perfectly good words who eventually agree to take on new names."

"But what does Drow want?" asked Edwin, becoming more fascinated by the minute.

"Drow wants to rewrite our story," said Peter sadly. "And if we don't stop him soon, *we* won't have a story to tell. Our lives will be over."

"I see," said Edwin, concerned.

"That's why we reacted so strangely when you said 'joshing.' The word 'joshing' does not exist in our story," said Peter.

"We're sorry if we scared you," said Beatrice, trying to comfort Edwin. "But we're all a bit paranoid right now."

"Look, don't get me wrong," continued Peter. "It's not that we don't like other words. We actually do. It's just that Drow wants to rewrite our story with *all* new words. His words haven't proven themselves in our story nor have they stood the test of time the way we have," he said, his eyes tearing up.

Everyone, including Edwin, felt uneasy and awkward.

"Look, Edwin," said Peter, wiping his eyes. "If we are to save our story, we must stop Drow. But to be honest, we need your help! All the words that have joined Alphabet Soup need to be told they are still useful and that our story is still worth telling. But only you can convince them of that, Edwin. You must be prepared to tell them that people from the outside world still like a good book like ours."

At that moment, the door of the Contents Room burst open and in walked a man wearing a white lab coat and little spectacles on his nose. In his jacket pocket, he carried a large assortment of pens and pencils.

彼得叹了一口气。"卓尔是一个主动动词，不知道从哪一天开始，他就出现在这本书的内套上了。我猜可能是哪个顽皮的孩子上英语课时，在书上随手写下了'卓尔'这个词。反正，卓尔就这样侵入了我们的世界。不久，他就成立了一个名为'字母汤'的秘密军团。他集结了一大帮爪牙到处游说，胁迫那些善良正派的单词们改名。"

"卓尔到底想要做什么呢？"埃德温变得更好奇了。

"卓尔想要改写我们的故事，"彼得伤心地说，"如果不立即阻止他，我们的故事就将这样结束了，而我们的生命也将走向终点。"

"我明白了。"埃德温努力表现出关心的样子。

"这就是为什么当你说'寻开心'，我们的反应如此奇怪的原因。我们这本书里压根就没'寻开心'这个词。"彼得说道。

"要是我们吓到你了，我真的很抱歉，"碧翠丝努力安慰着埃德温，"但是，我们现在都有点草木皆兵了。"

"希望你没有误会我的意思，"彼得继续说道，"倒不是说我们不喜欢外来的单词，事实上我们挺喜欢他们的。但是卓尔企图用新的单词取代我们这些老单词，那些单词并不适用于我们的故事，而且并不像我们这样久经考验。"他说着，两眼泛出泪光。

埃德温和在场的其他人都面面相觑。

"所以啊，埃德温，"彼得揉了揉湿润的眼眶，说道，"如果我们要拯救我们的故事，就必须制止卓尔。不过，我就实话说了吧，我们需要你的帮助！我们应该设法通知那些加入了字母汤军团的单词，让他们知道自己并非一无是处，我们的故事也从未被人遗忘。但是，埃德温，只有你才能说服他们相信这些事实。你应该心里准备好就去告诉他们，人类对我们这类优秀的著作仍然津津乐道。"

就在这一刻，目录室的门突然开了，一名相貌滑稽的男子走了进来，他身着白大褂，鼻梁上还架着一副眼镜。上衣口袋内装带一大排各式各样的钢笔和铅笔。

As this strange person walked across the room, he seemed completely unaware of Edwin and the others. He kept walking until he plowed right into a wall on the opposite side of the room. But he didn't stop there. His feet kept moving even though his body was pinned against the wall. He looked like a stuck battery-operated robot.

"Oh, my! Oh, dear!" cried Peter. "Thomas! Beatrice! Quickly! Before the Professor hurts himself."

Peter rushed over to the man, followed by Thomas and Beatrice who were carrying a stretcher.

"There, there, Professor. Don't worry. We'll help you," cried Peter.

The Professor mumbled something unintelligible and tried to keep walking even though his body was firmly against the wall.

Thomas and Beatrice placed their stretcher behind the Professor. With a tap of his finger, Peter pushed the Professor backward. PLONK! The Professor landed securely on the stretcher. No sooner was he prostrate, Thomas and Beatrice turned the stretcher around and lunged it forward. The Professor flew gracefully through the air and landed on his feet.

"Welcome! Welcome!" called out Peter.

"Ah, Peter, there you are. I was just looking for you down the hallway over there."

"I don't see a ha . . ." said Edwin.

"Shhhhh!" said Thomas, interrupting Edwin in mid-sentence. "You must pretend there is a hallway. Unfortunately, the Professor is in a world of his own. He's so focused on his material that at times he's completely oblivious to what's going on around him. We don't want to hurt his feelings."

"Yes, Professor, that certainly is a long hallway," said Peter, winking at the others. "Anyway, we are very glad you're here. Edwin, this is Professor I.N. Dex. The Professor has travelled all the way from the back of the book. He can help you prepare for your mission."

这名行迹古怪的男子大步穿过房间，似乎完全无视埃德温和其他人的存在。他径直走到对面的墙边，但是并没有停下脚步，即使身体已经贴着墙面，他的腿却还在往前踏步，看上去活像一个卡了壳的电动机器人。

"噢，天啊！噢，我的天！"彼得大声喊道，"托马斯！碧翠丝！快啊！别让教授伤着自己。"

彼得赶忙到那名身着白大褂的男子身边，托马斯和碧翠丝抬着担架紧随其后。

"好啦，好啦，教授，别紧张，我们会帮您的。"彼得大声说道。

教授只是含糊不清地喃喃自语着，虽然身体不能动弹，双脚却继续踢打着墙壁。

托马斯和碧翠丝把担架放到教授身后。随后，彼得轻轻把教授往后一推。**扑通**！教授猛地一下躺到了担架上，托马斯和碧翠丝立即把担架掉过头来，往前一摇。教授从空中划过一道弧线，稳稳地站在了地上。

"欢迎！欢迎！"彼得大声说道。

"啊，彼得，原来是你呀。我正在走廊那头找你呢。"

埃德温顺着教授指的方向看去。

"我没看到一条走……"埃德温答道。

"嘘！"托马斯急忙打断了埃德温说，"你必须假装那有一条走廊就行了。可怜的教授总是沉浸在他自己的世界里。他对自己的研究太过专注，有时完全忽视了身边的人和事。我们不想伤害他。"

"是的，教授，那可真是一条长长的走廊啊，"彼得向其他人使了个眼色，"不管怎么说，我们很高兴在这儿见到您。埃德温，这是I.N.德克斯教授。他是从封底不远万里赶到这里来的，他可以帮助你为你的使命行动做准备。"

"Hello, Mr. Professor, sir," said Edwin, not knowing the proper way to address a professor.

"Well, he—llo, young boy," said the Professor. "A pleasure, indeed."

The Professor extended his hand to Beatrice, thinking she was Edwin. Beatrice gently pushed the Professor's hand toward Edwin, who quickly grabbed it.

"Well, now that all the important introductions are over, we must work quickly," said Peter. "The Professor is the only person who knows everyone and everything that exists in this book. He will be able to tell us the whereabouts of Drow."

The sound of snoring suddenly filled the room.

"Wake up, Professor," cried Peter, shaking him.

"Wha . . . ? Who . . . ? Where . . . ?"

"Drow, sir. You were going to tell us about him," said Peter politely.

"Oh, yes, yes, of course. Drow! He has taken over much of our story," said the Professor. "If my memory serves me correctly, Drow first appeared on the inner sleeve of the book. He then started to lure words away from their sentences by offering them a better life. Once he had recruited enough words to create his own sentences, he entered our book and disappeared. He hasn't been seen since. But even though nobody knows the exact whereabouts of Drow, the force of his power can be felt throughout the book. Slowly, ever so slowly, he is rewriting our story."

"Rotten stuff, this Drow," said Peter grimly. "But Professor, how can we go after Drow if we don't know where he's holding out?"

The Professor bent his head toward the ground and started pacing back and forth. He looked like a world leader contemplating the fate of his nation. The rest of the group watched the Professor like spectators at a tennis match. Suddenly, he stopped and looked up at the group.

"If you really wanted to go after Drow, I think a trip to the Neergreve Forest is in order."

"您好，教授先生，呃，先生。"埃德温不知如何称呼这位教授才算得体。

"啊，你……好啊，孩子，"教授说道，"见到你实在是荣幸之至。"

这位教授把碧翠丝错当成埃德温，把手伸了过去。碧翠丝轻轻地把教授的手推向埃德温，埃德温立刻握住了教授的手。

"好了，既然大家都已经见过面了，我们最好马上开始该做的工作，"彼得说道，"只有教授对这本书里的一人一物、一草一木了若指掌，他能帮我们查出卓尔的下落。"

房间里突然响起了一阵鼾声。

"醒一醒，教授。"彼得喊道，试图把他从梦中摇醒。

"什……么？是……谁呀？这是……在哪儿？"他吞吞吐吐地问。

"卓尔，先生。您刚才正打算说出他的藏身之处。"彼得毕恭毕敬地回答。

"哦，是的，是的，没错。卓尔！他已经改写了大半个故事。"教授说道，"如果我没记错的话，卓尔最早只是出现在这本书的内套上。不久，他就软硬兼施，欺骗书里的单词说要带他们过上更优渥的生活，以此诱惑他们离开句子。他集结了大批单词组建了自己的句子，在我们的书里到处为非作歹，然后就凭空消失了，再也没有露面。不过，即使别人不知道他的确切下落，我仍然能隔着厚厚的书页闻到他霸占高位时散发出的那股子腐臭味，他正在一步步慢慢改写着我们的故事。"

"卓尔真是个可恶的家伙，"彼得咬牙切齿地说，"但是，教授，如果他下落不明，那我们怎样才能找到他呢？"

教授低下头来，在原地来回踱着步。他就像一位伟大的领袖，正在思考着江山社稷的兴衰存亡。房间里的其他人就像网球比赛中的观众一样急切地等待着教授揭晓答案。突然，教授陷入了沉默，转眼看着身边的人。

"如果你们真的想要追捕到卓尔，那么肯定得去尼尔格雷夫森林一趟。"

"The Neergreve Forest!" exclaimed everyone in unison.

"Yes, rumour has it that Drow's headquarters are located deep in the Neergreve forest but alas, that has not been confirmed."

"But I don't remember such a place, Professor," said Peter. "I am sure our Table of Contents has no information about a forest with that name."

"Yes, you are right. The whole forest is uncharted. It was created after Drow took over a number of chapters in the middle of the book. Very little is known about the place. But mark my word: Drow will do everything in his power to prevent you from getting near him. Legend has it that if Drow is exposed to a sentence that does not contain one of his words, he will turn into an 'et cet er a' and float off into oblivion."

"Oooooooh," said Peter.

"You must therefore travel in a sentence," continued the Professor. "If any one of you gets separated from the group, it could spell doom for you all. There are Alphabet Soup spies everywhere! They call themselves 'The Mumbojumbos'. Some of them are animals. They will do everything they can to win you over."

The Professor stopped talking and dozed off again, occasionally muttering the word "Drow" between snores.

"Oh, my! Oh, dear! Let me see. We have an Article and an Adjective. Thomas and Beatrice, you had better get packing," said Peter, pacing the floor. "But we still need the two most important words in a sentence."

Suddenly Edwin recalled something his English teacher often repeated during writing class. "If you don't have a Noun and a Verb, you don't have a sentence."

"I know!" blurted Edwin. "The two most important parts of a sentence are the Noun and the Verb."

"That's right," said Peter. "Oh! Thomas! Before you rush off, would you please call in Felix and Bartholomew?"

"尼尔格雷夫森林！"众人异口同声地惊叫起来。

"是的，传说卓尔的总部就是位于尼尔格雷夫森林的深处，但是，唉，我们并没有证据证明这点。"

"但我从没听过有这样一个地方，教授，"彼得说道，"我敢肯定目录室并没有这片森林的相关信息。"

"是的，你说得没错，地图上并未显示这片森林。卓尔攻占了这本书中间的部分章节后，就开辟了那片森林，很少有人知道那个地方。但是，记住我的话：卓尔肯定会竭尽全力阻止你们接近他的。传说如果卓尔遇到一个并非由他的爪牙组成的句子，他就会化为'乌有'，烟消云散。"

"哦哦哦……噢。"彼得说道。

"所以，你们必须组成一个句子才能前往那片森林，"教授继续说道，"期间如果有任何单词脱离了句子，将会给其他单词带来灭顶之灾。字母汤军团的间谍无孔不入！他们自称'胡言军团'，他们中有些人残暴凶狠，一定会不惜一切代价反你们的。"

这时，教授再次陷入沉默，打起了瞌睡，在呼呼的鼾声中不时听见"卓尔"两个字从他嘴里蹦出来。

"噢，天啊！噢，我的天！让我想想：我们这儿有一个冠词和一个形容词。托马斯和碧翠丝，你俩最好现在去打点行装。"彼得一边在房间里来回踱着步，一边安排着说，"但是，如果没有句子里最重要的那两个单词，我们根本没法上路啊。"

就在这时，埃德温想起了英语老师曾在写作课上总是反复强调地这么说："如果没有名词和动词，就无法构成一个完整的句子。"

"我知道了！"埃德温脱口而出，"一个句子最重要的部分是名词和动词。"

"说得没错，"彼得说道，"哦！托马斯！麻烦你在出发前，把菲利克斯和巴塞洛缪找来好吗？"

So Thomas headed off in one direction while Beatrice—after busily assembling combs, brushes, hair dryers, and make-up kits—dashed off in the other direction, calling out, "But I have nothing to wear and my hair's a mess!"

Edwin, completely engrossed in the story of Drow, had forgotten where he was. But as soon as everyone started to leave, he realized he had been in the Contents Room an awfully long time.

"Excuse me, Mr. Preface," he said, "but can we start this mission soon? I have to get home for supper."

"What's that? Pardon?" said Peter, not really paying too much attention to Edwin.

"When are we going on this mission?" Edwin asked impatiently.

"Oh, ahh . . . tomorrow, right after breakfast," said Peter, pacing back and forth.

"TOMORROW!!!" cried Edwin. "I can't stay in here until tomorrow! My uncle will be worried! My mother will ground me for a century!"

Peter realized Edwin was getting himself into an awful state.

"Don't worry, Edwin. You should know that time in books is not at all the same as your time. Each minute of your time equals one week in book time."

"Wow!" said Edwin. "That means . . . "

"Right, that means if you spent a year in this book, you would have wasted only 48 minutes in your time."

Edwin smiled. He was glad he didn't have to go home yet.

随后，托马斯和碧翠丝就分头行动——碧翠丝忙着整理她的梳子、刷子、吹风机和化妆包——使劲地往另一个方向去，嘴里不停地嚷嚷着："我没有漂亮的衣服可穿，而且，我的发型简直就是一团糟呢！"

卓尔的故事彻头彻尾地迷住了埃德温，他几乎忘了自己身在何方。但是看着身旁忙着打点行装的单词，他突然意识到自己已经在这里待了很长一段时间。

"很抱歉，前言先生，"他说道，"我们能不能马上开始行动呢？我还得赶回家吃晚饭呢。"

"什么？你说什么？"彼得对埃德温的问题漫不经心随口答道。

"我们什么时候开始行动呢？"埃德温再次问道，心里多了几分不耐烦。

"哦，啊……明天，早餐过后。"彼得还在来回踱着步。

"**明天**！"埃德温失声大叫起来，"我可不能在这儿过夜！叔叔会担心我的！母亲要是知道了，没准会罚我永远不准出门呢！"

彼得抬起头来，看出了埃德温焦躁的情绪。

"别担心，埃德温。你要知道，人类世界的时间观念和咱们书里可完全是两码事啊。外面的一分钟相当于咱们这儿的一个星期呢。"

"哇！"埃德温吃惊地说："那不就意味着……"

"没错，那意味着，即使你在这本书里待上一年，外面的世界也不过才过了48分钟而已。"

埃德温释然了。现在不用着急回家的事了，这让他松了一口气。

6

FELIX AND BARTHOLOMEW

The door of the Contents Room burst open and Thomas walked briskly back into the room carrying a knapsack on his back. He looked like an overgrown Boy Scout. He saluted Peter and said, "Ready for your command, sir!" Then Beatrice arrived with her luggage—about eighteen suitcases on wheels and tied together to form a chain.

"And WHAT do you think all of that is?" demanded Thomas, pointing to Beatrice's suitcase entourage.

"Well," said Beatrice, pondering the contents of each case. "This suitcase has all my morning wear; this one has my late-morning wear; this one contains all my old clothes that I don't really care about; and . . . "

"I didn't realize you owned any OLD clothes," said Thomas sarcastically.

"Oh, yes! I bought them yesterday. They're really quite worn out. But, if we get captured or tortured, I won't have to worry that they will be ruined."

"Of course not," said Thomas, slapping his head in complete disbelief.

Suddenly, there was a bang, then a thump.

"Gangway, everybody!"

The door of the Contents Room flew open. There, standing on the threshold was a short, muscular man in a mechanic's outfit with a tool kit around his waist.

"Ah, Felix. So glad you could make it. Welcome! Welcome! Welcome!" said Peter.

"So we're finally going after Drow, are we?" said the man with a long drawl.

6

菲利克斯和巴塞洛缪

目录室的门突然开了，托马斯迈着轻快的步伐走了进来。他背着一个背包，看上去就像是一名超龄童子军。他向彼得敬礼后说道："一切准备就绪，就等您的指令了，先生！"就看见碧翠丝也拖着行李走了进来。

她带来了18个滚轮行李箱，一个连着一个鱼贯而入。

"你这大费周章都是些**什么**东西呀？"托马斯指着碧翠丝的一大排行李箱问道。

"哦，"碧翠丝一边努力回想着每个箱子里的行李，一边解释道，"这个箱子装的是我所有的晨衣，这个是上午的裙装，这里是我所有的旧衣服，反正破了也不心疼，至于那个嘛……"

"你居然还有**旧**衣服啊，我还不知道呢。"托马斯挖苦道。

"那肯定啦！是我昨天买的，都是些又破又旧的衣服。不过，如果我们被俘或受刑，我就不用担心那些旧衣服被糟蹋了。"

"说得还有点道理。"托马斯拍了拍自己的脑袋，一副完全不信的表情。

突然，响起砰的一声，然后是沉闷的撞击声。

"让一让！大家让一让！"

目录室的门被猛地撞开了，门口站着一位个子不高但体格健壮的男子。他身着机修工工作服，腰间别着一个便携工具包。

"啊，菲利克斯，你能来我太高兴了。欢迎！欢迎！欢迎！"彼得说道。

"这么说，我们终于要去追捕卓尔了，是吗？"这名男子拖长着音调说道。

"Yes! Yes! At last," said Peter.

"Edwin, I would like you to meet Felix Fix. He is the Verb who will be accompanying you on your mission. He loves doing things. He will prove very useful if you ever get into trouble."

"Good to meet you, Ed. Glad to have you aboard," said Felix, as he smacked Edwin on the back, almost causing him to fall flat on his face.

"Thh . . . ank you," said Edwin, getting his wind back.

"Now, all we need is our Noun and we're set," said Peter confidently.

"Who is our Noun, Pete?" asked Felix.

"Hi, everybody! I'm here!"

They all turned in the direction of the door. There stood a short, pudgy boy with large black-rimmed glasses with tape wrapped around the part that sat over his nose. His pants seemed too short and his jacket too small. His belt, buckled very tightly around his waist, carried a portable calculator. A long pencil was perched on his right ear.

"OH, NO! IT'S BARTHOLOMEW BOOK!" cried Felix.

"Now stop that, Felix," asserted Peter. "We need a good Noun like Bart. He's intelligent, he's resourceful . . . "

"And he's a nerd!" exclaimed Felix.

"The fact that you have to use an immature word like 'nerd' instead of a nice, respectable word like, say . . . 'gauche', simply shows that you and your tool kit are unfit for this mission. So there!" Bartholomew exclaimed.

Felix raised his fists. His face looked like a fat beet about to explode. Peter and Thomas quickly held him back.

"Look!" cried Peter, becoming quite flustered. "I'm counting on all of you to work together as one unified sentence. You must put your differences aside. Now shake hands and make up!"

Felix, who was kicking and pulling like a mad bull, finally said, "Alright, alright. As long as HE doesn't get in my way!"

"I wouldn't dream of it!" Bartholomew said sarcastically.

"是的！是的！终于等到这一天了。"彼得说道。

"埃德温，请容我向你介绍菲利克斯·修理。他是一个动词，这次行动他将陪伴在你左右。他很有两把刷子，如果你陷入困境，他一定能助你脱险。"

"很高兴见到你，小埃。能与你能一同参与这次行动，我感到很荣幸。"菲利克斯在埃德温的后背猛地拍了一掌，震得埃德温差点摔了个狗啃泥。

"谢……谢您！"埃德温说道，好不容易定了定神。

"好了，只要名词一到，我们就万事俱备了。"彼得胸有成竹地说道。

"你找的哪个名词呀，老彼？"菲利克斯问道。

"嗨，大家好！我来啦！"

众人转过身看向门口，门口站着一个胖鼓鼓、矮墩墩的男孩。他戴着大大的黑框眼镜，眼镜的鼻梁上缠着胶带。他的裤子短得吊在腿上，外套也显得紧巴巴的。他的皮带紧紧地勒在腰间，上面还别着便携式计算器，右耳后夹着一支细长的铅笔。

"**哦，不会吧！你居然找来了巴塞洛缪·书**！"菲利克斯大叫了起来。

"少来这套了，菲利克斯，"彼得叫道，"我们需要小巴这样优秀的名词，他的脑筋灵活，又足智多谋……"

"还是个十足的书呆子呢！"菲利克斯叫道。

"听听，出口就是'书呆子'，连'学究'这些礼貌用语都不懂，看得出像你这种肤浅粗鲁的家伙还有你的工具完全不适合参加这次的行动。鉴定完毕！"巴塞洛缪揶揄道。

菲利克斯攥紧了拳头，他气得涨红了脸，好像随时都要爆炸了。彼得和托马斯赶紧拉住了他。

"好啦！"彼得神色紧张地大声说道，"我还指望你们能团结一致，组成一个句子共同进退呢，你们必须把对彼此的不满都暂且放下。现在，握手言和吧！"

菲利克斯一开始就像头疯牛似的又是推搡又是挥拳，最后不得不退让了一步地说："好吧，好吧，只要**他**答应不挡我的道。"

"我要是你就不会抱这种幻想！"巴塞洛缪讽刺道。

The two begrudgingly shook hands and Thomas and Peter cautiously let go of Felix.

"Good! Now, that's settled, would you all please stand in a line so I can arrange you into a sentence," said Peter.

"Let's see! FIX BEAUTIFUL THE BOOK? No, no, no, no! Change positions!"

All the words moved to different places in the line while Peter took another look.

"BEAUTIFUL THE BOOK FIX? Oh, dear, that won't work either," said Peter, quite disgruntled.

"I've got it!" shouted Edwin. "How about FIX THE BEAUTIFUL BOOK!?"

"Yes! Marvellous! You're brilliant, Edwin!" cried Peter.

The words immediately rearranged themselves to form the sentence FIX THE BEAUTIFUL BOOK!

"But wait!" cried Thomas, "We forgot to include Edwin."

"Yes, of course, of course. How silly of me to forget," said Peter.

"No problem," cried Bartholomew, "Just make it FIX THE BEAUTIFUL BOOK, EDWIN!"

"Marvellous! Very forceful! Full of confidence! Yes, I like it," exclaimed Peter.

"Lucky guess," grumbled Felix.

"Then we're all set!" said Peter.

"Felix, how long will it take to prepare the F.L.A.B.?"

"It will be ready by tomorrow, Pete."

"The F.L.A.B.?" asked Edwin.

"That's right, Ed. **F**elix's **L**ong-winded **A**ir **B**alloon! I'm rather proud of it. It can take us anywhere in the book. Once it starts, it just keeps on going," said Felix proudly.

"Is that how we're getting to the Neergreve Forest?" asked Edwin.

看到两个人极不乐意地握了握手，托马斯和彼得才小心翼翼地放开了菲利克斯。

"好了！现在，旧账一笔勾销，请大家站成一排，我要把你们编成一个句子。"彼得说道。

彼得将所有单词排成一排。

"我来看看！**修复美妙的这本书**？不行，不行，不行，不行！交换位置！"

所有单词互换了位置，然后重新排成一排，以便彼得再次过目。

"**美妙的这本书修复**？哦，天啊，这更说不通了。"彼得气恼地说。

"我知道了！"埃德温大叫起来，"**修复这本美妙的书，大伙儿觉得怎么样**！？"

"妙哉！妙哉！你真是个天才，埃德温！"彼得大声说道。

所有单词迅速列队，组成了新的句子：**修复这本美妙的书**！

"且慢！"托马斯说道，"我们忘了把埃德温放进句子里了。"

"是呀，对呀，对呀。我怎么把这茬给忘了，真是糊涂。"彼得说道。

"没关系啦，"巴塞洛缪叫道，"**修复这本美妙的书，埃德温**！这不就行了吗？"

"妙极了！太棒啦！很有气概！我太喜欢这个句子了。"彼得赞叹道。

"我不过是随口说说的。"菲利克斯低声嘟囔道。

"现在，万事俱备了。"彼得说道。

"菲利克斯，准备气球需要多长时间？"

"明天就能弄好，老彼。"

"气球？"埃德温问道。

"没错，小埃。由我菲利克斯一手打造的超级无敌热气球！那可是我的骄傲啊，它可以把我们送去这本书里的任何地方。一旦升上天空，就可以一直往前飞行。"菲利克斯的口气颇有几分得意。

"我们要搭乘热气球前往尼尔格雷夫森林吗？"埃德温问道。

"It's the quickest way, Ed. We should be there in three days."

"Wow!" said Edwin. "I've never been in an air balloon before!"

"这是最快的交通工具了，小埃。三天后我们就能到那里了。"

"哇！"埃德温坦承，"我以前还从来没有搭乘过热气球呢！"

7

THE F.L.A.B.

By late the next day, Felix's Long-winded Air Balloon appeared beside the Table of Contents. Edwin couldn't believe his eyes. The majestic machine towered toward the ceiling. It was much bigger than he had expected and it was decorated with every colour of the rainbow. Around the balloon were big orange letters that spelled the initials F.L.A.B.

Felix had worked all morning and afternoon preparing the balloon. He had filled it with helium and put boxes of food and supplies into the balloon's basket. The most difficult job had been loading Beatrice's luggage. Her eighteen suitcases had to be strapped around the outside of the basket.

"Well, Beatrice!" said Thomas, looking at the cases. "Are you sure you don't need anything else?"

"Well, now that you mention it . . ."

"FORGET IT! It's going to be hard enough to get off the ground as it is!"

"Actually," said Bartholomew, punching figures into his calculator, "this balloon has a gravity force of 20,000 Newtons. When the balloon is filled with helium, it can easily overcome a gravitational force of 30 Kilo Newtons. So really, we won't have any difficulty getting off the ground."

"Thank you, Mr. Know-it-all!" said Felix, busily making last-minute adjustments to the balloon's controls. "I'm quite aware of the strength of my balloon."

"Felix, it's getting late in the day. How long until you are ready?" asked Thomas.

7

菲利克斯的超级无敌热气球

第二天傍晚，菲利克斯的超级无敌热气球终于在目录室现身了。埃德温简直不敢相信自己的眼睛。这架庞大的机器直冲天花板，比他想象的可要大多了，机身被点缀得五彩斑斓。热气球四周吊挂着一圈橙色的大字：菲利克斯的超级无敌热气球F.L.A.B.。

菲利克斯花了整整一个白天收拾热气球，将氦气筒、食品和日用品装满了整个篮筐。但装运碧翠丝的行李才是最麻烦的事。菲利克斯不得不将她的十八大箱行李紧紧捆绑在篮筐外。

"哎呀，碧翠丝！"托马斯看着她满满当当的行李箱，说道，"你是不是还有什么东西忘拿了？"

"对呀，经你这么一提醒……"

"**得了吧**！光这些行李都已经很难起飞了！"

巴塞洛缪一边啪啪地敲打着计算器按键，一边说道："实际上，热气球自身有20,000牛顿的重力。充满氦气后，它可以很轻松地克服3万牛顿的重力。所以，起飞是没有任何问题的。"

"谢谢您啦，万事通先生！"菲利克斯一边忙着对热气球控制器做最后的调整，一边揶揄道，"我很清楚我的热气球的承重力。"

"菲利克斯，天色不早了。你还要准备多久呀？"托马斯问道。

"About 10 minutes, Tom. All we need are directions from the Professor."

Peter and the Professor were seated at the Table of Contents, studying a large map of *A Student's Guide to the Great Adventure Story*.

Peter was writing down the directions the Professor was giving him but he was beginning to get a little concerned. The Professor was changing his mind every 2 minutes. Peter had more scribbles than directions. At last, he and the Professor seemed satisfied that they had designed the best possible route, even though neither knew exactly where the Neergreve Forest was located.

Peter rolled up the maps and the directions and handed them to Felix, while the Professor prepared himself for his afternoon nap.

"Oh, by the way, Felix," said the Professor, looking over his shoulder. "Here is an envelope that contains some important information about Drow and his group. You will find this very useful."

Just then, a large horn sounded.

"All aboard!" screamed Bartholomew. "The balloon is ready for lift-off."

"十来分钟吧，小汤。现在就差教授的路线图了。"

彼得和教授正坐在目录室里。他们正在研究《〈伟大的探险〉学生导读本》里的大地图。彼得正忙着记录教授的路线图。但他开始担心起来，因为教授每隔两分钟就改变一次主意。彼得的本子上只留下了一堆乱七八糟的文字。尽管俩人都不知道尼尔格雷夫森林的具体坐标，但他们还是很满意最后绘制出的最佳路线图。

彼得把地图和路线图卷起来交给了菲利克斯，而教授则去享受他的午睡时光了。

"哦，对了，菲利克斯，"教授扭着头说道，"这个信封里是卓尔和他的部下的重要信息，我想你们肯定能用得上。"

就在这时，响起了一阵嘹亮的高音喇叭声。

"所有人听令，登上热气球！"巴塞洛缪叫道，"热气球准备升空。"

8

OFF TO THE NEERGREVE

"Goodbye, Edwin," said Peter, crying.

"Don't cry, Mr. Preface. We'll be back!" said Edwin, trying to console him.

"I know, I know," said Peter blowing his nose. "It's just that I'm so used to introductions that I've never had to say goodbye before."

"Don't worry," said Thomas. "We'll get this book back on the shelves," he said, patting him on the back.

"Yes, Peter. Please don't worry," said Beatrice, as she kissed him gently on the cheek.

With a handkerchief in his hand and tears rolling down his cheeks, Peter watched and waved as the group made their way toward the balloon.

Already on board, Felix and Bartholomew dropped a ladder for the others. Felix steadied it while Bartholomew stood like a flight attendant ready to check off names.

"Oh, dear, I should have put on my old clothes," said Beatrice, struggling up the ladder and catching her high-heeled shoes on the rungs.

"Your turn next, Edwin," said Thomas.

Edwin climbed easily up the ladder, followed by Thomas. When he reached the top, he looked at his new surroundings. This was no ordinary air balloon! It was simply enormous! It looked more like the deck of a ship with a control platform that housed all sorts of dials and hanging levers. Felix was already hard at work pushing and pulling the levers and turning the various knobs.

8

前往尼尔格雷夫森林

"再见了，埃德温。"彼得泣不成声地说道。

"别伤心了，前言先生。我们一定会回来的！"埃德温试图安慰着他。

"我知道，我知道，"彼得擤着鼻涕，"只是我习惯了与别人见面，可从来没有跟人道过别。"

"别担心，"托马斯说道，"我们一定会让这本书重新回到书架上的。"他一边说着，一边轻拍着彼得的背。

"是的，彼得。别担心。"碧翠丝也说道，轻吻了一下他的脸颊。

彼得拿着一块手帕不停地擦拭着顺着脸颊滚滚而下的泪珠，目送着小分队向热气球走去，依依不舍地挥了挥手。

早已登上热气球的菲利克斯和巴塞洛缪从上面抛下一架绳梯，菲利克斯牢牢地抓住绳梯，而巴塞洛缪则像乘务员一样准备清点乘客名单。

"哦，天啊，我应该早点换上旧衣服的。"碧翠丝气喘吁吁地爬着绳梯，生怕自己的高跟鞋会掉下去。

"该你了，埃德温。"托马斯说道。

埃德温跟在托马斯身后轻松地爬上了绳梯。登上热气球后，埃德温扫视了一圈周围的新环境。这可绝不是个普通的热气球！这里真是大得惊人！篮筐内的控制台内设有各类控制板和操纵杆，看起来活脱脱就像一艘船的甲板。菲利克斯已经在忙着操作那些操纵杆和旋钮了。

"Everyone is on board," cried Bartholomew, checking off the names of Edwin and Thomas.

A few moments later there was a large hissing noise and the sounds of boards creaking.

"Ladies, gentlemen, and Bart. Prepare yourselves for lift-off!" chuckled Felix.

"Oh, really! What an exceedingly immature comment!" grumbled Bartholomew.

Edwin could feel the excitement building up inside him. Just then, the roof of the Contents Room opened like the doors of an elevator. The room became very bright as a golden ray of sunlight filtered through the opening.

"Good afternoon, ladies and gentlemen," announced Bartholomew, holding his nose. "Welcome aboard Felix's Long-winded Air Balloon. Our Captain today is Captain Felix Fix and our estimated maximum altitude will be 9,000 metres, and . . ."

"Will someone put a cork in his mouth!" said Felix. "He's giving me an awful headache. Here," he said, handing Bartholomew a knife. "Take this and give me a hand!"

Felix and Bartholomew quickly started cutting all the ropes holding the balloon in place. Then Felix pulled a large lever and turned a big round knob.

Then came a lurch.

And a series of squeaks.

Then more hissing sounds.

The balloon started to rise into the air.

"Goodbye and good luck!" yelled Peter, getting smaller and smaller to the group by the second. "We're counting on you, Edwin," he screamed.

Edwin suddenly felt very important.

"Goodbye, Mr. Preface. I'll do my best!" Edwin cried out.

The balloon climbed higher and higher into the air.

It passed the open doors in the ceiling of the Contents Room and

"所有人都已经顺利登上热气球了。"巴塞洛缪点完埃德温和托马斯的姓名后，大声宣布。

过了一会儿，热气球响起了嘈杂的咝咝声和木板的嘎吱声。

"女士们，先生们，还有那个谁谁谁。我们要准备升空了。"菲利克斯乐不可支地宣布。

"不是吧！你非得这么幼稚吗！"巴塞洛缪嘟囔着。

埃德温能感觉到他已经越来越兴奋了。就在这时，目录室的天花板像电梯门一样打开了。金色的阳光从敞开的天花板上倾泻而下，房间内一时间变得通透明亮。

"下午好，女士们，先生们，"巴塞洛缪捏着鼻子说道，"欢迎大家登上菲利克斯超级无敌热气球。今天的队长是菲利克斯·修理，我们的预计最大高度将会达到9,000米，还有……"

"拜托来个人把他的嘴堵上吧！"菲利克斯说道，"他一开口我就头疼。来，"他递给巴塞洛缪一把刀，"拿着这个，快来帮我一把！"

菲利克斯和巴塞洛缪很快割断了所有连接热气球与地面的绳索。随后，菲利克斯拉下了一个巨大的操纵杆，然后转动了一个大旋钮。

篮筐猛地倾斜了一下。

随后是一串"吱吱声"。

然后是一阵"咝咝声"。

热气球开始缓缓升空。

"再见，祝你们好运！"彼得大声喊着。不久，他就逐渐消失在众人的视野中。

"全靠你了，埃德温。"他尖叫道。

埃德温突然感到大任在肩。

"再见了，前言先生。我一定会尽力的！"埃德温大声喊道。

热气球越升越高，穿过了目录室的天花板，一路继续上升。

continued rising.

Edwin peered over the side. There were houses everywhere and he could see the Contents Room beneath him. It had a domed roof like the Taj Mahal in India that he had seen in a picture.

"So! What do you think, Edwin?" asked Thomas.

"It's wonderful. It really is," said Edwin.

"No, it's not!" cried Beatrice. "The wind is picking up and my hair is getting blown all over the place. Can't you drive this thing any slower?"

Bartholomew looked at the balloon's dials. After making some quick calculations, he said, "The wind is coming from the west at 80 knots. But, according to the drop in barometric pressure, it will be moving due south within the hour."

"Oh, brother," said Felix. "Now he thinks he's the weatherman. Our expert here is trying to tell us we're due for a storm. I'll try to get us above the clouds before it hits. But all of you had better go downstairs."

"Downstairs?" asked Edwin.

"Yes, Ed. The F.L.A.B. is the only balloon in the world to have a downstairs," said Felix proudly.

"Here! Follow me, Edwin," said Beatrice. She liked the idea of getting out of the wind.

Edwin followed Beatrice over to a small trap door in the floor of the balloon's basket. Beatrice pulled and pulled but the wind was simply too strong. She couldn't pry it open.

Thomas finally gave Beatrice a hand and eventually the two of them heaved the door back. It flew open and slapped against the floor.

As he peered down through the hole, Edwin expected to see clouds and empty space. Instead, he saw a set of wooden stairs.

"Follow me," said Beatrice.

Edwin followed Beatrice.

埃德温向四周看去，地面上到处都是房子，他能看到脚下的目录室。从空中俯瞰下去，目录室让他想起了曾经看过的一张印度泰姬陵的照片。

"哎！你在想什么呢，埃德温？"托马斯问道。

"这实在是太美妙了。真的很美。"埃德温说道。

"才不是呢！"碧翠丝大叫道，"风越来越大了，我的头发都吹得乱成一团了。你就不能让它飞慢点吗？"

巴塞洛缪看了看热气球的控制板，他在大脑中飞速运算后说道："现在是西风，风速80节。不过，根据下降的气压推算，一小时内就会转正南风了。"

"哦，老天爷啊，"菲利克斯说道，"你还真把自己当成天气预报员了。万事通先生的意思是说，我们即将遇上一场暴风雨，我会在暴风雨来临前尽力把热气球升到云层之上。但是，大家最好都到下层去。"

"下层？"埃德温不解地问。

"是的，小埃。这可是全世界唯一的双层热气球。"菲利克斯自豪地说。

"到这边来！跟着我，埃德温。"碧翠丝似乎很乐意躲开这恼人的风。

埃德温紧跟着碧翠丝来到了篮筐地板上的一扇小活板门前。碧翠丝使劲拉了又拉，但风实在太强了，她费尽力气也打不开那扇门。

托马斯帮了碧翠丝一把，俩人终于合力打开了门。门被打开后，门板大力拍打着地板。

埃德温透过地板上洞开的大门朝下层看去，还以为能看到云彩和空旷的空间呢。相反，他只看到了一排木楼梯。

"这里，埃德温，跟我来。"碧翠丝说道。

埃德温跟着碧翠丝走下楼梯。

As they neared the bottom, Beatrice took out a match and lit a large lantern that hung from the wall. Edwin could not believe his eyes. There, in front of him, was a huge room panelled in beautiful dark wood. The floor was covered with a deep, red carpet with huge, soft, round couches around it. Hanging from the walls were beds you would find on a ship.

A small area separated by a counter had been made into a kitchen. A large dining room table stood by a set of curtains. Beatrice pulled back the curtains to reveal a gigantic bay window that looked out into the sky. The whole room filled with brilliant light.

Edwin looked out the window. He felt he was in a big piece of cotton wool; it was one of the most beautiful sights he had ever seen.

"Breathtaking, isn't it?" said Beatrice.

Edwin was at a loss for words. For the next few hours, he sat at the dining room table, staring out the window and marvelling at nature's beauty. Finally, as the light of the day began to give way to nightfall, the picture window turned to black.

"Time for some supper!" announced Thomas. "Beatrice, you and Edwin set the table. I'll put on the stove and start preparations."

Edwin and Beatrice laid spoons, napkins, and mats on the table while Thomas poured some liquid, vegetables, and noodles into a big brass pot. The wind was now howling and the balloon was beginning to sway from side to side. Despite the noise of the wind, the three of them could hear Felix and Bartholomew arguing up on deck.

Finally, Thomas sounded a big gong, signalling supper was ready. The door to the deck flew open and Felix and Bartholomew made their way down the stairs. The sound of the wind was now deafening so Felix sealed the door tightly shut before going over to the table.

"What's for supper, Tom?" he asked.

"Alphabet soup!" announced Thomas, carrying a big soup tureen to the table.

快到达楼梯底部时，碧翠丝取出一根火柴，点燃了挂在墙上的大灯笼。埃德温简直不敢相信自己的眼睛，他面前是一个镶嵌着精美护墙板的大房间。地板上铺着深红色的地毯，房间四周陈列着巨大而舒适的圆沙发。墙上挂着的吊床是只有在船上才有的。

吧台将一块小区域分隔开来成为一个厨房，窗帘旁摆放着一张宽大的餐桌。碧翠丝拉开窗帘，露出一扇视野开阔的飘窗，可以看到窗外的天际线，整个房间内异常明亮。

埃德温透过飘窗向外眺望，觉得好似在一大片云海里飘荡。这是他有生以来所见过的最美丽的景色之一。

"真是太美了，对吧？"碧翠丝说道。

埃德温内心的激动难以用言语形容。接下来的几个小时里，他就这么坐在餐桌旁盯着窗外出神，沉醉在这片美如梦境的云海奇观之中。随着夜幕降临，窗外渐渐变成了漆黑一片。

"该吃晚餐了！"托马斯突然说道，"碧翠丝，你和埃德温负责摆桌子。我来生炉子，准备晚餐。"

埃德温和碧翠丝将勺子、餐巾和餐垫一一摆到桌子上，托马斯则将水、蔬菜和面条倒入一口大铜锅中。狂风在窗外呼啸，热气球开始摇摆不定。虽然狂风大作，但是他们三个仍然能听到菲利克斯和巴塞洛缪在上面拌嘴的声音。

一切准备就绪，托马斯鸣锣通知他俩下来吃饭。通向上层的活板门猛地开了，菲利克斯和巴塞洛缪走下楼来。同时传来震耳欲聋的风声。菲利克斯紧紧地关上了门，然后向餐桌走过来。

"晚餐吃什么，小汤？"他问道。

"字母汤！"托马斯捧着一大盖碗汤走到桌前。

"Don't you think it's rather ominous to be eating a soup with that name?" asked Beatrice.

"Don't worry, Beatrice. For goodness sake!" said Thomas. "We need our energy This soup will strengthen your letters and keep you healthy."

As he sipped the hot soup and listened to the cold wind blowing outside, Edwin began to get goose bumps.

"She's really blowing now," said Felix, taking a big slurp of soup. "But still, if we can make it through the clouds, we might be able to miss the full force of the storm."

"The storm is too strong," said Bartholomew. "We won't have time to get above those cumulonimbus clouds," he said, sipping his soup like a gentleman.

"Well, we've got to try!" snapped Felix. He lifted up his bowl and tipped it toward his lips like a cup. With one large gulp, he swallowed what was left.

"Sorry for being so rude, but I've got to get back upstairs." He put his bowl down on the table, wiped his mouth with his sleeve, and excused himself. "Come on, Bart! Give me a hand!"

"You do realize it's a complete waste of time," said Bartholomew, as he cleaned his empty bowl. "But if you must persist, I'll help. Keep the soup warm, Thomas. We'll be back in a jiffy."

"Smarty pants!" exclaimed Felix.

Felix and Bartholomew made their way back up the stairs to the deck. Edwin could hear them struggling with the trap door and the howling wind.

"How safe is a balloon in a storm?" asked Edwin.

"Oh, don't worry, Edwin. The F.L.A.B. is a strong air ship. She can handle just about anything," said Thomas.

At that moment, the balloon gave a sudden lurch to the left. Beatrice, who had been admiring her reflection in the window, fell off her high-heeled shoes and started to roll toward one of the couches. Her shoes flew through the air and their high heels stuck themselves in the wall. They looked like darts on a dartboard.

"喝这种名字的汤你就不怕触霉头吗？"碧翠丝问道。

"别瞎操心了，碧翠丝。看在老天爷的分儿上！"托马斯说道，"我们需要能量，这个汤可以强筋健骨，让大家的身体更健康。"

一边喝着热汤，一边听着窗外咆哮的寒风，埃德温不禁打了个寒战。

"这风可刮得真带劲儿啊，"菲利克斯咕噜咕噜地大口喝着汤，"不过，只要我们升到云层之上，我们或许就能躲过这场暴风雨。"

"风暴太大了，"巴塞洛缪说道，"我们没有足够的时间升到积雨云的上空。"他一边说着，一边像个绅士一样轻轻地喝了一口汤。

"不管怎么说，我们总得试试吧！"菲利克斯抢白道。他像端茶杯一样把碗举到嘴边，把剩下的汤一口全喝光了。

"对不起，我表现得太粗鲁了，不过，我得赶紧回到上层去。"

他把碗放回桌上，用袖子擦了擦嘴角，就准备退席了。"那个谁，少装蒜了！过来帮我一把！"

"你明知道这完全就是在浪费时间吧，"巴塞洛缪说着，也把碗内的汤喝光了，"不过，既然你执意要这么做的话，我乐意效劳。托马斯，用火温着汤，我们去去就回。"

"自以为是的家伙！"菲利克斯不屑地叫道。

菲利克斯和巴塞洛缪顺着楼梯回到了上层。埃德温听到他们费力地打开活板门，还有呼呼作响的风声。

"热气球在暴风雨中的安全性有多高？"埃德温问道。

"噢，不用担心，埃德温。菲利克斯超级无敌热气球可是条超级牢固的飞艇。不管多么恶劣的情况都能应付自如。"托马斯说道。

话音未落，热气球突然猛地向左一斜。正在窗边欣赏自己的倒影的碧翠丝一脚踩空，高跟鞋掉落，她在地板上滚了起来，滚到沙发旁。高跟鞋甩到了半空中，最后直直地钉在了墙上，向上看去就像插在圆靶上的飞镖。

The balloon gave another lurch.

Edwin and Thomas slid off their chairs and rolled smack into Beatrice who had just picked herself up.

The door to the deck flung open again as Felix and Bartholomew went back downstairs.

"I don't want to hear one word about 'how you told me so', " said Felix, imitating Bartholomew's speech. "It was still worth a try."

"You just don't want to admit you were wrong and I was right," said Bartholomew.

"Not one word!" ordered Felix.

The two peered over at the dining room table and the pair of high-heeled shoes stuck in the wall.

"This is no time to be rolling around on the floor," said Felix, looking at the pile of bodies. "I want all of you to get into your beds. We're expecting a bit of rough weather—foreshadowing, I'd say."

"He's right!" remarked Bartholomew. "There are force-four winds coming from the south, due to meet a northerly cold front."

"Look," said Felix, "If I want the weather forecast, I'll turn on the radio. Now help me get these land-lubbers up!"

With the help of Felix and Bartholomew, Edwin untangled himself from Thomas who untangled himself from poor Beatrice. She was now in an awful state! Her dress was crumpled, her hair was all over the place, and her shoes had become wall hangings.

"Look at me. I'm a complete mess!" wailed Beatrice.

"You look normal to me," said Thomas.

"Very funny, Thomas The. Your last name is not Beautiful. You don't have to worry about keeping up an image as I do."

"Alright, everybody. Listen!" ordered Felix. "The balloon has been put on automatic pilot for the night. Its compass will keep us on course. The safest place for all of us is in bed."

接着热气球又是狠狠一震。

埃德温和托马斯从椅子上摔下来，直接撞到了好不容易才爬起来的碧翠丝身上。

当菲利克斯和巴塞洛缪走下楼来时，通向上层的活板门再次被推开。

"我不想听那套'我早就告诉过你了'的鬼话。"菲利克斯模仿着巴塞洛缪的口气说道，"不试你怎么知道呢。"

"你不过是不愿意承认自己错了，而我是对的罢了。"巴塞洛缪说道。

"你给我闭嘴！"菲利克斯吼道。

两人隔着餐桌看到了插在墙上的那两只高跟鞋。

"现在可不是滚着玩的时候，"菲利克斯对着乱作一团的他们说道，"我要你们现在就上床去。我们将遇上一场狂风暴雨，现在还只是个开场而已。"

"他说得对！"巴塞洛缪也说道，"四级南风马上就要和北方冷锋相遇了。"

"得了吧，"菲利克斯说道，"如果我想听天气预报，我自己会打开收音机的。赶紧帮我把这几个笨手笨脚的家伙拉起来。"

菲利克斯和巴塞洛缪把埃德温从托马斯身上扶了起来，然后又把托马斯从碧翠丝身上扶了起来，可怜的碧翠丝可被压得够呛！她的衣服皱巴巴的，发型一团糟，高跟鞋也早已经飞到墙头上去了。

"看看我吧，简直是一塌糊涂！"碧翠丝伤心地哭了起来。

"我觉得这样挺好。"托马斯说道。

"一点儿也不好笑，托马斯·这个。你的姓氏不是美丽。你压根就不必像我这样费心思保持形象。"

"好了，大家都注意听！"菲利克斯开始下达指令，"今天晚上热气球将启用自动驾驶模式，罗盘系统将按设定航向飞行。对大家来说，最安全的地方就是待在床上。"

Everyone followed his orders and made their way to the bunks. Everyone, that is, except Beatrice.

A few minutes later, the group had crawled under their warm sheets.

"Where's Beatrice?" asked Thomas.

"Here I am," she replied.

Thomas started to laugh hysterically. Beatrice's face was covered with mud and her hair was full of rollers.

"Ahhhhhh, it's the Boogie monster!" screamed Thomas.

"Laugh if you must, but I would like you to know this is special beauty mud. It's guaranteed to enhance my looks."

"Well, it's certainly an improvement," continued Thomas, laughing so hard it hurt.

"Oh! Why do I put up with you?" sighed Beatrice. And with that, she turned down the lanterns and threw herself on her bunk. "Good night, everybody."

"Good night," everyone said in unison.

The F.L.A.B. swayed and rocked all night as the wind and rain played melodies outside.

Everyone slept, except Edwin. He lay in his bed thinking about all that had happened and imagining what Drow would look like. He wondered whether his mother would approve of his flying off in an air balloon with a group of strangers. Then again, he thought, whenever he had watched a bit too much television or played a few too many video games, his mother would always say, "Why don't you go and spend some time with a book!" He chuckled to himself. He was certainly taking his mother's advice to heart.

The balloon was rising and falling now. Edwin felt as if he was on a roller coaster. His stomach had a strange, almost sick feeling. His friends were snoring away. Each person's snore sounded like a different instrument. When

所有人都听从菲利克斯的指令，乖乖上了床，除了碧翠丝。

几分钟后，大家都躺在了温暖的床上。

"碧翠丝哪儿去了？"托马斯问道。

"我在这儿。"她答道。

大家看向厨房，托马斯歇斯底里地笑了起来。碧翠丝的脸上涂满了黑泥，头发上则粘满了卷发筒。

"哎呀呀，怪物来啦！"托马斯尖叫着讽刺道。

"想笑你就笑吧，但是我得告诉你，这是专用的美容泥，可以让我变得更美。"

"嗯，现在看上去的确美了不少。"托马斯继续说道，这会儿他的肚子都要笑痛了。

"哦！为什么我非要忍受你这个讨厌的家伙？"碧翠丝叹了口气。话音刚落，她就吹灭了灯笼，钻到了床上。"大家晚安。"

"晚安。"其他人异口同声地说道。

热气球在狂风暴雨中剧烈地摇摆了一整夜。

每个人都进入了甜美的梦乡——除了埃德温。他躺在床上，回忆着今天发生的事，不禁好奇那个卓尔到底是什么模样。他想知道，母亲会不会反对他跟着一帮陌生人搭乘热气球呢。然后，他又想起，每当看到他长时间看电视或玩电子游戏时，母亲总会说："你为什么不去看一会儿书呢！"他轻声地笑了起来，这一回他可是听了妈妈的话了。

热气球现在一会儿上升，一会儿下降，就像坐在过山车上一样。埃德温有一种奇怪的、近乎恶心的感觉。他的朋友们似乎都睡得很安稳，还打起了呼噜，每个人的鼾声都像一种不同的乐器。此起彼伏的鼾声交织成了一支

they all snored together, it made a comforting sort of tune. Edwin listened to the sounds and at last his eyes began to feel heavy. Before long, Edwin Bellamy was fast asleep.

催人安眠的小夜曲。埃德温听着这些声音，眼皮也开始打架了。很快，埃德温·贝拉米也进入了梦乡。

9

COMPASS PROBLEMS

The next morning Edwin awoke to find the whole room filled with light. The storm had passed but he could see out the big bay window that it was still gray and overcast.

He climbed down from his bunk and walked over to the dining room table. There he found his friends sitting glumly with their heads in their hands.

"What's the matter?" asked Edwin.

Without looking up, Felix reached across the table and picked up a large metal object and shoved it in front of Edwin.

Edwin's heart sank. He knew what it was. It was the balloon's compass. And it was full of water. Edwin's stomach felt weird. Without the compass, they would certainly get lost.

"Can't you fix it, Felix?" Edwin asked.

"Yes, but I can't calibrate it unless I know what direction we are heading," said Felix.

"And we can't know that without the compass," said Bartholomew.

Edwin walked away from the table. Now he felt scared and, for the first time, a little homesick. He sat down on one of the big couches and stared at the bookcases built into the wall. They were full of dictionaries and word games like Scrabble. There was also a small portable radio. Edwin got up and turned it on.

"Good Morning and welcome
to the Word Today News Hour."

9

罗盘出问题了

第二天早晨，埃德温醒来时发现天已经亮了。暴风雨在夜里已经平息了，他透过大飘窗看到外面仍是灰蒙蒙的阴天。

他从床上爬下来，走到餐桌前，他看见朋友们坐在桌旁，个个都闷闷不乐地用手托着额头。

"发生什么事了？"他问道。

菲利克斯头也不抬地从桌子对面拿起一大块金属推到埃德温面前。

埃德温看了一眼，心里一沉，他很清楚这是什么——热气球的罗盘。但此刻，罗盘却全部湿透了。埃德温心里很不舒服，如果没有罗盘，他们肯定会迷失方向。

"你不能把它修好吗，菲利克斯？"埃德温问道。

"能倒是能，但是如果不知道前进的方向，根本就没法校准罗盘啊。"菲利克斯说道。

"没有罗盘，又怎么可能知道前进的方向呢。"巴塞洛缪接着说道。

埃德温转身离开餐桌。这一刻，他感到很害怕，而且第一次觉得有点想家了。他在一个大沙发上坐了下来，盯着嵌在墙上的书架发呆。书架上摆满了字典和拼字游戏，还有一台小型便携式收音机。他站起身来，打开收音机。

"早上好，欢迎收听今日一小时的单词新闻节目。"

Edwin played with the radio, not paying much attention to the voice coming from the speakers. Then suddenly his ears perked up. The weatherman had started talking.

"There are strong winds coming from the east and the temperature is expected to reach... ."

"That's it!" he shouted. "Hey, everybody! I've got it!" cried Edwin.

"What is it, dear?" asked Beatrice kindly.

"The weatherman just said the winds are coming from the east."

"So?" said Felix.

"Of course!" screamed Bartholomew. "How silly of me not to realize such a basic solution to our enigmatic situation."

"Translation, please!" said Felix, tapping his fingers on the table.

"Felix! Don't you see?"

"Quite honestly . . . NO!"

"Look!" said Bartholomew excitedly. "If we know from which direction the wind is coming, we can figure out the direction we are heading."

"By golly, you're right!" said Felix, suddenly springing to life. "We can also fix the compass. As long as we know where east is, it's very easy to figure out the other points," he cried jubilantly.

"Three cheers for Edwin!" yelled Beatrice.

Everyone sang out, "Hip! Hip! Hurrah!" and Edwin was hailed as a jolly good fellow.

"Well, everybody! What are we waiting for?" cried Thomas.

They all rushed up the stairs to the deck. They wet their fingers and stuck them in the air, trying to determine the direction of the wind. After everyone agreed, Felix began emptying the water-logged compass. Within minutes, the compass needle was spinning again and the balloon was back on course.

Because of Edwin's smart thinking, Felix had allowed him to pull the levers, turn the dials, and do all the neat stuff that made the balloon work. Edwin felt very pleased with himself.

埃德温把玩着收音机，对播放的内容不甚在意。突然，他竖起了耳朵，只听得天气预报员说道：

"本地将出现强烈的东风，温度预计将达到……"

"我知道啦！"他大叫了一声，"嗨，大家注意！我知道该怎么办了！"埃德温兴奋地大叫起来。

"怎么了，亲爱的？"碧翠丝柔声问道。

"天气预报员刚才说，咱们这儿将出现东风。"

"所以呢？"菲利克斯满腹狐疑地问道。

"对呀！"巴塞洛缪也叫了起来，"我真是太糊涂了，居然没想到可以用这么简单的方法对付现在这个复杂的局面。"

"请说人话！"菲利克斯用手指敲了敲桌子。

"菲利克斯！你难道还不明白吗？"

"老实说……**没明白**！"

"你瞧！"巴塞洛缪兴奋地说道，"只要知道了风向，我们就知道正要前进的方向了呀。"

"天哪，你说得对！"菲利克斯一下子回过神来，"我们可以修复罗盘了。只要我们确定了东边方向，其他方向的问题就迎刃而解了。"他兴高采烈地喊道。

"为埃德温喝彩吧！"碧翠丝大叫道。

大家伙儿齐声高唱"嘿！嘿！万岁！"，还管埃德温叫作福星小子。

"好了，大家还在等什么呢？"托马斯说道。

所有人都冲到了篮筐上层，他们站在风中，努力辨别着风向。最后，他们终于就风向达成了一致意见，随后菲利克斯开始排干罗盘内的水。只过了一会儿工夫，罗盘的指针就重新开始转动，热气球又重新回到了正轨。

菲利克斯见识到了埃德温的厉害，让他帮着控制操纵杆和控制板以及其他飞行工作。埃德温对自己的表现也很是得意。

"Well, Ed. I think you know what you're doing," said Felix as he leaned over Edwin's shoulder to check the readings.

"Just keep your eye on the compass and make sure she stays on course. I'm going downstairs to take a look at the Professor's maps. You're in charge!"

"好了，小埃，我想你知道该怎么做了。"菲利克斯一边越过埃德温的肩头观察着仪表的读数，一边说道。

"只要随时关注罗盘的数据，确保它保持正确的航向就行了。我要下楼去看看教授的地图。这里就交给你了！"

10

EDWIN'S STRANGE SIGHTING

Edwin had a warm feeling inside. He'd never had such a big responsibility before. He was enjoying his new job. He particularly liked flying through big, white clouds. Whenever that happened, everything turned white—even the deck. Sometimes he couldn't even see his feet!

He also liked playing with the levers. He could make the balloon go up into the clouds by pushing the levers and he could bring it back out again by pulling on them. Then the balloon would make a funny sound—a sort of "omm pat pat, oom pat pat, ppsssst."

He pushed and pulled the levers and hummed a little tune to the various sounds of the balloon.

"We're Felix's Fabulous Air Balloon, sharing the sky with the sun and the moon.

With Beatrice, Thomas, Bartholomew, too, Felix and I are in charge of the crew."

But just as Edwin was about to sing of Drow, he became aware of a new sound. He stopped humming and listened carefully. The sound was like a flag flapping in the wind. Edwin looked up. Sitting on top of the balloon was a bird.

Edwin picked up a pair of binoculars and focused on the bird. Suddenly his heart missed a beat. He gasped to get his breath. He was looking at one of the ugliest and strangest birds he had ever seen. Its purple feathers surrounded a fat, blubbery body. Its head, which seemed to lack any type of neck, mushroomed into a plumage of red and orange that made it look on fire. But what was

10

埃德温的新发现

埃德温感到内心有一股暖流涌过，他从来没有承担过这么重要的责任，他很喜欢这个新任务。在漫天的云海中飞行让他格外开心，热气球过处，一切都变成了白色——甚至连整个篮筐上层都散发出炫目的白光，他的脚在白云中时隐时现！

他很喜欢操作那些操纵杆。轻轻一推，热气球就直飞入云端，再轻轻一拉，热气球又飞离了云海。同时，热气球还会发出"呜啪啪、呜啪啪、噗咝咝咝咝"这样好玩的声音。

他在不停地推和拉操纵着操纵杆时，还和着这些声音哼着小调。

"我们是神奇的菲利克斯热气球，

与太阳和月亮共享一片蓝天。

与碧翠丝、托马斯和巴塞洛缪并肩战斗，

菲利克斯和我是快乐的掌舵人。"

埃德温正准备接着唱卓尔的歌，却突然听到了一个异样的声音，他停止了哼唱，认真地听着。那个声音就像一面旗帜在风中飘扬，猎猎作响。埃德温抬头看了看，热气球的顶部站着一只小鸟。

埃德温拿起双筒望远镜，仔细看过去。突然，他心里一惊，倒抽了一口凉气。他看到了一只生平见过的样貌最丑陋、最古怪的鸟。它胖乎乎的身体四周环绕着一圈紫色的羽毛，似乎没有脖子，圆嘟嘟的蘑菇头上长满了红色

most peculiar was its beak, pink and shaped like the letter "U." The beak's tip pointed up into the air.

If that wasn't weird enough, the strange creature had one long and solitary hair hanging from its head and reaching down toward the ground. At the end of the thin strand was something that resembled a toilet plunger!

The bird had a fiendish look. It grinned at Edwin in an evil way. Edwin dropped his binoculars and ran downstairs, screaming for the others.

"Felix! Thomas! Bart! Beatrice! Quick! Come and see!"

The group looked up from busily mulling over some of the Professor's maps.

"What is it, Ed?" asked Felix. "Is there something wrong with the balloon?"

"I don't know. You've got to come and see," cried Edwin.

The group followed him upstairs. When Edwin got back on deck, he looked up at the top of the balloon. The bird was gone.

"What is it, Edwin?" asked Beatrice.

"A bird! A fat bird with an upside-down beak and a toilet plunger hanging from its head," Edwin said excitedly.

Felix started to laugh. "I think you've been out here a bit too long, Ed. Maybe you've got vertigo. Why don't you go downstairs for a rest!"

Edwin was about to accept the fact that he was seeing things when he heard the sound again. He looked up. Where the bird had been, he saw a small hole and a torn piece of balloon flapping in the air.

"I think Edwin must have seen something. What else could have caused that hole?" said Thomas, peering through the binoculars.

"But, Tom," said Felix, "who has ever heard of a bird with an upside-down beak?"

"Not to mention a toilet plunger hanging from its head?!" exclaimed Beatrice.

和橙色的羽毛，看上去好像顶着一头燃烧的火焰。它的喙呈粉红色，形似字母U，顶部尖尖的向上直戳着，令人瞠目结舌。

这还不算呢，这个怪模怪样的家伙脑后还有一根长长的羽毛一直拖到地板上，这根细长的羽毛末端居然还吊着一个形似皮搋子的东西！

这只鸟目露凶光，嘴角带着一丝不怀好意的微笑，盯着埃德温。埃德温放下了双筒望远镜，他跑下楼，大声疾呼着其他人的名字。

"菲利克斯！托马斯！小巴！碧翠丝！快来呀！快来看呀！"

其他四位正忙着研究教授的地图，这时纷纷抬起头来。

"怎么了，小埃？"菲利克斯问道，"热气球出了什么问题吗？"

"一时半会儿说不清楚，你赶快过来看看吧。"埃德温大声说。

其他人跟着埃德温一路走上楼来。埃德温回到上层后，迅速抬头看向热气球的顶部。但是，那只鸟却不见了。

"到底怎么了，埃德温？"碧翠丝问道。

"是一只鸟！胖乎乎的，头上吊着一只皮搋子那样的东西，它的喙就像倒着长的一样。"埃德温激动地说。

菲利克斯笑出声来："我觉得你是在热气球上待得太久，脑筋有点不清楚了吧，小埃。你不如下楼去好好休息一会儿吧。"

埃德温也觉得可能是自己眼花看错了。可就在这时，他又听到了那个旗帜在风中猎猎作响的声音。埃德温抬头看了看，在刚才那只鸟站立的地方，出现了一个洞，一块被撕裂的热气球布在空中翻腾。

"我觉得，埃德温看到的肯定不是幻觉，不然怎么可能会出现这个洞呢？"托马斯拿起望远镜，一边仔细观察，一边说道。

"但是，小汤，"菲利克斯说道，"哪有鸟的嘴巴是倒着长的呢？"

"更别说它头上还吊着一个皮搋子了。"碧翠丝附和道。

While the group argued and Edwin stood there trying to defend himself, Bartholomew went downstairs to search through some of the papers Professor I.N. Dex had given them. A few minutes later, he reappeared with what he had been seeking.

Felix exclaimed, "Look! We're losing pressure. There must have been something sharp on that bird."

"Yes, but what, Felix?" said Thomas impatiently.

"I wonder if I might say something useful," said Bartholomew, clutching a pile of papers.

"Yes, I've often wondered that myself," said Felix, watching the pressure gauges drop.

"No, really! Look at this!" ordered Bartholomew.

Everyone glanced at the notes he was holding in his hand. There in the middle of the page was a picture of the same bird Edwin had seen.

"That's it!" cried Edwin. "That's the bird that was on the balloon."

"What does it say?" asked Beatrice, scanning the page.

"Let's see," said Bartholomew. "Ah, yes! Here we are. It's called a Rekcus Bird. It's indigenous to the Neergreve Forest region. And it's a Mumbojumbo. Characteristics include a U-shaped beak and a long hair with a toilet plunger on the end."

"Look what else it says," said Thomas, peering over Bartholomew's shoulder. "Any direct contact with the bird could result in Unoitis."

"Unoitis?" exclaimed Edwin.

"Yes," continued Bartholomew. "Unoitis. That bird has the ability to suck every idea from your brain. Slowly, ever so slowly, you develop an inability to describe anything without using the expression 'like, you know.' Drow makes sure all of his captured words develop Unoitis until he is ready to issue them one of his new names. It prevents the words from mutating and creating their own sentence fragments."

"But what does all of this mean?" said Beatrice.

在大家争论不休、埃德温忙着为自己辩护的当口，巴塞洛缪跑到楼下，去搜索I.N.德克斯教授临行前交给他们的一些文件。几分钟后，他又回到了上层，手里拿着大家都迷惑不解的答案。

"瞧！我们的浮力正在逐渐减小。一定是那只鸟捣的鬼。"菲利克斯懊丧地叫喊着。

"就算是它，那又怎么样呢，菲利克斯？"托马斯不耐烦地说。

"我不知道说这些话有没有用。"巴塞洛缪拿着一堆文件走过来说。

"没关系，反正你的话大部分时候都没啥用。"菲利克斯眼看着压力表的数字以难以置信的速度飞速下降，不满地讽刺道。

"真的，我没开玩笑！大家看看这个！"巴塞洛缪指给大家看。

每个人都看向他手里拿着的笔记本。在笔记本中间的一页，画着一只与埃德温的描述一模一样的鸟。

"就是它！"埃德温大叫起来，"这就是刚才那只站在上面的鸟。"

"这上面是怎么说的？"碧翠丝扫了一眼笔记本，问道。

"让我看看哈，"巴塞洛缪说道，"啊，我懂了！是这么回事的，这只鸟叫作雷克斯鸟，是尼尔格雷夫森林的特有物种，而且它隶属于胡言军团。U形喙和吊着皮撅子的细长羽毛是它的典型特征。"

"还有别的吗？"托马斯探过巴塞洛缪的肩头，看了一眼笔记本。

"任何与这只鸟有直接接触的人都会患上失语症。"

"失语症？"埃德温惊叫起来。

"是的，"巴塞洛缪继续说道，"失语症。这只鸟可以从你的大脑里吸光所有语言能力。感染失语症的人会慢慢丧失语言能力，只会反反复复地重复表达一句话——'就像，你知道的吧。'卓尔会故意让被俘虏的单词感染失语症，直到给他们分配新的名字，以此防止单词变化或者组成句子。"

"但这些到底意味着什么呢？"碧翠丝问道。

"It means we are getting closer to the Neergreve Forest," said Felix.

"I'm afraid it also means we have been spied on," said Bartholomew grimly.

"That bird was a spy?" Edwin exclaimed.

"I'm afraid so, Ed," said Felix. "If that Rekcus Bird reports back to Drow that it has seen a sentence without one Drow word in it, our lives will be in grave danger."

"You see, Thomas!" said Beatrice. "I knew I would need my old clothes. We ARE going to be tortured."

"Thank you for that pleasant prediction, Miss Optimism!" said Thomas.

"I'm just trying to be realistic, Thomas. You never appreciate me. You are always making fun of me. Why I . . . "

"Fine!" yelled Thomas. "I'm sorry. You're right! We are going to be tortured. Drow will probably put us all in a blender and make P soup out of us. Or steep us in a T pot. Or better still, put us through a food processor and serve us with C-zer salad and R-tachokes!"

"You're making fun of me again!" said Beatrice, stamping her foot.

"Now stop this bickering—both of you!" ordered Felix. "Remember what Peter Preface said. We have to work together—as a team."

"Uh, Felix, if my calculations are right, we should be directly over the Neergreve Forest by breakfast tomorrow," said Bartholomew, playing with his calculator and looking at some of the Professor's papers.

"Good thing, too!" said Felix. "The balloon is losing pressure by the minute because of that stupid bird. It has only about a day's worth of helium left."

"这意味着我们离尼尔格雷夫森林已经越来越近了。"菲利克斯说道。

"恐怕也意味着我们已经被盯梢了。"巴塞洛缪一脸严肃地说。

"那只鸟是间谍吗？"埃德温问道。

"恐怕是的，小埃，"菲利克斯答道，"那只雷克斯鸟肯定很清楚我们组成的句子里不包含卓尔的爪牙，如果它向卓尔告密的话，那我们就非常危险了。"

"看吧，托马斯！"碧翠丝说道，"我就知道那些旧衣服肯定能派上用场，严刑拷打看来是**免不了**了。"

"多么美好的前景啊，谢谢你啦，乐观小姐！"托马斯揶揄道。

"我只是实事求是而已，托马斯。你就只会打击我，挖苦我。为什么我……"

"好啦！"托马斯喊道，"我道歉就是了，你说得对！严刑拷打是免不了的。卓尔肯定会把我们所有人丢到搅拌机里，然后做成一大锅豌豆汤；要不就是把我们倒进茶壶里泡成一壶好茶。说不准还会把我们一股脑儿都扔进食物加工机，然后就着恺撒沙拉和洋蓟饱餐一顿呢。"

"你又挖苦我了！"碧翠丝跺着脚气恼地叫着。

"别吵了，你们俩！"菲利克斯正色道，"你们忘了彼得·前言的嘱托了吗？我们必须同心协力，共同战斗。"

"呃，菲利克斯，如果我的计算无误，明天早餐前我们就应该能飞到尼尔格雷夫森林的上空了。"巴塞洛缪一边研究教授的资料，一边敲打着计算器的按键说道。

"还想听好消息吗？"菲利克斯说道，"都怪那只可恶的鸟，热气球的浮力正在逐渐下降，我们剩下的氦气最多只够用一天了。"

11

INTO THE NEERGREVE FOREST

The next day, Edwin and the others packed some overnight bags with food and supplies. As Bartholomew stood, clutching clipboard and pen in hand, Felix started calling out the names of the items the group had assembled on the floor.

"One map," yelled Felix.

"Check!" replied Bartholomew.

"Five bags of food."

"Check!"

"Five rolls of toilet paper."

"Check!"

"Twenty-three assorted hair brushes."

"Che . . . What?" cried Bartholomew.

"How did these get here?" asked Felix.

Thomas looked over at Beatrice. "Well?!" he said, a smug look on his face. Poor Beatrice turned as red as a radish.

"Well, that should be about it," said Felix, rubbing his hands together. "Everyone take a bag and head upstairs. We'll be landing any minute now."

As the group reached the deck, Edwin rushed over to the side of the basket. The balloon was very low now and had barely enough helium left to keep it aloft. There directly beneath him lay a dark and spooky forest . . . hundreds of tall, spidery trees, with spindly branches reaching like overgrown fingers. In the middle of the forest was a wide black stream with dead tree stumps protruding from its stagnant water. A mist hovered above the water

11

潜入尼尔格雷夫森林

第二天，埃德温和其他伙伴开始打包过夜的食物和日常用品。巴塞洛缪手里拿着笔记本和钢笔站在一旁，菲利克斯则开始清点地板上大家整理出来的行装。

"一张地图。"菲利克斯大声说。

"齐了！"巴塞洛缪答道。

"五大包食物。"

"齐了！"

"五卷卫生纸。"

"齐了！"

"二十三套梳子。"

"齐……什么？"巴塞洛缪大声问道。

"怎么会有这些玩意儿？"菲利克斯问道。

托马斯看了看碧翠丝，说道："你说呢？！"他的脸上带着一丝幸灾乐祸的微笑。可怜的碧翠丝脸涨得通红。

"都好了，应该就是这些了吧，"菲利克斯搓着手说道，"每个人背一个袋子，上楼去。我们随时准备着陆。"

回到上层后，埃德温走到篮筐一侧。因为氦气不够，所以现在热气球的高度非常低，在空中摇摇欲坠。他从篮筐一侧向下俯瞰，在他的脚下，是一片阴森黑暗的森林。成百上千棵高耸入云的古木擎着细长如手指的树枝，巨

like a protective shield and the sounds of slithering and crawling and creeping and clawing creatures emanated from hidden areas within.

"That's Drow's Stream of Consciousness," said Bartholomew, standing beside Edwin. "All of Drow's Mumbojumbos sail off down that stream to different parts of the book, telling everyone the terrible things Drow has on his mind. They don't even use the help of the Punctuation People to guide them. They just travel on and on, not really knowing where they are heading."

"Wow!" said Edwin.

"Where are we going to land, Felix?" asked Thomas, surveying the forest with his binoculars.

"Over there!" said Felix, moving beside Thomas and pointing to a small clearing in the trees. "The balloon will be well hidden if we have to leave in a hurry and there's enough room to maneuver ourselves out."

"What if it's marshland?" asked Beatrice. "We'll sink into the ground, never to be seen again!"

"That's a chance we'll have to take," said Felix. "The balloon has lost too much pressure as it is. Going on any further will put our lives in jeopardy."

And so, with some pushing and pulling of levers, some turning of dials, and a lot of hissing, the balloon floated gently down into the depths of the Neergreve Forest. As it neared the clearing, everything suddenly turned dark. The group held their breath in anticipation, waiting to see if indeed they would sink into a bottomless marsh.

But that was not to be.

There was a bit of a rumble.

Then a crunch!

Then a snap!

And at last a sort of kerplonk!

The balloon landed securely on hard ground.

大的树冠如蛛网般重重叠叠，令人不寒而栗。在整片森林的中央，有一条宽阔的河流，枯死的树桩在腐臭的黑色河水中直愣愣地矗立着。河流上空飘荡着重重迷雾，好似那些潜藏于水下的未知生物的保护神，为幽暗的河水笼罩上层层阴影。

"那就是卓尔的意识之河，"站在埃德温的巴塞洛缪说道，"卓尔的胡言军团从那里顺流而下，在这本书的每一个角落神出鬼没，到处散播卓尔那套假仁假义的理论。他们甚至都不需要标点符号为他们引路，只是到处游荡，走到哪儿算哪儿。"

"哇！"埃德温说道。

"我们要从哪儿降落，菲利克斯？"托马斯问道。此刻他正忙着用双筒望远镜打探森林的地形。

"那边！"菲利克斯走到托马斯身旁，指着树林里一小块空地说道："那里可以将热气球很好地掩护起来，以便我们匆忙撤退，而且地方也足够宽敞，便于我们部署作战计划。"

"可是如果那是一片沼泽呢？"碧翠丝问道，"那我们将会沉下去，永不见天日了！"

"那我们也得冒险一试，"菲利克斯说道，"热气球的浮力不够了。我们如果再不着陆，随时都可能有生命危险。"

于是，他们忙而不乱地操纵着操纵杆和控制板，热气球伴随着一阵咝咝声缓缓降落到了尼尔格雷夫森林的深处，就在快要抵达那片空地时，四周突然陷入了一片黑暗。每一个人都屏住了呼吸，祈祷着千万不要陷入一片无底的沼泽之中。

幸好厄运并没有降临。

只听得轰隆隆一阵巨响。

然后是嘎吱嘎吱的声音！

随后瞬间传来啪的一声脆响！

最后是扑通一声！

热气球稳稳地停在了坚硬的地面上。

The sounds of the forest seemed louder now. Echoes made it difficult to tell their source. Everyone began to get the feeling they were being watched.

"Alright, everybody, listen carefully!" ordered Felix. "We have to find Drow before he finds us. If we run into anyone or anything, we'll have to disguise our sentence. Drow will have told all his spies to capture members of sentences that do not contain Drow words. We must, therefore, be extremely careful."

Edwin began to shiver uncontrollably. He was homesick again and felt uneasy and unsure about the situation.

"Don't worry, Edwin," said Beatrice, noticing his trembling. "You'll be perfectly safe with us. You stay close to me. I'll make sure no harm comes to you. I promise."

Edwin smiled at Beatrice in a loving way. She now seemed more like his mother than a beauty queen. For the first time, he could see that her beauty was not just in her clothes.

After a quick lunch beside the balloon, the group was ready to begin the really dangerous part of their mission.

"Attention, everybody!" ordered Thomas, reassuming his Boy Scout role. "Follow Felix. Forward . . . MARCH!"

"But where are we heading?" asked Beatrice.

"I saw a road from the balloon. It's through the set of trees over there, I think," Felix said, pointing to an overgrown swamp. "It's probably about a six-kilometre walk."

"Actually, Felix," said Bartholomew, "it's a six-point-eight-kilometre walk, assuming there are no areas of elevation."

"As I said. About a six-kilometre walk!" grumbled Felix.

And so the group started their six-point-eight-kilometre walk through the woods. At first, the trek reminded Edwin of some of the lovely hikes he had taken as a Cub Scout. But as the walk wore on, it began to turn into a miserable experience. The only thing the same was the necessity to "Be

林间各种古怪的声音愈加震耳，但阵阵缥缈的回声让他们难以分辨声音究竟从何而来。每个人都感觉似乎被无数双眼睛监视着。

"好了，大家都听好了！"菲利克斯指令道，"我们必须得先找到卓尔，以防我们被他先发现。一旦碰到任何人或异常情况，我们都要把组成的句子掩盖起来。卓尔肯定已经下令，所有部下只要看到任何尚未归附的单词组成的句子一律逮捕。所以，我们必须格外小心。"

埃德温一时控制不住，颤抖了起来。他又有点想家，又感到不安，也不知道下一步局势将如何发展。

"别担心，埃德温，"他的紧张没有逃过碧翠丝的眼睛，"和我们在一起，你是绝对不会出事的。你跟着我就行，我一定会保护你，我保证。"

埃德温充满感激地向碧翠丝笑了笑。她现在看起来更像他的母亲而非一位美丽的女王，他第一次发现原来她的美不仅仅局限于外表。

在热气球旁简单地用过午餐后，大家准备开始行动了。

"大家注意了！"托马斯俨然一副童子军的架势，"大家都跟着菲利克斯。齐步……**向前走**！"

"我们这到底是要去哪儿啊？"碧翠丝问道。

"在热气球上时，我就看准了这里有一条路。我想，应该是从那边的那排树穿过去，"菲利克斯指着一片杂草丛生的沼泽说道，"步行大约需要走6公里。"

"其实吧，菲利克斯，"巴塞洛缪补充道，"考虑到海拔差，应该是6.8公里。"

"我再重复一遍。步行大约需要走6公里！"菲利克斯愤愤地说道。

于是一行人等开始了6.8公里的林间穿越之旅。刚开始时，埃德温还觉得这就像之前参加的幼童军旅行一样有趣。但随着时间的推移，他越来越感到力不从心。他现在觉得，二者唯一的相同点就是"准备吃苦"的心态。可是

Prepared." For what, he wasn't quite sure!

The ground was swampy, making it difficult to walk without sinking right up to the ankles. On more than one occasion, Edwin had seen slithery reptiles oozing and slurping through the mushy quagmire.

Then, of course, there was the problem with Beatrice! Her high-heeled shoes were not what you would call ideal replacements for hiking boots. With each step she took, they got stuck. Felix would have to take out his crowbar and pry each stuck foot loose until she took her next step.

Finally, the group was so fed up, they decided to carry poor Beatrice. Thomas and Edwin held her arms, while Felix and Bartholomew—who by this time were arguing about the direction they were heading—held her feet.

Then it started to rain!

Edwin was convinced that if someone looked up the definition of "miserable" in the dictionary, he or she would surely find a picture of this awful experience. It was wet, cold, dark, and almost impossible to walk. Edwin's lip began to quiver. He knew he was going to cry. There was nothing he could do to stop a flood of tears.

But, instead of crying, he froze!

Something was on his leg. At first, he thought he had caught himself on a root but he quickly realized it couldn't be a root because whatever it was had wrapped itself around his ankle. It was alive!

他何故要吃这个苦头呢，连他自己都说不清了！

　　湿滑的路面使得更难以行走，每一脚踩下去，都沾满了深及踝部的泥泞。埃德温不止一次看到滑溜溜的爬行动物在脚下蠕动或在黏巴巴的泥浆里穿行。

　　然而，这些对碧翠丝就更是高难度了！她的高跟鞋跟登山靴相比可差远了。每走一步，都要在泥浆里卡上半天。菲利克斯不得不拿出撬棍把她深陷在泥泞里的脚撬出来，直到她能够跨出下一步脚。

　　最后，大家都烦透了，于是他们决定抬着碧翠丝继续前进。托马斯和埃德温一人抓住一只胳膊，而菲利克斯和巴塞洛缪——他们此刻正为该朝哪个方向前进而争论不休的——则各抬着一只脚。

　　就在这时，天空突然下起雨来！

　　埃德温觉得，如果有人要描述"悲催"在字典里的含义，他们此时这副狼狈相真是再合适不过了，要在这条潮湿阴冷的幽暗小道上继续前行几乎是不可能的。埃德温的嘴唇开始颤抖起来，他知道自己忍不住要哭了，他无法抑制住自己喷涌而出的泪水。

　　但是，还没待他哭出声来，他突然惊得不敢动弹了！

　　他的脚踢到了什么东西。起初，他还以为只是一截木桩。但他很快意识到不可能是木桩，因为他的脚踝已经被牢牢缠住了，它是活的！

12

THE YA

"Help!" screamed Edwin. But it was too late. An enormously fat-looking gray snake—about the length of a garden hose—had coiled itself around Edwin's foot. Edwin dropped Beatrice in the mud while Thomas pulled on Edwin's arm, trying to yank him away from the creature.

"Oww," yelled Edwin.

"You can't do that, you idiot." said Beatrice, getting up out of the mud. "You'll pull off his arm."

"Help!" cried Edwin again.

This time the snake started making sounds. At first Edwin didn't understand what they were. Then he recognized them as distinct "Ya" sounds. With every twirl and coil around Edwin's body, with every slither, slather, and squeeze, the gruesome reptile would cry out a victorious "YA"!

Coil, coil, "YA"!

Squeeze, squeeze, "YA"!

Slither, slather, slither, slather, "YA YA YA!" went the snake as it wrapped itself higher around Edwin's body.

"Let go, you beast!" ordered Beatrice.

"YA," yelled the beast. But it didn't let go.

"Felix! Do something!" cried Beatrice.

Felix fumbled in his tool kit while Bartholomew flipped through the Professor's papers, trying to discover what this thing was.

"Help me! Please!" screamed Edwin.

12

遭遇攻击

"救命啊！"埃德温狂叫起来。但为时已晚，一条与花园水管一般粗的大灰蛇已经紧紧地缠住了埃德温的脚。埃德温随手将碧翠丝往泥浆里一扔，托马斯赶紧上前拉着埃德温的胳膊，试图将他拖出那条蛇的攻击范围。

"嗷呜呜！"埃德温大叫起来。

"快住手，你这个笨蛋。"从泥浆里爬起来的碧翠丝说道，"你会把他的胳膊拉断的。"

"救命啊！"埃德温再次尖叫起来。

这一次，蛇开始发出攻击的声音。起初，埃德温还没弄明白这个声音的含义。随后，他听出了清晰的"呀"声。每当它围绕埃德温多缠绕一圈或者勒紧一下，这条可恶的大蛇就发出欣喜若狂的"**呀**！"

缠呀缠，"**呀**！"

挤呀挤，"**呀**！"

滑呀滑，滑呀滑"**呀呀呀**！"大蛇在埃德温的身体上越缠越高。

"放开他，你这只野兽！"碧翠丝大声叫道。

"**呀**！"大蛇回敬她道，丝毫没有要放松的意思。

"菲利克斯！快想办法啊！"碧翠丝哭喊起来。

菲利克斯在工具包里摸索着，巴塞洛缪飞快地翻着教授的文件，试图找到对策。

"救救我！求求你们啦！"埃德温大声哭喊着。

"Oh, goodness gracious!" said Beatrice, quite annoyed with the lack of action to save poor Edwin. She whipped off one of her high-heeled shoes and, with all her might, whacked the snake across its head.

The snake immediately cried out, "YA," which quickly turned into "Yow." Before you could say "reptilian," the snake had slipped off Edwin and submerged back into the marsh.

Thomas and Felix looked at each other in disbelief.

"Well, a lot of good you two turned out to be," said Beatrice, helping Edwin get up off the ground.

"I'm alright now," said Edwin. "Thank you for saving me."

Beatrice put her arm around him and squeezed him lovingly. "What did I tell you, Edwin? I said I'd look after you."

"What was it?" asked Edwin, starting to shiver again.

"Some sort of snake, Ed," said Felix.

"Ya," said Bartholomew.

"But it was bigger than a snake," said Beatrice.

"Ya," said Bartholomew.

"Well, maybe it was a sea monster," said Thomas.

"Ya," said Bartholomew.

"Will you put a lid on it!" cried Felix. "Why must you keep saying 'Ya'?"

"Because Ya is what that was," answered Bartholomew.

"What?" said Felix.

"Ya," said Bartholomew.

"Blessed balloon-head!" screamed Felix. "What is the matter with you?"

"Ah, Felix. I think Bart is trying to tell us the creature is called a Ya," offered Edwin.

"Oh," said Felix. "Well, for goodness sake, why didn't he just say so?"

"哦，天哪！"碧翠丝看到可怜的埃德温如此受罪，大家却都手足无措，心里大为光火。她猛然抽起一只高跟鞋，拼尽全身力气朝蛇头一阵猛砸。大蛇大吼一声"**呀**"，未及出口，就被一声痛苦的"哟"盖过。说时迟那时快，那条大蛇迅速从埃德温身上滑落，遁入沼泽之中。

留下托马斯和菲利克斯面面相觑。

"很好，关键时刻你俩还真是帮了大忙。"碧翠丝一边揶揄道，一边将埃德温扶起身来。

"我没事了。"埃德温说道，"谢谢你救了我。"

碧翠丝抱住他的肩膀，疼爱地抚摸着他："还记得我说过什么吗，埃德温？都说了我会保护你的。"

"刚才那个到底是什么东西？"埃德温问道，想起来又开始再次颤抖了。

"一种蛇，小埃。"菲利克斯说道。

"呀。"巴塞洛缪说道。

"它比蛇可大多了。"碧翠丝说道。

"呀。"巴塞洛缪说道。

"哎呀，说不准是海怪什么的。"托马斯猜测着。

"呀。"巴塞洛缪重复着这个字。

"你就不能闭上嘴吗？"菲利克斯大叫了起来，"为什么你要一直不停地说'呀'？"

"因为呀就是它的名字。"巴塞洛缪答道。

"什么？"菲利克斯惊奇地问。

"呀。"巴塞洛缪又重复了一次。

"你好个烦人的家伙！"菲利克斯不耐烦地尖叫起来，"你这是怎么回事了？"

"哎呀，菲利克斯，我想小巴的意思是说，刚才那条蛇的名字就叫犽。"埃德温解释道。

"哦，"菲利克斯说道，"哎呀，看在老天爷的分儿上，他直接说不就得了吗？"

"What do your papers say about it, Bart?" Edwin asked inquisitively.

"Let's see," said Bartholomew, flipping through the Professor's notes. "Oh, yes! Here we are!" he said, flattening out a crumpled piece of paper. "The Ya is another creature that is indigenous to the Neergreve Forest. Yas look like long snakes that range in length from two to three metres. Drow created the Yas to help lure words into his Stream of Consciousness. Extended exposure to Yas may result in your agreeing to do anything anyone asks of you."

"I see!" said Felix gloomily. "Another one of Drow's creatures. We must be more careful. Keep your eyes open for anything that appears out of the ordinary."

"Forward MARCH!" ordered Thomas.

And so the group continued on, trudging through the Ya-infested swamp and still carrying Beatrice. After her brave efforts, she deserved a free ride.

They walked and walked and then walked some more until finally the ground began to get a bit harder.

"文件上怎么说的，小巴？"埃德温好奇地问道。

"让我看看。"巴塞洛缪翻看着教授的附注。

"哦，对啦！上面是这么说的！"他抚平了一页皱巴巴的纸，解释道，"犽也是尼尔格雷夫森林的一种特有生物，外形与蛇类似，体长可达两到三米。卓尔创造了犽，以便将单词们诱入意识之河。长时间与这种生物接触的人将会丧失自主意识。"

"我懂了！"菲利克斯愁眉不展地说，"又是卓尔制造的一种邪恶生物，看来我们得加倍小心谨慎了，大家一定要留神身边出现的任何异常事物。"

"齐步，**向前走**！"托马斯发出了指令。

于是大家伙儿在遍地滋生着犽的沼泽地中继续前进。不过这一回，大家抬着见义勇为的碧翠丝，心里再也没有了埋怨。

他们走啊走啊，一直走到一片更为崎岖的地形之上。

13

A HOUSE IS SPOTTED

"What's that?" said Thomas, pointing into the air. "It looks like smoke."

The group looked up. Sure enough, rising through a clump of trees was a stream of gray smoke.

"I don't see anything," said Beatrice, lying flat in the arms of the others.

"Take our word for it," snapped Thomas. "There's smoke!"

"Oh, great!" exclaimed Beatrice. "The forest is on fire!"

"No, no," said Felix. "That looks like chimney smoke to me. We must be nearing the road. There's probably a house over there."

Edwin perked up. He couldn't imagine anyone living around here. He had given up hope of ever seeing civilization again. But this might be a chance to dry off and warm up before a roaring fire.

"Let's go and see," said Edwin excitedly.

"Wait!" said Bartholomew. "Felix, are you thinking what I'm thinking?"

"Oh, I'd hate to be doing that," said Felix sarcastically. "But, yes, I know what you mean."

"What?" said Edwin.

"That house probably belongs to one of Drow's spies," said Felix. "We can't just go waltzing up to the door and expect to be met with open arms."

"Oh," said Edwin sadly.

"Bart, here's your chance to do something useful for a change. It's time for a transformation."

"What's he going to do?" said Edwin, perking up again.

13

一座房子

"那是什么？"托马斯指着半空中问道，"看起来像是一团烟。"

大家纷纷抬起头来。果然，在一排树丛中升起一团灰色的烟雾。

"我可什么也没看到。"碧翠丝四仰八叉地躺着，说道。

"我说是就是咯，"托马斯厉声说道，"是烟！"

"哦，那就太好了，"碧翠丝叫道，"森林肯定是着火了。"

"才不是呢，"菲利克斯说道，"我倒觉得那看起来像是烟囱冒出来的烟，我们肯定是接近大路了，估计那边是一座房子。"

埃德温心头一喜，他无法想象居然有人居住在这一带，他早就放弃了可以再度看到文明的幻想了。说不定他们还能坐到熊熊燃烧的炉火前烤烤衣服，暖和暖和呢。

"我们去看看。"埃德温激动地说。

"等等！"巴塞洛缪说道，"菲利克斯，你是不是也在想我正在考虑的问题？"

"哦，我不愿意那样做的，"菲利克斯刻薄地说，"不过，是的，我懂你的意思。"

"你们说什么呢？"埃德温问道。

"那房子的主人很可能就是卓尔的间谍之一，"菲利克斯解释道，"难道你还想优哉游哉地走过去，受到贵宾般的热情接待不成？"

"哦。"埃德温感到一阵失落。

"小巴，这可是你立功的好机会，该你大显身手了。"

"你要他去做什么？"埃德温的精神头儿又回来了。

"As you know, Ed, Nouns can be persons, places, or things. Bart here, being a Noun, has the power to change into just about anything."

"What are you going to become?" Edwin asked, looking over at Bartholomew.

"A Drow word!" announced Bartholomew. With that, he mumbled a few words and stuck his finger in his left ear. POOF! He was suddenly enveloped in a cloud of smoke. A few minutes later, as the smoke began to dissipate, Bartholomew came back into view.

The group stared in amazement! Bartholomew the Nerd was now Bartholomew the Cool Dude. No longer was he dressed in his short pants with the tight belt and horn-rimmed glasses with tape wrapped around the middle. He wore a leather jacket with a very strange picture on the back—a man sitting on a motorcycle with his large pet snake wound around his head.

Bartholomew's hair had also changed. It was now spiked. And to complement the whole image, a large silver earring hung from his left nostril.

"Hey, man! Like what d'ya think?" said Bartholomew.

"Very cool, Bart!—I mean, Dudly Dude," said Felix, chuckling at this new spectacle.

"Let's have a look at our sentence now," Thomas said excitedly.

The group arranged themselves and everyone looked from left to right to see what it said.

FIX THE BEAUTIFUL DUDE, EDWIN.

"A rather strange sentence," said Thomas. "But it will have to do. Come on! Let's push on," he continued. "Forward MARCH!"

And so Felix Fix, Thomas The, Beatrice Beautiful, Dudly Dude, and Edwin Bellamy headed toward the rising column of smoke. As they walked among the trees and over a couple of embankments, in the distance they gradually saw the shape of a small cottage with smoke bellowing from its chimney.

"你知道的，小埃，名词可以代表人物、地点或事物。你眼前的这个名词，小巴，他可是具有千变万化的魔力喔。"

"你打算变成什么呢？"埃德温看着巴塞洛缪问道。

"卓尔的单词！"巴塞洛缪说道。话音刚落，他就把手指插入了左耳中，口中念念有词。**噗**！只见一团烟雾笼罩在他周围，几分钟后，烟消雾散，巴塞洛缪走了出来。

每个人都被惊得目瞪口呆！书呆子巴塞洛缪一瞬间成了大帅哥巴塞洛缪。短得吊在腿上的裤子、紧勒在腰间的皮带还有缠着胶带、破破烂烂的眼镜架都不见了。他穿着一件皮夹克，夹克后印着怪异图案——是一位男士坐在一辆摩托车上，他的头上缠着一条长长的宠物蛇。

巴塞洛缪的头发也已改变成帅气的缪莫霍克发型，与之前简直判若两人，他的左鼻孔上挂着一个银色的大鼻环，为整款造型画龙点睛。

"嘿，兄弟们！觉得咋样啊？"巴塞洛缪问道。

"酷毙了，小巴！——我是说，达德利·伙计。"菲利克斯看着巴塞洛缪的新造型笑出声来。

"现在，让我们看看我们的句子。"托马斯激动地说。

大家伙儿重新列队，从左向右看齐，以确定句子的意思是否无误。

修理这个美丽的伙计，埃德温。

"这个句子有点怪啊，"托马斯说道，"不过，只要说得通就行了，来吧！我们继续前进。"他说道："齐步，**向前走**！"

于是，菲利克斯·修理、托马斯·这个、碧翠丝·美丽、达德利·伙计，还有埃德温·贝拉米一齐向那团冉冉升起的烟雾走去。他们走过一排树木和几座护堤，一座小别墅在远处若隐若现，一团团烟雾从它的烟囱里袅袅升空。

"There it is," said Edwin, pointing to the little house.

"All right, listen carefully!" ordered Felix. "We must proceed with extreme caution. We'll pretend we're a sentence that has lost its way."

"A run-on sentence," said Edwin.

"Yes—that's it!" said Felix approvingly. "We're a run-on sentence."

The group climbed down a steep bank and walked gingerly toward the cottage. As they neared the front entrance, Edwin caught sight of a little sign hanging on a low picket fence that surrounded the garden.

"Look! A sign," he said.

"What does it say? What does it say?" said Beatrice, still lying flat in the group's arms.

"It says THE GEEKS," said Edwin.

"The GEEKS?" said Beatrice. "Must be some of Thomas's relatives."

"Ha! Ha," grumbled Thomas.

"Well, at least we know they work for Drow," said Felix. "There are no geeks in our story."

"Then let's get out of here!" said Beatrice, struggling to free herself from the group's grasp.

"Not so fast!" ordered Felix. "We have nothing to worry about as long as Bart remains Dudly Dude. I say we check out these Geeks and see whether we can get some information from them on the whereabouts of Drow."

"Fine," said Thomas. "Who's going in first?"

"Not me," said Beatrice.

"I'll go," said Edwin, "if you really want me to."

"That's alright, Ed. I think Dudley here should lead the way," said Felix, pointing to Bartholomew. "Just to be on the safe side."

"Hey, man, like what are we waitin' for?" said Bartholomew jokingly. "Let's check out this cool pad."

"就在那儿。"埃德温指着那座小别墅说道。

"好吧,大家都听好了!"菲利克斯正色道,"我们必须谨慎行事,我们要假装成一个迷路的句子。"

"一个不连贯的句子。"埃德温说道。

"是的,就这意思!"菲利克斯赞许地说道,"我们就装成一个不连贯的句子。"

大家爬下陡峭的河堤,小心翼翼地朝别墅走去,靠近前门时,埃德温突然注意到花园的小栅栏上挂着一块小牌子。

"快看!看那块牌子。"埃德温说道。

"上面写了些什么呀?写了些什么呀?"碧翠丝四仰八叉地躺着,急切地问。

"写着:**老怪物**。"埃德温也好奇起来。

"**老怪物**?"碧翠丝重复道,"准是托马斯家的亲戚。"

"哈!哈!"托马斯假笑道。

"嗯,现在我们至少可以确定他们是卓尔的手下了,"菲利克斯说道,"我们的故事里没有老怪这个单词。"

"那咱们还是离开这儿吧。"碧翠丝试图从其他人手里挣脱出来。

"急什么!"菲利克斯正色道,"只要小巴伪装成达德利·伙计,咱们就没什么可担心的。我说,咱们不妨上这老怪物家探一探,看看能不能从他们这里打听到有关卓尔的下落。"

"行。"托马斯说道,"谁第一个进去呢?"

"别找我。"碧翠丝说道。

"我去吧,"埃德温自告奋勇地说,"如果你们同意的话。"

"没关系啦,小埃,我觉得应该让达德利打头阵,"菲利克斯指了指巴塞洛缪说,"为了大家伙儿的安全考虑嘛。"

"嗨,哥们儿,那咱们还在这儿废啥话呀?"巴塞洛缪半开玩笑地说道,"现在就进去看看。"

And so Bartholomew, Felix, and Edwin walked up to the front door of the house, followed by Beatrice and Thomas who huddled together, peering apprehensively over each other's shoulders.

When Bartholomew got to the door, he lifted the big knocker and rapped three times. No sooner had he let go of the knocker, he realized the door was already open. He eased it open a bit more and the hinges began to creak. Warm air rushed over the group's faces, reminding them they were still wet and longing for some warmth. Felix and Edwin followed Bartholomew into the front hall and surveyed the surroundings.

It was a cozy little house with crooked walls plastered with white stucco. The roof was held up with huge wooden beams. Beyond the narrow staircase at the entrance, there were large French doors and to the right of the stairs was a living room with a big stone fireplace, complete with a marvellous roaring fire.

"Hey, there! Anyone home?" cried Bartholomew.

There was no answer.

"Well, that's too bad," said Beatrice turning around in a hurry. "I guess we'll just have to go."

As she reached the open door, a thump, thump, thumping noise started coming from upstairs. The group froze. Their hearts raced as the thumping noise moved down the stairs.

于是，巴塞洛缪、菲利克斯，和埃德温向大门走去，碧翠丝和托马斯两人缩手缩脚地跟在后面，隔着彼此的肩膀忧心忡忡地向前瞟。

当巴塞洛缪走到大门前，抬起门环敲了三次，他刚放下门环，大门吱呀一声就开了。他轻轻推开大门，听到铰链吱吱作响，迎面拂过一阵暖风，他们这才想起自己身上还是湿漉漉的，多想围着炉火暖和一下啊！菲利克斯和埃德温紧跟着巴塞洛缪来到了前厅，谨慎地扫视着周围的环境。

别墅内部温馨宜人，歪歪斜斜的墙壁上粉刷着白色的灰泥。巨大的木梁支撑着整个屋顶，透过在入口处窄长的楼梯，可以看到若干宽大的法式落地玻璃门，在楼梯右侧是一间起居室，有一个巨大的石制壁炉，炉内的火正熊熊燃烧着。

"嘿！有人在家吗？"巴塞洛缪大声问道。

没人回答。

"哎呀，太不巧了，"碧翠丝匆忙转过身说道，"看来我们得走了。"

正当她准备伸手去拉门时，从楼上传来一阵扑通、扑通、扑通的声音，所有人都屏住了呼吸，随着这个声音从楼梯上拾级而下，他们的心也吊到了嗓子眼儿。

14

THE GEEKS

Suddenly, a head peeked out around the corner of a wall halfway up the stairs. Then out popped another head. Then a body emerged—a body with two heads.

Edwin and the group gasped.

"It's all right," whispered Bartholomew. "It must be a compound word. Those two have to stick together."

Edwin started to feel quite uncomfortable. He had never seen anything like that and didn't know what to think.

"Who are YOU?" asked one of the words suspiciously.

"We're a run-on sentence that has lost its way," said Felix.

"Oh, that's a shame," said the other twin. "Please, do come in. Allow me to introduce ourselves. I'm Gonna Geek and this is my brother Gimme Geek. I don't know if you have noticed but we are a compound word."

"Oh, yes . . . yes, so you are," said Felix, trying to be polite.

Gimmegonna ushered the group forward. As it waddled toward the living room, its two heads bounced up and down like the heads on a marionette.

"Where did you get those . . . LOVELY names?" said Beatrice, half sarcastically. No sooner had she asked the question, the answer became obvious.

"Gimme that chair," cried Gimme, pulling at the arm of a big overstuffed chair.

14

老怪

楼梯中间的拐角处突然探出一个脑袋，接着，又探出了一个脑袋。然后，整个身体也站了出来——原来是一个双头怪。

埃德温和其他人吓得连大气也不敢出。

"别紧张，"巴塞洛缪压低声音说道，"它肯定是一个复合词。所以两个词才会粘在一起的。"

埃德温觉得很不舒服，他可从来没见过这么奇怪的事，一时半会儿竟没了主意。

"**你们**是谁？"其中一个脑袋用怀疑的眼神打量着他们，问道。

"我们是一个不连贯的句子，现在迷路了。"菲利克斯犹犹豫豫地说道。

"哦，可怜的，"另一个脑袋说道，"进来吧，别见外了，请允许我向大家做个自我介绍，我是吉纳·老怪，这是我弟弟吉米·老怪。不知道你们是否留意到了，我们是一个复合词。"

"哦，是的……是的，我们看出来了。"菲利克斯尽量表现得礼貌得体地说。

两兄弟领着一行人等往里走，摇摇摆摆地走进了起居室，往前走的时候，两个头就像提线木偶的脑袋一样上下晃悠着。

"你们怎么会有这么……**可爱的**名字呢？"碧翠丝半是嘲讽地问道。她话音还没落，就从兄弟俩的行为中看出了端倪。

"把椅子给我！"吉米抓着一把软垫椅的扶手，跟哥哥大声争吵了起来。

"No!" cried Gonna, pulling the other arm, "I want it, OK? Let go or you're gonna get it."

"Gimme, gimme, gimme!" screamed Gimme.

"You're gonna gimme that chair or else I'm gonna smash you on the head, OK?" yelled Gonna.

But Gimme did not let go. And both of them continued to scream at each other and to pull and tug on the poor old chair until finally the inevitable happened. The chair broke in half. Each member of the compound word was suddenly left holding one of the chair's broken arms. When they realized what had happened, they simultaneously began to bawl like babies. The group looked at each other and shrugged, not knowing what else to do.

"Excuse me, Mr. Geek and Mr. Geek," said Edwin. "Why, when you are both sharing the same body, would you want to fight over a chair? Wherever one of you sits, the other one has to sit there, too."

Gimmegonna stopped sobbing and looked at the broken chair and then each head looked at the other one.

"The boy is right, huh?" screamed Gimme.

"So he is!" said Gonna. And with that, they both burst out laughing.

"You're a smart boy," said Gonna. "What is your name?"

"Edwin, sir. Edwin Bellamy."

"Well, Edwin Bellamy, because of your helpfulness in pointing out this very important fact about chairs to Gimme and me, we would like you and your friends to stay for supper, OK? Isn't that right, Gimme?"

"Yes! Yes! Most definitely," said Gimme excitedly. Edwin looked over at Felix, who quickly nodded his head in approval.

"Yes, that would be lovely," said Edwin.

"Good," said Gonna. "Now, what are all your names?"

"Well," said Edwin, pointing in turn to each member of the group, "This is Felix Fix, Beatrice Beautiful, Thomas The, and Dudley Dude."

"不行！"吉纳紧抓着另一边的扶手，大声叫道，"我要坐，不行吗？再不放手，我就要砸碎你的头。"

"给我，给我，给我！"吉米尖叫着。

"你给我放手，否则我就打破你的头，听见了吗？"吉纳大叫着说。

但是，吉米死也不肯撒手，两个人继续互相嘶吼，紧抓着那把可怜的旧椅子又是拉又是拽，直到最后悲剧发生了，椅子被硬生生扯成了两半。兄弟俩手中各拿着一半残缺不全的椅子扶手，当他们明白过来时，兄弟俩像任性的孩子似的同时放声痛哭起来。其他人面面相觑，无奈地耸耸肩膀，不知拿他们如何是好。

"很抱歉，大老怪先生和小老怪先生，"埃德温突然说道，"可是，你俩不是只有一个身体吗？干吗还为了一张椅子争得头破血流呢？只要一个人坐着，另一个不就也坐下来了嘛。"

兄弟俩停止了哭泣，看了看四分五裂的椅子，然后又看看对方。

"这孩子说得没错，对吧？"吉米尖声说道。

"是没错！"吉纳也承认。话音刚落，兄弟俩都止不住大笑起来。

"你真是个聪明的孩子，"吉纳说道，"你叫什么名字？"

"埃德温，先生。埃德温·贝拉米。"

"好吧，埃德温·贝拉米，感谢你帮我和吉米认清了一个重要的事实，不知你和你的朋友们是否愿意赏脸共进晚餐，可以吗？怎么样，吉米？"

"太棒了！太棒了！这主意太妙了！"吉米激动地说。埃德温抬眼看了看菲利克斯，菲利克斯飞快地点了点头算是同意了。

"好的，那就却之不恭了。"埃德温说道。

"太好了，"吉纳说道，"对了，请教各位尊姓大名呀？"

埃德温指着伙伴们一一介绍："嗯，这位是菲利克斯·修理，这位是碧翠丝·美丽，这位是托马斯·这个，还有这位是达德利·伙计。"

Gonna started shaking the hand of each group member when suddenly Gimme cried out, "Hey, gimme a chance to shake their hands, huh?"

Gonna turned to Gimme with rage on his face.

"Look, when are you gonna learn some manners?" said Gonna, bonking Gimme on the head. "Now why don't you run off to the kitchen and make our guests some food."

Gimme turned bright purple as a large bump began to emerge from his head. He turned around and stormed toward the kitchen.

"Hey, wait," cried Gonna realizing his own two feet were running down the hall. "I don't wanna go, too!"

Unfortunately, once again, Gonna had forgotten he shared the same body as Gimme. And despite his yelling and screaming, Gonna's body continued tearing toward the kitchen.

"Stop!" screamed Gonna, his head spinning around in circles.

"Go back!" he ordered.

"Freeze!" he demanded.

"Help! Police!" he yelled.

But his screaming and yelling were to no avail. At last the noise subsided as the compound word made its way into the kitchen at the back of the house.

"Now what?" said Thomas.

"Shhh," said Beatrice, falling into a large red couch. "Felix knows what we're doing. Hey, Felix, what are we doing?"

"We're going to stay for supper and get some information out of these Geeks. We've got to ask them about Drow."

"Say what?" said Bartholomew. "Hey, man, like, I say we split this pad. These dudes are nothing but geeks; I mean REAL geeks."

"Good, then. You should feel right at home here," said Felix glibly.

"Droll, man, very droll!" said Bartholomew.

"Shhh," said Edwin, "I think I hear them coming back."

吉纳和众人一一握手，突然吉米大声叫了起来："嘿，也给我留个机会跟他们握手吧，哼？"

吉纳转过身，满脸愠色地看着吉米。

"瞧瞧你那德行，你什么时候才能懂点儿礼貌呢？"说着，吉纳冲着吉米的脑门儿弹了一记响崩："你干吗不去厨房给客人们弄点好吃的呢。"

吉米的脑门儿上立刻鼓起了一个青紫色的大包。他转过身去，怒气冲冲地朝着厨房冲了过去。

"嘿，等一下，"吉纳看着自己的两条腿向着楼下大厅飞奔，不由得怒吼道，"我可不想去！"

不幸的是，他好像又忘了兄弟俩共享的是同一个身体。尽管吉纳一路大喊大叫着表示抗议，但他的身体仍然朝着厨房发足狂奔。

"停下！"吉纳尖叫着，开始转着圈摇晃起自己的脑袋来。

"回去！"他命令道。

"不许动！"他继续说。

"救命啊！警察先生！"他大喊道。

但是，无论他怎么大喊大叫都无济于事。直到兄弟俩扭打着冲进别墅后方的厨房里，歇斯底里的吵闹才算告一段落。

"现在怎么办？"托马斯问道。

"嘘，"碧翠丝悠闲地往一个红色的大沙发上坐下去。碧翠丝问道："菲利克斯知道该怎么做。嘿，菲利克斯，现在该怎么办啊？"

"我们留下吃晚饭，看能不能从老怪兄弟俩口中打探点有用的信息。我们得问问他们有关卓尔的事。"

"你说什么？"巴塞洛缪问道，"嗨，哥们，照我的意思，咱们不如把这里拆个稀巴烂。这些家伙就是些怪物，**不折不扣**的怪物。"

"那好吧，那您就请自便吧。"菲利克斯油嘴滑舌地说道。

"跳梁小丑，自以为是，真是滑稽！"巴塞洛缪说道。

"嘘，"埃德温说道，"我好像听到他们往回走的脚步声了。"

The group quickly sat up straight. The sound of more arguing could be heard down the hall.

"Gimme that tray. I prepared the food so I should serve it, OK?" cried Gimme.

Gimmegonna rounded the corner and stood in the doorway of the living room.

"You're gonna give me that tray or else," ordered Gonna, pulling on the tray of food balanced on Gimme's hand.

"Or else what?" demanded Gimme.

"Or else . . . or else I'll make myself a garlic sandwich and I won't brush my teeth for a week. Then, when we go to sleep at night, I'll sleep with my head turned in your direction."

"You wouldn't!"

"Oh, yes I would!" screamed Gimme.

"All right stinko, here! Take your silly tray!"

"Thank you," said Gimme smugly.

The compound word entered the living room with a tray of various-shaped pieces of brown food.

"What is that?" said Beatrice under her breath.

"Hmmm," said Felix, "It looks like . . . "

"Please, don't say it," said Beatrice.

"Chocolate!" cried Edwin.

"Chocolate?" said Beatrice.

"Yes, yes," said Gimme, hearing the word chocolate. "We have chocolate pizzas, chocolate-chip stew, chicken dipped in chocolate sauce, and chocolate liver bits."

The group looked at each other in complete horror and each turned greener than grasshoppers.

"And if you think that's good," continued Gonna, "you'll love what's for dessert. There's broccoli cake, broccoli ice cream, broccoli pie, and broccoli greenies."

大家伙儿都正襟危坐，只听得大厅那头传来更激烈的争吵声。

"把托盘给我，我做的饭，就该我来端，懂吗？"吉米嘶吼道。

吉米、吉纳转过大厅的拐角，走到了起居室的门口。

"把托盘给我，否则……"吉纳命令道，就伸手去抢吉米手中的一盘食物。

"否则怎样？"吉米挑衅地问道。

"否则……否则我就做一个蒜味三明治塞进嘴里，然后一个星期也不刷牙，晚上睡觉的时候，我就脸冲着你那边儿，熏死你。"

"你敢！"

"哦，我就敢！我就要这么做！"吉米尖叫道。

"好吧，大臭蛋，给你！拿着你可笑的盘子吧！"

"那我就不客气了！"吉米得意地说道。

兄弟俩拿着一盘形状各异的棕色食物走进起居室。

"那是什么呀？"碧翠丝压低声音问道。

"嗯……"菲利克斯说道，"看上去像是……"

"拜托，别说了。"碧翠丝说道。

"巧克力！"埃德温大叫道。

"巧克力？"碧翠丝问道。

"是的，没错，"吉米听到了他们的话，说道，"我们有巧克力、比萨、巧克力炖菜、巧克力蜜制鸡柳，还有猪肝拌巧克力酱。"

大家伙儿面面相觑，个个脸色铁青。

吉纳继续说道："如果这些菜合你们的胃口，那么你们肯定会喜欢我们的甜品有：西蓝花蛋糕、西蓝花冰激凌、西蓝花馅儿饼，还有西蓝花绿蛋糕。"

"Don't you mean brownies?" asked Edwin.

"No, I mean greenies. If you want brownies, you have to use rotten broccoli. I could make you some if you'd like, OK?"

"Ah, no thank you. Greenies will be fine," said Edwin humbly.

"Good, then," said Gonna. "We'll eat in here in front of the fire."

The group politely nibbled on the chocolate morsels, wondering how they were going to eat them all without throwing up.

Gimmegonna solved that problem. Without caring the least bit about being polite hosts, the two of them gobbled down the whole tray of food in 2 minutes flat.

"Oh, boy, am I ever full!" said Gimme, letting out a large burp.

"Me, too," groaned Gonna, wiping his chocolatey mouth with his sleeve.

"Yes, we're all full, too, aren't we?" said Thomas, winking desperately at the others.

"Yes, quite, quite full, thank you," said Beatrice, sticking her piece of chocolate pizza down the side of the couch.

"你是指巧克力蛋糕吧？"埃德温问道。

"不，我说的是绿蛋糕，做巧克力蛋糕得用烂掉的西蓝花。如果你想吃，我可以给你做一点儿，你要吃吗？"

"啊，不用，谢谢。我吃绿蛋糕就行了。"埃德温很有礼貌地说道。

"很好，那么，"吉纳说道，"我们就在这边的炉火前就餐吧。"

大家伙儿都象征性地咬了几口巧克力甜点，拼命抑制住反胃的感觉。

不过，这兄弟俩显然吃得很尽兴，不到两分钟就把整个餐盘内的食物瓜分得一干二净，完全没有考虑到礼让客人的规矩。

"哦，天啊，我从没吃得这么撑过！"吉米打了个大饱嗝儿，说道。

"我也是。"吉纳一边用袖子擦拭着嘴角的巧克力，一边心满意足地说道。

"是呀，我们也都吃饱了，对吧？"托马斯不停地冲大家使着眼色。

"没错，吃得好饱呀，谢谢你们的盛情款待！"碧翠丝悄悄地把手里的巧克力比萨丢到沙发一侧。

15

MORE ABOUT DROW

"Well, now that supper is over, we can talk," said Gimme. "You say you're a run-on sentence that has got lost. Where exactly were you heading?"

Felix realized this was the opportunity he had been waiting for.

"We were on our way to visit a man called Drow," said Felix.

Suddenly Gimmegonna's heads shot up like turtle heads coming out of their shells. Their eyes began to bulge out of their sockets.

"What's the matter?" asked Felix.

Gimme tried to compose himself. "You . . . you said you were going to VISIT Drow?"

"Yes, that's right," said Felix. "We . . . we have to attend to some business. Is there something wrong with that?"

"No one ever VISITS Drow," said Gonna seriously.

"Why not?" asked Edwin, now very interested in the conversation.

"Be . . . b . . . because Drow isn't a nice person. HE'S the one that does the visiting," said Gonna.

"Yes, and when you least expect it," said Gimme gravely.

"What do you mean?" said Thomas, throwing himself into the conversation.

"Drow's Mumbojumbos. They're hiding everywhere. They're just waiting to convert you to Drow."

"We know!" said Felix. "We've encountered a couple of them already."

"Were you converted to Drow?" asked Edwin, turning to Gimme and Gonna.

15

卓尔的传说

"好了，晚餐吃完了，咱们来聊聊天吧，"吉米说道，"你们不是说自己是不连贯的句子，现在迷路了吗，敢问几位这是要上哪儿去呀？"

菲利克斯意识到这可是他一直在等待的机会。

"我们正打算去拜见卓尔先生。"菲利克斯说道。

兄弟俩的两个脑袋立刻像探出头的乌龟一样竖了起来，两人都把眼睛瞪得圆圆的。

"怎么了？"菲利克斯问道。

吉米努力使自己镇定下来："你……你说，你们要去**拜见**卓尔？"

"是的，没错，"菲利克斯说道，"我们……我们跟卓尔之间有点儿业务往来，有什么不妥吗？"

"卓尔可不是你们想见就能见的。"吉纳一脸严肃地说道。

"为什么不？"埃德温对这段对话非常感兴趣。

"因……因……因为卓尔可不是什么上等君子。**他想**见你时，自会找上门的。"吉纳说道。

"没错，而且往往是在你最意想不到的时候。"吉米也严肃地说。

"什么意思？"托马斯也被这个话题吸引了进来。

"卓尔的胡言军团四处潜伏，无处不在，随时准备着把你们这样的单词转化后进献给卓尔。"

"我们早有耳闻了！"菲利克斯说道，"我们已经跟好几个胡言军团的人打过照面了。"

"你们是被卓尔转化的单词吗？"埃德温转过头问兄弟俩。

"We sure were!" said Gonna. "I used to be the word 'going' and Gimme used to be called 'give'." But one day we were walking through the forest when all of a sudden, something hit us on the head. Sort of like an idea, you know. Anyway, at first, all we could say was 'like you know'. Then, one day we woke up and we were stuck together the way you see us now."

"Not only that," said Gimme, "but taped to the front of our body was a new birth certificate saying we were now called Gimmegonna Geek."

"I see," said Felix grimly.

"By the way, how did you become a Drow word?" said Gonna, turning to Bartholomew.

"Oh, him," said Felix. "This is really Bartholomew Book. He's a Noun. We had him undergo a transformation because we thought you might have been spies for Drow. He's not really a Drow word. Come on, Barty Baby, show your stuff!"

Bartholomew muttered a few words, stuck his finger in his ear, then POOF, he was back to himself again—complete with glasses, pencil, and clothing that was too small for him.

"Mmmm," said Felix, surveying the change. "I think I liked you better as a dude."

"Holy cow!" screamed Gimme. "You're really a sentence without one Drow word in it. Do you realize what that means?"

"Yes, we do," said Bartholomew. "It means if we can get close to Drow, he will turn into an "et cet er a" and float off into oblivion."

"You should be glad you have the ability to transform. It could prove very useful. If Drow already knows your sentence exists, he will do everything possible to stop you from ruining his master plan," said Gimme.

"Master plan?" asked Thomas, concerned.

"Yes," added Gonna. "Rumour has it that Drow wants to convert all the words in the book to Drow. You guys are in great danger."

"How can we find this Drow?" asked Felix.

"当然啦！"吉纳说道，"我本名叫'将'，而吉米原名叫'给'。有一天，我们穿过森林时，突然就被什么东西砸到了头，确切地说，就像是某个想法突然被植入了我们的头脑中一样，你们明白吧。反正刚开始那段时间，我们就只会翻来覆去地重复'你知道的吧'这句话。后来，有一天我们醒来后，就发现我俩的身体被粘在一起了，就是现在你们看到的这副样子。"

"还不止这些呢，"吉米补充道，"我们胸口上还贴着一张出生证明，上面写着我们的新名字：吉米吉纳·老怪物。"

"原来如此啊，"菲利克斯冷冷地说。

"对了，你是怎么变成卓尔的单词的？"吉纳转过头来问巴塞洛缪。

"哦，他呀，"菲利克斯慌忙打圆场，"这位先生的大名叫巴塞洛缪·书，是一个名词。我们本来担心你们是卓尔的间谍，所以就让他变形了，其实他并不是卓尔的单词。好了，亲爱的小巴巴，让他们看看你的真实面目吧！"

巴塞洛缪把手指插入了耳中，口中不断地念着咒语，只听得**噗**的一声，他又变回了老样子——戴着眼镜，夹着铅笔，穿着小得可笑的衣服。

菲利克斯端详着变回原样的巴塞洛缪，说道："嗯，我觉得还是刚才那个样子更讨人喜欢。"

"我的老天啊！"吉米尖叫道，"你们还真是完全没有一个卓尔的单词的句子呀。你们知道这意味着什么吗？"

"当然，我们知道，"巴塞洛缪说道，"这意味着，如果我们能成功接近卓尔，他就会化为'乌有'，烟消云散。"

"幸好你懂得变形这一门绝技，这招儿可太管用了。如果卓尔已经知道你们的句子存在，他肯定会尽一切努力阻止你们，以免你们坏了他的大计。"吉米说道。

"什么大计？"托马斯忧心忡忡地问道。

"没错，"吉纳补充道，"有传言说，卓尔想要转化这本书里所有的单词给他自己。你们现在的处境非常危险。"

"我们怎样才能找到卓尔呢？"菲利克斯问道。

"Like I told you," said Gimme. "You don't find Drow. He finds you."

"Yes, but suppose somebody wanted to find Drow first. Where would he go?"

"That's easy," said Gimme. "You'd go up Drow's Stream of Consciousness. But I've never heard tell of anyone who ever did that. The stream is full of Yas and other bizarre creatures."

"Oh, well, Felix," said Beatrice, turning toward the front door. "I guess we'll just have to go home, right?"

Edwin, not very keen on meeting another Ya, looked over at Felix hopefully.

"Wrong!" said Felix adamantly.

"I was afraid you were going to say that," said Beatrice, slumping back into the couch.

"Gimme, do you know where we can get hold of a boat?" asked Felix.

"Sure! We have a boat. Hasn't been used in years. It's an old rowboat but I'm sure it still floats. You can have it, if you want."

"That's very generous of you," said Felix.

"What are you gonna do if you find Drow?" asked Gonna.

"We want to make him turn over the chapters of the book he has captured and allow us to return the book to the way it used to be."

"Wow, that sounds great!" said Gonna, "but you're never gonna be able to get near him. He has spies everywhere. Drow has simply become too powerful."

"Maybe so, but we still have to try," said Felix. "We promised a good friend of ours that we'd do everything we could. Anyway, I think you should know that Edwin here is from the outside world. Do you know that he has to read books in school—books like our Story?"

"I don't believe it!" said Gimme.

"That simply can't be true!" said Gonna.

"No, really. And not only that! Once we confront Drow, Edwin is going

"不是告诉你们了吗，"吉米说道，"你们找不到他，他自会找上门的。"

"话是没错，但如果我们想先发制人，应该去哪儿找他呢？"

"此事倒也不难，"吉米说道，"你们只要顺着卓尔的意识之河逆流而上就行了。不过，我可从来没听说有人成功过。那条河里充满了犷和各种千奇百怪的生物。"

"哦，这下可好了，菲利克斯，"碧翠丝转过身向前门走去，说道，"我看咱们该老老实实回家了，对吧？"

埃德温也很害怕再遇到犷，他满怀希冀地抬眼看了看菲利克斯。

"错！"菲利克斯的语气不容置疑。

"早就猜到你会这么说了。"碧翠丝说道，她颓然坐回到沙发上。

"吉米，你知道在哪儿可以弄到船吗？"菲利克斯问道。

"当然知道了！我们就有一艘船呀，不过很多年没用过了，虽然是一条旧划艇，但我敢打包票，用起来是一点问题都没有的。你们要的话，就送给你们了。"

"你真是太慷慨了。"菲利克斯说道。

"就算找到了卓尔，你们又打算怎么办呢？"吉纳问道。

"我们要他把书里已改写的章节恢复到原来的模样，让我们回到以前的生活。"

"哇，这主意不赖！"吉纳说道，"但你们可能永远都无法接近卓尔，他的间谍无处不在，卓尔的势力实在是太强大了。"

"这么说是没错，但我们还是要试一下，"菲利克斯说道，"我们曾对一位挚友许下过承诺，一定会竭尽全力完成任务。对了，我还要告诉你们，埃德温来自外面的世界，你们有所不知，他在学校里就经常读书，我是说——像我们的故事这一类的书。"

"我不信。"吉米说道。

"这绝对不可能。"吉纳也说道。

"真的，我没开玩笑！好戏还在后头呢！一旦我们见到卓尔，埃德温会

to tell everyone in this book that they're still loved, they don't need Drow, and that our story is still worth telling!" gushed Felix.

"This is awesome," said Gimme to Gonna.

"It's fantastic!" said Gonna. "To think we might start feeling like ourselves again, all because of this incredible Edwin from the outside world.

Edwin thought about Gonna's phrase "from the outside world" and began thinking about his mother and school and all his friends. Small tears started to roll down his cheeks. Beatrice, noticing poor little Edwin's distress, held his arm tightly and smiled warmly at him. That loving gesture was all he needed. He gave a sniff, wiped his tears, and said triumphantly, "We'll get that Drow. Just you watch!"

Beatrice grinned and Felix cried out, "Here! Here" That's the spirit, Ed. We'll get him, all right!"

"This is absolutely amazing," said Gonna.

"It's simply outrageous," said Gimme. "To think we may not have to be stuck together any longer. The thought of it sends tingles down my spine."

"Mine, too!" said Gonna.

"You guys must rest up for this remarkable mission," said Gimme. "There are enough beds for all of you upstairs. Tomorrow at sunrise, we will carry the boat to the Stream of Consciousness where you can make an early start."

"This is all very kind of you," said Felix.

"Our pleasure!" said Gonna. "If you can turn our book back to the way it used to be, we'll do anything to help you."

"Well, we'll try our best, Gimmegonna," said Felix. "Alright, Thomas, lead the way!"

"Right, Felix!" said Thomas. "Everybody! Forward MARCH—upstairs!"

告诉这本书中的每一个人他是爱他们的，他们不需要卓尔，而且我们的故事还是值得讲述的！"菲利克斯快速地说道。

"这真是太好了！"吉米转头对吉纳说道。

"太棒了！"吉纳附和道，"有了这位来自外界的埃德温的大力相助，我们终于有机会做回自己了。"

埃德温听着吉纳的形容提到"外面的世界"，不由得怀念起了母亲、学校和他所有的朋友，一滴滴泪珠从他的脸颊上悄然滑落。碧翠丝看着可怜的小埃德温，紧紧地搂住他的胳膊，冲他友善地笑了笑，这些温馨的举动足以给埃德温带来抚慰。他吸了一下鼻子，然后擦了擦眼泪，信心满满地说："我们一定会找到卓尔的，大家就等着瞧吧！"

碧翠丝被他逗乐了，菲利克斯也兴奋地大叫起来："就是这样！就是这样！要的就是这个精气神！小埃，咱们一定能抓住他！"

"这感觉真是太妙了！"吉纳说道。

"太令人兴奋了。"吉米也说道，"想想看，我们可能再也不用粘在一起了，一想到这些，我就激动得直发抖。"

"我也是！"吉纳附和道。

"你们几位应该在任务开始前好好休息休息，"吉米说道，"楼上有足够的床位，大家请自便。明天日出时分，我们就会把船抬到意识之河的岸边，好让大家早些上路。"

"两位真是太周到了！"菲利克斯说道。

"我们很乐意效劳！"吉纳说道，"如果你们能让我们的书恢复到以前的模样，我们愿意为你们做任何事。"

"嗯，我们一定会尽全力的，吉米、吉纳，"菲利克斯说道，"好了，托马斯，开路吧！"

"遵命，菲利克斯！"托马斯说道，"大家注意了！目标——楼上！齐步，**走**！"

16

THE VISIT

And so the group marched upstairs where they found an open room containing a series of beds, just enough beds for everyone. Before any of them had a chance to say good night, they were fast asleep. Even Gimmegonna was snoring away on the big double bed. Everyone was deep in his and her own little dream world.

Night had crept in. The bedroom was dark, except for the faint glow of moonlight coming through a small window above Edwin's bed. Everyone seemed peaceful, nestled in their warm blankets . . . so peaceful that none heard the quiet creaking of the window as it opened.

Nor could they see a shape, which some might say looked exactly like a toilet plunger, ease its way down the wall, secured by only a single strand of hair.

Not even Edwin heard the slurp of the plunger-shaped object as it secured itself to his head and slowly—ever so slowly—pulled him from his cozy little bed to the open window.

By the time the window had closed, the only evidence that something had transpired was the moonlit silhouette of a strange bird clasping a small boy as it flew into the night sky.

16

偷袭

一行人来到楼上，宽敞的房间内摆放着一排床铺，刚好一人一个床位，大家伙儿都累得来不及道晚安就昏昏入睡了。吉米、吉纳在大号双人床上鼾声震天，其他人也沉入了甜美的梦乡。

夜色深沉，微弱的月光透过埃德温床头的一面小窗洒进昏暗的卧室内。每个人都蜷在温暖的床上安静地睡着，大家都睡得太死，以至于谁都没有听到窗户被顶开时吱吱的响声。

更没有人看到一个形似皮撬子的物体顺着墙边悄然潜入，只靠一缕头发固定。

甚至连埃德温也完全不知道那个不明物体是如何把自己从小床上好慢——慢慢地—— 一点点拉到窗外的。

窗户啪嗒一声再次关上，一切似乎又恢复了平静。一只外形古怪的大鸟用爪子紧抓着一个小男孩飞向夜空，瞬间消失得无影无踪，只有模糊的剪影留在苍茫的夜色中。

17

EDWIN IS MISSING

Morning finally arrived. Sunlight softly nudged Beatrice's eyes open. At first, she did not realize where she was. But as she sat up, she caught sight of Gimmegonna, contentedly snoring away with smiles on its faces.

Ah, yes! thought Beatrice. Our two inseparable hosts. She turned toward Edwin's bed. She felt somewhat maternal about his well-being. When she noticed he wasn't there, her first thought was he had gone off to the bathroom. As time wore on, she became more concerned. Finally, some of the other group members started stirring and Beatrice leaned over to Felix's bed.

"Felix! Wake up!" she whispered, shaking him gently.

"What is it?" said Felix, rubbing his eyes.

"I can't find Edwin anywhere. He's . . . he's gone!"

Felix bolted upright, making so much noise that he woke Thomas and Bartholomew.

"What is it?" said Tom, sitting up on his bed.

"It's Ed . . . he's missing," said Felix, already running around the top floor.

"Oh, my goodness!" said Bartholomew as he threw on his clothes. "I'll take a look outside. Maybe he just went for a walk or something."

The sounds of doors being opened and closed echoed through the house.

"Ed! Ed! Where are you?" called Felix.

As the slamming of doors got louder and Felix's calling became more desperate, the enormity of the situation hit Beatrice and the others.

"It's all my fault," cried Beatrice. "I promised I would look after him. Now look what's happened!"

17

埃德温不见了

　　终于天亮了，阳光照进了卧室，丝丝暖意将碧翠丝从甜梦中唤醒，她一时忘了自己身在何处。她坐起身来，看到面带笑意的吉米、吉纳老怪兄弟俩正轻轻地打着鼾。

　　啊，对了！碧翠丝暗想着，我是在这对连体兄弟家呢。然后，她充满爱意地转过头看向埃德温的床，想看看他休息得怎么样。她发现埃德温不在床上，便猜他肯定是上卫生间去了。但是，随着时间的推移，她发现越来越不对劲了。最后，连其他人也开始担心起来，碧翠丝赶紧走到菲利克斯床边。

　　"菲利克斯！快醒醒！"她一边低声说道，一边轻轻摇醒他。

　　"怎么了？"菲利克斯问道，他揉了揉眼睛。

　　"我到处都找不到埃德温。他……他不见了！"

　　菲利克斯猛地站起身来，他的动静太大，一下子把托马斯和巴塞洛缪都吵醒了。

　　"发生什么事了？"托马斯从床上坐起来问道。

　　"是小埃……他不见了！"菲利克斯一边说道，一边在顶楼四处搜索。

　　"噢，我的天哪！"巴塞洛缪匆忙套上衣服，说道，"我去外面看看，也许他只是出去散散步什么的。"

　　一阵乒乒乓乓的开关门声传遍了整栋别墅。

　　"小埃！小埃！你在哪儿呀？"菲利克斯大声喊道。

　　听着开关门声和菲利克斯徒劳的叫喊声，碧翠丝和其他人终于意识到了事态的严重性。

　　"这都是我的错，"碧翠丝哭了起来，"我答应过要好好照顾他的，现在却发生了这种事。"

"Don't blame yourself," said Thomas, putting his arm around her shoulder. "You have been very caring with Edwin. I've been watching you. So let's just wait and see whether we can find any clues to his whereabouts."

"Okay," said Beatrice sniffling. "Thank you, Thomas."

By this time, Gimmegonna had risen and was outside helping Felix and Bartholomew check the garden and the banks that surrounded the house. Eventually the search party returned with sullen faces. Everyone sat on the edge of their beds, looking very glum.

Just as Beatrice was about to flop down and bury her head in her pillow, she caught sight of an orange feather by the bedroom window. She thought nothing of it at first, but got up to admire its colour. As she plucked the feather from the window's grasp, Gimmegonna let out a horrible scream. Thinking she had done something terribly wrong, Beatrice dropped the feather and she screamed, too. Then Felix, Bartholomew, and Thomas, who did not really know what was going on, started screaming.

The screaming went on at least a minute, until Felix, seeing how stupid the whole situation was, yelled, "STOP!!!"

Suddenly, there was dead silence.

"Now," said Felix. "Would someone mind telling us why we were all screaming like raving idiots?"

"It was because of this," said Gimme, holding up the orange feather.

"Are you saying we were all screaming because of this KILLER feather?" said Felix, snatching the feather from Gimme's hand.

"No," said Gonna. "Not because of the feather itself, but because of who owns it."

"Yes," said Gimme. "That feather is from a Rekcus Bird. Sometime during the night, one of those birds must have sneaked in here."

"你也别太过自责了，"托马斯拍着她的肩膀说道，"对埃德温一直非常尽心，你的所作所为大家都看在眼里。让我们看看能不能找到什么线索，好查出他的下落。"

"好吧，"碧翠丝抽泣着说道，"谢谢你，托马斯。"

此时，吉米、吉纳老怪兄弟俩也已经起床，正帮着菲利克斯和巴塞洛缪在花园和别墅附近的河岸边搜寻埃德温的踪迹。最终，大家都一无所获，只得一脸阴沉地回到了别墅，大家都闷闷不乐地坐在自己的床边。碧翠丝正准备扑倒在床上，把脸埋到枕头里痛哭一场，夹在床边窗户上的一根橙色羽毛却引起了她的注意。起初她并没往深处想，只是想拿起来欣赏一下这根羽毛漂亮的颜色。她刚从窗户上拔出这根羽毛，吉米、吉纳老怪兄弟俩就发出了可怕的尖叫声，碧翠丝误以为自己做了什么傻事，吓得将羽毛一扔，也开始高声大叫。然后，菲利克斯、巴塞洛缪和托马斯也不明就里地跟着尖叫起来。

尖叫声持续了至少一分钟，菲利克斯终于意识到大家的行为有多愚蠢，于是喊道："**别叫了！**"

房间内一时陷入了死一般的寂静。

菲利克斯问道："刚才大家干吗都像白痴似的尖叫呀？谁来解释一下？"

"都是因为这个。"吉米捡起了那根橙色的羽毛。

"你的意思是，大家尖叫就是因为这根带着**杀气**的羽毛？"菲利克斯从吉米手里一把抢过那根羽毛。

"不是的，"吉纳解释道，"不是因为羽毛本身，而是因为这根羽毛背后所代表的黑手。"

"没错，"吉米附和道，"这根羽毛来自雷克斯鸟，这种鸟有时会趁着夜色偷偷潜进来。"

"Of course, the Rekcus Bird," said Felix, remembering Edwin's sighting on the F.L.A.B. and the picture in the Professor's book.

"Oh, my," said Beatrice, "Edwin has been captured by one of those horrible Likeyouknow things. He'll get Unoitis! Drow's going to change that lovely boy into something revolting!" she said, bursting into tears once more.

"Where would that bird be heading?" asked Felix, turning to Gimmegonna.

"To Drow, of course," said Gimme. "That bird is the head of the Mumbojumbos. Edwin will certainly be transformed by Drow or I'm not a Geek."

"Not if we can help it," said Felix. "Bart! Tom! Beatrice! We must head up Drow's Stream of Consciousness immediately. We are going to save Edwin, even if it's the last thing we do!

"我想起来了，雷克斯鸟！"菲利克斯回忆起埃德温在热气球上的所见所闻以及教授文件里的图片。

"噢，天啊，"碧翠丝说道，"埃德温肯定被这种迷人心智的怪鸟抓走了。他要是得了失语症可怎么办！卓尔一定会把那个可爱的小男孩变成可怕的怪物的！"她再次放声大哭起来。

"那只鸟会飞到什么地方去呢？"菲利克斯转头问吉米、吉纳老怪兄弟俩。

"肯定是去卓尔那里了，"吉米说道，"那只鸟是胡言军团的头领，任何落到卓尔手里的人都在劫难逃，包括埃德温，不然我也不会变成这副怪胎样了。"

"有我们在，埃德温就不会有事，"菲利克斯说道，"小巴！小汤！碧翠丝！我们必须现在就赶往卓尔的意识之河。哪怕这是我们能做的最后一件事，我们也一定要帮埃德温逃离魔爪！"

18

EDWIN MEETS DROW

About the same time that Felix and the others were saying goodbye to Gimmegonna Geek and launching their boat into the Stream of Consciousness, Edwin Bellamy was beginning his descent from the sky—the sky where he had spent the last 10 hours flying.

It had not been a good night for him, what with waking up and finding himself hanging from a toilet plunger and having to experience the cold night air blowing against his face. He had wondered if, just maybe, he was in the ultimate nightmare.

It had not taken him long to figure out what was going on, particularly when he looked up and saw the vivid colours of the Rekcus Bird reflected in the moonlight. All he could do was wait and wonder. He didn't cry—he couldn't, really—and yet he knew where he was going and whom he was going to meet. It was an event he had envisioned with some trepidation. He knew the time had come to meet Drow face to face.

The sun had risen a little higher as he began to return to ground level and the glare made it difficult to see where he was going. Just as he began to catch sight of trees, his legs touched down on solid earth and he rolled forward. He placed his hands on his head and felt for the plunger. It had gone!

He stood up and surveyed the brown grass beneath his feet. As he raised his head, he saw a sight so incredible, he remained completely transfixed, staring in disbelief. There, directly in front of him, was one of the largest and most beautiful palaces he had ever seen. It was far more beautiful than

18

埃德温与卓尔面对面

菲利克斯和其他人与吉米、吉纳老怪兄弟俩道别后，就预备乘船从意识之河逆流而上，与此同时，那只抓走了埃德温·贝拉米的雷克斯鸟正准备从天空降落到目的地——他已经在天空上长途飞行了10个小时。

埃德温在这一夜可遭了不少罪，他突然醒来，发现自己被吊在一个皮撅子上，午夜的冷风把他的脸刮得生疼，他一度怀疑这，或许，只是个荒诞的噩梦而已。

然而，没过多久——尤其当他抬头看到月光映照下雷克斯鸟独有的鲜艳羽毛后，他就彻底清醒了，他唯一能做的就是静待事态的进一步发展。他没有哭——也哭不出来——着然，但他对自己要去的地方和要见的人却心知肚明，这正是他最害怕发生的一幕，因为他知道，与卓尔面对面的时候终于到了。

太阳爬得更高了，他感觉到雷克斯鸟正贴地飞行，但刺眼的光线使他无法看清前进的方向。他先是看到一排青葱的树木，接着感觉双腿碰到了坚硬的土地，惯性带着他往前滚去，他伸手去摸头上的皮撅子，不见了！

他站起身来，仔细观察着在他脚下黄褐色的草地。他抬起头来，一座富丽堂皇的宫殿映入眼帘，其恢宏的气势令人叹为观止。埃德温呆呆地看着，一时间震惊得无法言语，埃德温生平头一遭看到如此宏伟、如此美丽的

Buckingham Palace in England or the Palace of Versailles in France. Its gold-coloured stone walls twinkled in the sunlight and it had six huge castle-like towers, one at each corner and two at either side of the entrance. Surely it was the most impressive building in the world.

As he stood admiring this wonder, the door to the palace started to open. Slowly, a shadowy figure began to materialize. Edwin sensed an immense power in the air.

The sun was still glaring so he couldn't see the person's features. A human form began to move forward, stepping down the many stairs that led away from the entrance to the palace. Edwin watched, unable to move, as a man crossed the palace lawn and got closer and closer.

Before the ominous figure descended the final embankment, he stopped, still encased in shadow. Edwin could barely make out that he was holding a cell phone but he could hear him yelling at someone on the other end of the line.

"Look, just check the wording of the sentence, alright?! I'm not going to pay you for the sentence until it's complete . . . What do you mean you charge extra for idioms? . . . Fine, get on with it . . . Yes, I liked the other sentence you created . . . I laughed . . . I cried . . . It really moved me . . . Now do the same with this one! Anyway, we'll do lunch so we can talk about this further. Right! Bye now!"

The figure flicked the cover of his cell phone shut and attached the phone to his belt buckle.

"Editors!" he yelled. "What a pain!"

He looked up at Edwin.

"Who are you, dude?" said the figure, sounding very impatient. "Another misplaced word captured by my trusty Rekcus Bird? What's your name, kid?"

"E . . . d . . . win, sir!"

宫殿，令他大开眼界。眼前的景致使白金汉宫和凡尔赛宫都相形见绌。金色的石头与阳光相映生辉，六座形似城堡的巨型塔楼矗立在四个角落和大门两侧，埃德温想，这座宫殿绝对是全世界最令人惊艳的美景。

当他还在盯着这座华丽的宫殿出神时，正门却突然打开了，一个阴影从门后慢慢逼近，埃德温立即感觉到空气中弥散着凝重的气息。

阳光格外刺眼，使他无法看清来人的面庞，一个人形身影越来越清晰，从正门旁通向别处的台阶上快速走下来。埃德温一动也不动地注视着这个男人的动静，目视着他穿过宫殿前的草坪，越走越近。埃德温感觉到来者不善，好在他终于停了下来，与埃德温之间还隔着一道路堤。他浑身上下被一团黑色的阴影包围着，埃德温模模糊糊看到他正对着手机大喊大叫。

"听着，你只要检查句子的措辞就行了，知道了吧？句子要是不完整，你一个子儿都别想拿到……什么叫成语另收费？你什么意思？好吧，你继续就是了……没错，你造的另一个句子我确实挺满意……让我喜泪交加……真感人啊……这个句子你也要好好琢磨琢磨！好吧，咱俩一起吃个午饭，到时候再详谈。没错！再见！"

来人把手机合上，插入皮带搭扣中。

"编辑！"他大声感叹道，"真够烦的！"

他抬眼看看了埃德温。

"你是谁呀，哥们？"这名男子的声音听起来很不耐烦地说道，"忠诚的雷克斯鸟又抓了个走错地方的单词吗？孩子，你叫什么名字？"

"埃……德……温，先生！"

"Edwin?" said the figure, somewhat puzzled. "I've never heard of a word called 'edwin' before. Are you messin' with me?"

"I . . . I'm a boy," said Edwin.

"What do you mean you're a boy?" he said, annoyed. "You're either a boy or you're an edwin. Which one are you?"

"I'm both," said Edwin.

"Look! I'm a busy man. And I don't like you. You're givin' me a hard time. What part of the book d'ya live in, anyway?"

Edwin thought about the question. If he told him he was from the outside world, he would ruin any chance of his friends succeeding with their mission. He decided to lie.

"I live in the beginning of the book," said Edwin hesitantly.

"Then why are you here?" snapped the figure.

Edwin thought about that question, too, and was about to answer when the cell phone rang.

The figure whipped the phone from his belt and flicked his wrist so the phone's cover flung open.

"Yup . . . ? . . . What do you mean it doesn't work! . . . I told you to choose your words carefully . . . I'm already hearing rumours that the Punctuation People are threatening to go on strike unless we fix this problem . . . I'm gonna kick some butt if you guys don't pull this together . . . Send him an 'E' mail or better still, send him one of my 'FEE' mails. That'll get him moving! . . . Listen, we'll have a power lunch on Tuesday to discuss it . . . My people will be in touch with your people . . . I need to bring this story to a conclusion. Fast!"

The figure snapped his cell phone shut again and turned toward Edwin.

"Well, like I was saying. Why are you here?"

"埃德温？"这名男子一头雾水地看着埃德温，说道，"我从来没有听说过有叫'埃德温'的单词，你是在耍我吗？"

"我……我是个男孩。"埃德温说道。

"什么叫你是个男孩？"他看起来已经怒火中烧了，问道，"你要么是男孩，要么是埃德温，你到底是哪一个？"

"两者都是我。"埃德温回答道。

"得了！我可是个大忙人，我不喜欢你，你把我搞得头晕脑涨了，你住在这本书的哪个部分呀？"

埃德温埋头想了想，如果据实相告，那他的单词朋友们所做的努力都将付诸东流。所以，他决定捏造一个身份。

"我住在这本书里的开篇部分。"埃德温闪烁其词。

"那你为什么会到这里来？"这名男子厉声问道。

埃德温也有想到他会问这个问题，正要回答时，对方的手机突然铃声大作。

这名男子从皮带上一把抽出手机，甩了一下手腕，手机盖便啪地弹开了。

"什么……？……什么叫作不下去了？……我告诉过你，要你谨慎挑选单词……我早就听到风声了是有关标点家族威胁说，如果我们解决不了这个问题，他们就要罢工……你们几个要是搞不定，我要你们好看……给他写封邮件，要不就给他一封邮件送我的最大笔'费用账单'过去。总有办法解决吧！……听着，我们在星期二的高层会议上再详细讨论……我的人会联系你的手下……我要尽快了结这事，越快越好！"

这名男子啪地一声再次合上手机，转过身来看着埃德温。

"嗯，我们刚才说到……对了，你为什么会到这里来？"

Edwin remembered the Table of Contents Room and Chapter 4, which offered the opportunity to travel the world. That gave him an idea.

"I am travelling, just passing through on my way to visit Chapter 4. I want to . . . to travel the world," said Edwin, trying to appear sure of himself.

"You're lying. Nobody travels in this book anymore. Anyway, you already passed Chapter 4. Look, you don't seem to realize who you're talkin' to. I am the infamous Drow—the coolest Verb around. Man, I'm Active! Me and my people, the Mumbojumbos, will soon be the rulers of this book. So now, answer my question! Why are you here?"

Edwin decided to say nothing.

Drow began to move down the last embankment and was clearly in Edwin's view at last.

This was Drow himself and Edwin was ready for the worst. His heart started racing and his legs began to shake, the way they had when he had given a speech to his class on the history of the rhinoceros.

But when the figure eased down the final bit of grass and stood in front of him, Edwin realized his biggest problem was not going to be fear but holding back his laughter!

Drow stood no more than one-hundred-and-two-and-a-quarter-centimetres tall. In fact, his head only came up to Edwin's chin.

His hair was purple and plastered to his head with a pungent hair oil.

Then there were the rings—nose rings, earrings, and finger rings.

And that fearsome man was wearing one of the most ridiculous outfits imaginable!

He wore a white shirt with a red polka-dot bow tie and a pair of striped navy-blue dress pants held up with brightly coloured red chains that resembled Christmas streamers. The top parts of his white cowboy boots were so big, they came right up to his knees. All in all, Edwin thought Drow looked very peculiar.

埃德温想起了目录室里的第四章《环游世界》，他灵机一动，有了主意。

"我四处旅行……正准备拜读第四章的内容。我打算……环游世界。"埃德温试图表现得更有说服力。

"你撒谎。现在没人会在这本书里旅行了，不过看来你已经读过第四章了。小子，你还不知道自己在跟谁说话吧。我就是大名鼎鼎的卓尔，我是这里最酷的单词，我和我率领的胡言军团，很快就会成为这本书的统治者。所以，你现在最好给我老老实实回答问题！你为什么会到这里来？"

埃德温决定保持沉默。

卓尔从路堤上走下来，逐渐靠近埃德温。

埃德温很清楚这就是卓尔本人，心里已经做好了最坏的打算。他的心狂跳不已，双腿也开始不听使唤，就像以前他当着全班同学的面登台演讲犀牛的历史时一样。

不过，当卓尔穿过草坪走到他面前时，埃德温之前最担心的事反而不再是问题了，他甚至忍不住想大笑起来。

站在埃德温·贝拉米面前的卓尔还不到102.25厘米高。实际上，他的头只能够到埃德温的下巴。

他的发型就十分搞笑，刺鼻的发油将紫色的头发牢牢紧贴在头皮上。

而那些鼻环、耳环和指环等形形色色的环圈也非常滑稽，好笑的还远不止这些。

更别提他那让人忍俊不禁的服装了，简直跟传说中的恶魔完全沾不上边。

他身着白色衬衫配红色圆点点的领结和深蓝色条纹西裤，西裤上的鲜红色背带看起来好似圣诞节彩带。超大号的白色牛仔靴直到他的膝盖，卓尔全身上下的每一个细节都让埃德温觉得古怪至极。

Drow looked up at Edwin, revealing a fat little boyish face.

"I asked you a question, man. Why are you here?"

Edwin remained steadfast, refusing to say a word.

"Well, maybe my trusty Head of the Mumbojumbos will provide me with some answers," he said angrily.

Drow placed his two forefingers in his mouth and whistled. Suddenly, there was a flapping noise, the same sound Edwin had listened to all night long.

The Rekcus Bird appeared out of the sky and squatted gracefully beside Drow. Drow began whispering into its ear. What was even stranger, the bird appeared to whisper back.

After a few minutes of whispering, Drow looked up at Edwin. He had an evil look in his eyes and one of his eyebrows began to twitch.

"So, my trusty bird here tells me you are a member of the sentence that was spotted flyin' through the air yesterday—a sentence that did not contain one Drow word."

Drow raised his eyebrows and gave Edwin a penetrating stare.

"Well, we have ways of dealin' with the likes of you."

Drow pulled out a large dog-whistle and blew into it. Edwin heard nothing but a large animal came bounding out the palace door. It made its way to Drow and Edwin, then stopped.

Edwin realized it was not a regular household pet. He looked more like a two-metre-tall gorilla who had accidentally been born with a dog's face. Not any old dog, mind you. No, his head definitely had the look of a Schnauzer, complete with beard and pokey ears. And he wore horn-rimmed glasses.

Edwin watched as the creature bounced up and down on his big and fuzzy hind legs. Large globules of spit hung in strings from his mouth.

"Ah, Riffraff. There you are," said Drow smiling.

"Duhh, wath the madder, Bauths? Anuthur word mithbehavings?"

"No, Riffraff. This is a special case. This little twerp here has been seen

卓尔抬头看着埃德温，露出一个胖胖的小娃娃脸。

"我问你呢，小子，你为什么会到这里来？"

埃德温仍然一动也不动地装聋作哑。

"好吧，也许我那听话的胡言军团头领能透露点口风！"他气愤地说。

卓尔把两根食指伸到嘴里，吹了一声口哨，只听得传来一阵振翅之声。昨天一整晚，这个同样的声音一直在埃德温的耳边萦绕。

雷克斯鸟从天际飞来，优雅地停在了卓尔的身边。卓尔转过身对着它耳语一番，更奇怪的是，那只鸟似乎也在窃窃私语回应着卓尔。

说了几分钟的悄悄话之后，卓尔转过身来，抬头看着埃德温。他目露凶光，眉翼一侧微微抖动。

"这样子，那只我的亲信鸟告诉我，你和你的伙伴们组成了一个不包含卓尔单词的句子，他们昨天不远万里赶了过来。"

卓尔眉毛一扬，以锐利的眼神盯着埃德温。

"嗯，对付你们这种人，我自有妙计。"

卓尔拿出一枚大型犬笛，吹了一下。埃德温什么也没听到（犬笛嘛，人类自然是听不到的），但他看到了一只体型庞大的动物从宫殿正门冲了过来。它先是朝卓尔和埃德温发足狂奔，然后突然停了下来。

埃德温很快就意识到，它绝不是一只普通家养宠物。事实上，它看起来更像是一只两米高的大猩猩，只不过凑巧长了张形似狗的脸罢了。而且一看便知，这只狗正值盛年，从胡须和小耳朵等头部特征判断这可能是一只雪纳瑞，它还戴着一副角质框眼镜。

埃德温看着它拖着毛茸茸的、胖胖的后腿在四周徘徊。它在附近蹿上跳下，白花花的唾沫星子从嘴角飞溅出来。

"哎呀，混混，你来啦！"卓尔微笑着说。

"粗甚么四啦，老大？似不似又有单词闹四了？"（混混是非人类，其吐词不清）

"没呢，混混，只是一点小意外而已。这个烦人的小家伙组成了一个不

travelling in a sentence that does not have one Drow word in it."

Edwin lowered his head, although he didn't really believe he had done anything wrong.

"Wath? Drow, do you know wath thith meanths?"

"Of course I know what it means, bonehead. It means my fabulous master plan *and* my life are in danger unless I put a stop to all of this. That is why, Riffraff, you're gonna lock up this edwin or boy or whatever it is and put all the Mumbojumbos on Word Alert. I am sure the rest of his sentence will soon come lookin' for this misplaced word. And if, by some incredible fluke, they make it up my Stream of Consciousness, then and only then, Riffraff, may you do what you do so well."

"Eath my wordths!" said Riffraff.

"Yes, eat your words! Now, off with this wretch before I throw him over the cliff with the other dangling Participles."

"Where to, Bauths?"

"Put him in the Drower!" said Drow with a horrid laugh.

Riffraff pulled out a small collar and whipped it around Edwin's neck. The two ends of the collar snapped together, then he hooked Edwin to a long leash.

"Okay, leth go."

Edwin did as Riffraff said, although he had no choice in the matter.

They walked around the front of the huge palace for what seemed like ages, then finally came to a big cage with a sign on it.

THE DROWER: SPECIAL COMPOUND FOR WORDS

Riffraff took the huge key that hung from his neck and unlocked the big iron grate that served as the only entrance to the cage.

He gave Edwin a little push.

"Get in der," ordered Riffraff.

Edwin lunged forward and landed on the floor. The door slammed shut.

"Tho long," said Riffraff as he bounded away.

包含卓尔单词的句子。"

虽然埃德温没干任何坏事，但他还是低下了头。

"甚么？卓尔，你知道介意味着甚么吗？"

"我当然知道这意味着什么，笨蛋。这意味着，如果我不能及时制止他们，我的宏图大计就要泡汤了，说不定我自己的小命都保不住了。所以，我要你把这个叫埃德温，不，叫男孩，不，哎呀，总之把他给我关起来，然后出动所有胡言军团给我去搜。我相信，他的同伙很快就会来找他的。如果他们恰好要从意识之河逆流而上的话，那就是你混混大显身手的时候了。"

"刚柴的话就当我没嗦。"混混说道。

"哈哈，当你没说！现在，趁我还没把他和别的悬垂分词一起扔下悬崖时，赶紧把这小家伙给我关起来。"

"关哪儿，老大大？"

"就关在卓尔地牢好了！"卓尔的笑声让人不寒而栗。

混混赶紧掏出颈圈套在埃德温的脖子上，颈圈锁扣紧紧地卡在一起。然后，他用一根长长的皮带拴住了埃德温的颈圈。

"好了，我们抖（走）吧。"

埃德温别无选择，只得照做。

他们在这座古老的宫殿前绕了一大圈，来到一座巨大的牢笼前。笼子上挂着一块牌子，上书：

卓尔地牢：单词专用牢房

混混从脖子上取下一把大号钥匙，那是唯一能打开入口的铁栅门。

然后他把埃德温轻轻推了进去。

"进去吧！"混混命令道。

埃德温向前一扑，摔倒在地板上，门砰的一声关上了。

"宅见啦！"混混说着，扬长而去。

Edwin looked around. There were others in the cage, staring at him.

"Hi," said Edwin nervously, looking at all the faces.

"Hello, young boy," said a man extending his hand.

"Welcome to the Drower! My name is Mark Man, although my friends simply call me 'Man.' "

Man shook Edwin's hand, then turned to a person sitting beside him.

"This is my agent Horace He. Horace is from the eastern part of the book. He represents me on occasions when I'm too busy. He's a Pronoun, you see."

"Very nice to meet you," said Horace, bowing his head.

"Yes, nice to meet you, too, Mr. He," said Edwin.

"How long have you been here?" asked Edwin, staring at all the faces.

"We just got here!" said a fit woman joining the conversation.

"How are you, young boy?" asked the woman, extending her hand. "My name is Quintella Quickly. I used to be a trainer for Verbs. I'd try to get them to work a bit harder. But now that Drow is on the scene, the Verbs have become very lazy."

Quintella introduced Edwin to all the words in the cage. Some were already showing signs of Unoitis.

After everyone had said their piece, they shuffled off to various corners of the cage.

Edwin sat down and put his head on his hands. He wondered if his friends knew he was missing. Once again, thoughts of his mother and home and everything else he had been used to started flashing through his mind.

"Hi there," said a voice, catching Edwin off guard. He looked up. A small girl, dressed in a workman's hat and plaid shirt and pants with scruffy suspenders, stepped forward.

"Hello. My name is Tom," said the girl.

"Hi, I'm Edwin. Nice to meet you . . . Tom?"

"Yes, Tomboy, actually."

"Oh, I see," said Edwin.

埃德温朝四周看了看，铁笼里的其他人都好奇地盯着他。

"嗨！"埃德温看着一张张陌生的面孔，紧张地说道。

"你好，孩子。"其中一个人向他伸出手来。

"欢迎来到卓尔地牢！我叫马克·男人，不过朋友们一般都叫我'男人'。"

男人握了握埃德温的手，指了指他身旁的人。

"这是我的经纪人，贺拉斯·他，贺拉斯来自这本书的东部。我很忙的时候，很多事情就交由他代理。你看，他是一个代词。"

"很高兴认识你！"贺拉斯点了点头。

"我也很高兴认识您，他先生！"埃德温说道。

"你们在这里待了多长时间了？"埃德温看着身边的人问道。

"我们刚被关进来！"一位身形苗条的女士插话道。

"你没事吧，孩子？"女士一边说，一边把手伸向了埃德温，"我叫昆特拉·敏捷，以前曾是一位动词培训师，帮助他们培养积极的工作态度。不过自从卓尔掌权后，动词们都变得非常懒惰。"

昆特拉将埃德温一一介绍给牢房里的不同单词，其中一些单词已经出现了失语症的初期症状。大家互相认识后，又散到不同的角落各自休息去了。

埃德温双手抱头，静静地坐了下来。他想道：不知道朋友们有没有察觉到我失踪了。他想起了母亲、家人及其他熟悉的一切，一幕幕场景在他脑海里再次浮现。

"嗨，你好啊！"埃德温的耳边冷不防响起了一个声音，埃德温抬头看了看，一个头戴工装帽、身着格子衬衫和破破烂烂的背带裤的小女孩走到他面前。

"你好，我叫男孩。"小女孩向他伸出了手。

"嗨，我是埃德温，很高兴认识你……男孩？"

"没错，实际上，我全名叫假小子。"

"哦，我明白了。"埃德温说道。

"What's your name?" asked the girl.

"Edwin."

"Edwin?" said the girl. "Edwin what?"

"Edwin Bellamy."

"What's a bellamy?" she asked.

"Well . . . it's . . . it's the name of my family," said Edwin.

"What are you, then?" she asked.

"I'm a boy, of course," laughed Edwin.

"You can't be a boy. I'm the only boy who lives in this book. I was born Tomboy—a compound word on page sixteen in Chapter 3. But I'm sure there have never been any other boys in this book."

Edwin realized he had some explaining to do but wondered whether he could trust this Tomboy. Then again, he thought, now that he was being held prisoner, he had to confide in someone. That settled it. He would explain the whole story to Tom, even the part about discovering Cedric's secret library.

Tom listened attentively to Edwin's fantastic tale, occasionally gasping at the juicy parts. Just as Edwin was about finish the part about Gimmegonna Geek, something really strange started to happen to his body.

First, his face began to quiver.

Next, his legs began to shake.

Then, billows of black smoke started pouring out of his nose and ears.

"Tom! What's happening to me?" cried Edwin.

Tom watched and waited. The smoke started to dissipate and Edwin's body slowly stopped shaking.

"Do something! Please!" yelled Edwin.

"Edwin! Say, 'Isn't the weather nice today!' " ordered Tom.

"Like you know, isn't the weather, like you know, nice today!" repeated Edwin.

"你叫什么名字？"小女孩问道。

"埃德温。"他答道。

"埃德温？"小女孩继续问道，"姓什么呢？"

"埃德温·贝拉米。"

"贝拉米是什么意思？"小女孩不解地问道。

"嗯……这是……这是我们家族的姓氏。"埃德温不知道她为什么会提出如此奇怪的问题。

"那你到底是什么？"小女孩追问道。

"我当然是男孩啊！"埃德温笑着说道。

"你怎么可能是男孩呢？我是这本书中唯一的男孩。我是个复合词，打出生开始我就叫男孩这个名字了。虽然我从未离开过第三章第16页，但我敢肯定，这本书里绝不可能有其他的男孩。"

埃德温意识到他可能需要好好解释一番了，但他还不太肯定眼前这个假小子是否值得信任。他转念一想，既然都被关在牢房里了，他总得找一两位可以倾诉的朋友吧，就这么定了。他决定把整个故事一股脑儿地告诉假小子，甚至连误入塞德里克爵士的秘密图书馆的那件事也据实相告。

假小子认真地听着埃德温讲述他精彩的故事，有些刺激惊险的部分吓得她连大气都不敢出。正当埃德温准备讲述在吉米、吉纳老怪家发生的故事时，奇怪的事却在他身体上接踵而来。

首先是他的脸开始不由自主地颤动。

接着，他的双腿也开始不听使唤地抖动起来。

然后，他的鼻子和耳朵里开始呼呼地直冒黑烟。

"假小子！我这是怎么了？"埃德温大叫道。

假小子静静地看着他，什么也没说。随着烟雾逐渐消失，埃德温的身体也渐渐平静下来。

"帮帮我！求求你啦！"埃德温大叫着。

"埃德温！跟我说：'今天的天气真好啊！'"假小子严肃地说道。

"你知道的吧，今天的天气，你知道的吧，真好啊！"埃德温重复道。

"I knew it!" exclaimed Tom. "I just knew it!"

"Like you know, what?" asked Edwin.

"Don't you see?" asked Tom. "You have developed Unoitis. It was that Rekcus Bird."

Edwin looked down at his feet. "Like you know, Tom, what am I, like you know, going to do, like?"

"Do?" said Tom. "The only thing you can do is pray that your friends somehow succeed in getting rid of Drow. If they don't, you're cooked. First you'll be saying 'like ya know,' then finally Drow will assign you a new name, like 'jerk.' "

Edwin started to cry.

"Where are my friends?" he said quietly under his breath. "Where are they?"

"我就知道！"假小子大声地说，"我一猜就是！"

"你知道的吧，你在说什么呀？"埃德温问道。

"你难道还不明白吗？"假小子说道，"你已经患上了失语症，肯定是那只雷克斯鸟干的。"

埃德温低头看看自己的脚。"像你知道的，假小子，我现在，像你知道的，该怎么办，像？"

"怎么做？"假小子说道，"你唯一能做的就是祈祷，祈祷你的朋友们能想办法推翻卓尔的统治。如果他们没法抓住卓尔，那你就完蛋了。一开始，你会不停地重复'你知道的吧'，直到卓尔给你取一个新名字为止，像'衰人'。"

埃德温开始大哭起来。

"我的朋友们都在哪儿啊？"他静静地啜泣着说道，"他们都在哪儿呀？"

19

ACHOO

Edwin's friends were not having a good time! The Stream of Consciousness was a horrible place, as was just about everywhere else in the Neergreve Forest. The stream was dark, smelly, damp, and very meandering—with bends and curves every few metres. Dead tree stumps were scattered hither and thither; beside each of those obstacles, hidden a few centimetres below the misty water, were the remnants of the trees that had once towered over the area. With every stroke of the oars, there was the threat that the group's fragile little rowboat would slam into one of the solid pieces of driftwood and sink into the abyss.

"We're not getting anywhere!" said Beatrice.

"Actually, we've travelled eight kilometres or six-point-six nautical miles," said Bartholomew, discovering his trusty calculator.

"It's quite irrelevant how far we've travelled," Felix said angrily. "We're going to keep travelling until we find Ed."

"I'm with you, Felix," said Thomas. "I don't care how long we spend in this wretched stream. We're responsible for Edwin and it's our duty to help him."

"You're right. You're all right," said Beatrice sheepishly. "I was just thinking of myself. I want Edwin back just as much as anyone."

Beatrice lay back in the rowboat and began fiddling with her hair. She had not concerned herself with her beauty since leaving the F.L.A.B. and yet, she thought, it didn't really matter that she was dirty and unkempt for a change. There was no one to impress out here in this swamp.

19

阿嚏

　　埃德温的朋友们一路也并不轻松！意识之河的阴森恐怖，丝毫不亚于尼尔格雷夫森林的其他角落。这里幽暗崎岖，奇臭无比，波涛汹涌的急流险滩比比皆是。沿途散落着大量枯死的树桩，在云雾缭绕的水面下方数厘米处隐藏着一度高耸入云、如今却已枯朽不堪的树干。每一次划动双桨，这只弱不禁风的小划艇都有可能迎面撞上危险的浮木，将他们拖入黑暗的深渊。

　　"我们一直在原地打转呢！"碧翠丝说道。

　　"实际上，我们已经前进了8公里，或者说6.6海里。"巴塞洛缪一边看着他可靠的计算器，一边说道。

　　"我们走了多远并不重要，"菲利克斯没好气地说，"重要的是，我们将继续前进，直到找到小埃为止。"

　　"我同意，菲利克斯，"托马斯说道，"我不在乎我们在这条可恶的河里花了多长时间，埃德温这件事因我们而起，把他解救出来是我们的责任。"

　　"你说得对，你说得有道理，"碧翠丝羞愧地说，"我只考虑到我自己，我跟大家一样，希望早点把埃德温找回来。"

　　碧翠丝躺回划艇，无聊地抚弄着自己的头发。自从热气球着陆后，她就完全没心思管自己的外在形象了，她觉得，即使蓬头垢面也没多大关系。在这片沼泽地里，谁又会在乎她美不美呢。

She placed her arms along the gunwales of the boat and stretched out her feet. From there she watched as Felix and Thomas rowed and Bartholomew checked his compass and punched figures into his calculator. She dangled her hands over the boat, letting the water flow through her fingers.

The water was cold and slimy and she was beginning to get a funny tingling sensation in her arms. At first she thought maybe her arms had fallen asleep. But as she looked down, she didn't even question what she saw. She simply screamed as hard as she could.

"AHHHHHHHHHHHHH!!!"

The rest of the group whirled around. Clutching Beatrice's arms were two white tentacles covered with hundreds of little suction cups. Felix reached into his tool kit, whipped out a large crowbar, and started whacking another two tentacles at the stern that were causing the boat to bob up and down. Finally, the tentacles let go of Beatrice, but the others remained secured to the side of the boat.

"Oh, gross!!! Look at my arms!" cried Beatrice. "I'll never be able to wear sleeveless shirts again."

Beatrice's arms were covered with tiny red pockmarks where the suction cups had been attached. But no one had time to worry about appearances. Two more tentacles appeared at the bow of the boat. In complete unison, the four aquatic arms began to make the boat bob furiously in the water.

If that wasn't enough, there was a big SPLASH, then gurgling sounds, and a huge white globiferous head emerged. It had large, saucer-shaped eyes and when it opened its cavernous mouth, it revealed a perfect set of razor-sharp teeth.

"We're going to be eaten!" screamed Beatrice, leaning toward the back of the boat.

Bartholomew, who usually liked to offer his opinion on matters like this, remained quiet. He looked a bit gah gah, as if he was going into a state of shock.

她把手臂搭在船舷边，使劲伸展开双腿。她看见菲利克斯和托马斯正在费力地划桨，而巴塞洛缪则一边检查着罗盘上的方向，一边敲击着计算器的键盘。她把手伸向船舷外，手指轻轻地划过水面。

黏滑的河水冰寒刺骨，一阵说不清道不明的刺痛感袭上她的手臂。起初，她以为只是手臂麻了。但当她低头往下看时，她却被吓得连话都说不出来了，她拼尽全力高声尖叫起来：

"啊啊啊啊啊啊啊！"

其他人纷纷停下手中的工作，转过身来看着她，只见碧翠丝的胳膊上爬着两个白色的触角，上面布满了上百个小吸盘，在两只触角的拉扯下，小船不停地上下摆动。菲利克斯伸手从工具包里掏出一根长长的撬棍，冲上去对着触角奋力地抽打起来。最终，两只触角从碧翠丝的手臂上脱落了下来，但仍死死地吸附在小船的船舷上。

"哦，好恶心呀！看看我的胳膊！"碧翠丝失声叫了起来，"我再也不能穿无袖衬衫了。"

碧翠丝的胳膊上星星点点布满了吸盘咬过的红色瘢痕，但此刻大家哪还顾得上这些。就在碧翠丝甩脱触角后不久，两只更大的触角也爬上了船头。所有的触角同时猛烈地上下摇晃着船身。

祸不单行，只见一片激烈汹涌的**水花**，紧接着传来一声汩汩的水流声，平静的水面下浮现出一只巨大的白色圆头生物，它的碟形眼球大得惊人，血盆大口内齐整而锋利的獠牙更是令人毛骨悚然。

"我们要被吃掉了！"碧翠丝一边尖叫，一边朝船尾钻去。

一向最爱发表意见的巴塞洛缪此刻也安静得出奇。他目瞪口呆地矗立着，仿佛陷入了休克状态。

"Come on, people. Focus! Focus! Just hold on!" Felix ordered.

Suddenly the monster sneezed and uttered the words, "Okay? Okay?" then disappeared under the water.

"What was THAT?!" cried Thomas.

The group stood up to take a closer look as two tentacles re-appeared and the boat started bobbing again.

"Kneel down and grab the gunwales," ordered Felix.

A large black mass under the boat slowly lifted it right out of the water.

"This is a different creature!" exclaimed Thomas, peering nervously over the side. "I think we must be on top of a whale or something. Wh . . . a . . . at do you think, Bart?"

Bart looked up at Thomas, groaned, and uttered a series of high-pitched squeals. His eyes were glazed over and there was a look of terror on his face.

"Ye . . . yes! Whale! Bad whale!" he uttered. "A ba . . . bad whale, I think."

"It's a KILLER whale," screamed Beatrice, as a humungous black tail heaved itself out of the dirty water and spun like a garden sprinkler at the stern of the boat. As it twirled and flapped, it created a huge whirlpool, then sank back into the water. The vortex spun the rowboat around. It eventually slowed to a gentle turn.

Everyone felt dizzy and queasy. No sooner had the boat stopped, the water around the rowboat began to bubble and foam.

"What now?" screamed Beatrice. "I can't take much more of this!"

"Relax!" ordered Felix, trying to be calm. "There's nothing to . . ."

Just as he was about to say "worry about," the boat heaved backward and steam began to rise from the bubbles. Another head presented itself. This one was shark-like, with a large open jaw and slimy fangs oozing green slime.

At first the head emitted a roar that sent a spray of slime over the group.

"大家伙儿，加油啊，集中注意力！集中注意力！坚持住啊！"菲利克斯正色道。

这个怪物打了个喷嚏，然后突然说道："好吗？好吗？"然后就悄无声息地潜回水下了。

"刚才**那个**是什么东西？"托马斯大声问道。

众人站起身来想仔细查看一番，但那两只触角再度爬上了船头，就在此时，船身再次摇晃起来。

"蹲下！抓紧船舷！"菲利克斯命令道。

这时，一只黑色的庞然大物悄悄潜到船身下方，慢慢地把小船顶出了水面。

"又来了另一只怪物！"托马斯惊呼道，并小心翼翼地探出船舷看了一眼："我想我们大概是在一只鲸鱼或其他什么东西的身上。呃……你……你觉得呢，小巴？"

巴塞洛缪抬头看了看托马斯，一边呻吟着，一边发出一连串高声尖叫。他眼光呆滞，表情惊恐。

"是……是的！鲸鱼！可恶的鲸鱼！"他喃喃自语道，"我认为一定是一只非常坏……坏的鲸鱼。"

"是一只**杀**虎鲸。"碧翠丝尖叫着。这时，一条巨大的黑色尾鳍从船尾扫过。虎鲸将尾鳍从腐臭的河水中伸出，然后像花园内的洒水器一样疯狂地旋转起来，它不停地拍打和扇动着水浪，卷起了巨大的漩涡。过了好一阵子，它才无声无息地重新潜回水下。船身在漩涡中继续飞速旋转，最终慢慢停了下来。

每一个人都觉得头晕目眩，但还没等船停稳，众人就看见周围的水面开始浪花翻滚，泡沫飞溅。

"不会吧？还来？"碧翠丝大声叫道，"我实在是受不了了。"

"放松！"菲利克斯尽量镇定地说："没什么好……"

他那句"担心的"还没来得及说出口，船身就往后一倒，接着，从河面的泡沫中升腾出一缕缕蒸汽。另一只未知生物猛地从水中冒出头来，它外形酷似鲨鱼，长着强壮有力的下颚，恶心的绿色黏液从寒光森森的獠牙间不断渗出。

它发出震耳欲聋的嘶吼声，从血盆大口中朝他们喷射出黏稠恶臭的黏液。

Then it sneezed.

Finally, it called out "Okay? Okay?" and slid back into the stream.

"No! It's not okay!" yelled Beatrice hysterically. "Look at my clothes!" she said, wiping slime off her top. "I don't even suit green!"

Bartholomew realized he had to pull himself together. Quickly, he retrieved the Professor's papers from the bottom of the boat and leafed through them, searching for some clue about what was happening.

"Hmmm," he said, staring at one of the pages. "Achoo."

"Bless you," said Beatrice. "What have you found?"

"Achoo," repeated Bartholomew.

"Bless you! Are you getting a cold, Bartholomew?" asked Beatrice, giving him a strange look.

"I think Bart is trying to say the monster is called an 'Achoo,' " said Thomas. "Achoo is the monster's name, Beatrice."

"That's right," continued Bartholomew, as he thumbed through the Professor's notes. "This monster is another one of Drow's Mumbojumbos. Like the Ya, he pesters its victims by saying 'Okay' until you finally agree to join Drow's side. Its effects can be immediate, causing a quick word transformation."

"But why is it called an Achoo?" asked Beatrice.

"Every time an Achoo sneezes, it transforms itself into something else."

"Aha! So, there weren't two creatures after all," said Thomas. "There was just one Achoo trying to make us believe we were being attacked by two creatures. Interesting!"

"Achoos! Reckus Birds! Yas! Gimmegonnas! This is getting worse by the minute!" said Felix gravely. "Lord knows what's going to happen to poor Ed if we don't get ourselves out of this mess and save him."

The tiny rowboat was bouncing about like a hooked halibut.

"What are we going to do?" pleaded Beatrice.

然后，这只庞然大物突然打了个喷嚏。

随着一声"好吗？好吗？"，它也悄然隐退，潜入了暗流之中。

"不好！一点也不好！"碧翠丝歇斯底里地叫了起来，"看看我的衣服啊！"她一边抱怨，一边擦拭着外套上的黏液，"我最讨厌绿色了！"

巴塞洛缪抬起头来，意识到自己必须振作起来。他迅速从船身底部取出教授的文件，飞快地翻阅起来，希望能找到一丝线索。

"嗯，"他盯着一页资料，若有所思地说，"阿嚏。"

"愿上帝保佑你，"碧翠丝说道，"找到有用的信息了吗？"

"阿嚏。"巴塞洛缪重复道。

"愿上帝保佑你！你感冒了吗，巴塞洛缪？"碧翠丝看着他，露出异样的神情。

"我想，小巴是想说，那个怪物的名字就叫'阿嚏'，"托马斯说道，"'阿嚏'是怪物的名字，碧翠丝。"

"没错，"巴塞洛缪一边继续翻阅着教授的笔记，一边说道，"这只怪物也隶属于卓尔的胡言军团，像犸一样，它会一直缠着自己的猎物问'好吗？''好吗？'，直到对方最终同意加入卓尔的盟军为止。其效果立竿见影，可以在瞬间转化一个单词。"

"但是为什么叫阿嚏呢？"碧翠丝问道。

"每次阿嚏打喷嚏，它都能把自己变成另一种生物。"

"啊哈，我明白了！原来刚才看到的都是同一种生物啊，"托马斯说道，"这只是一个阿嚏想让我们误以为同时有两种不同的生物在攻击我们，有意思！"

"阿嚏！雷克斯鸟！犸！吉米、吉纳双头怪！情况越来越糟糕了！"菲利克斯严肃地说，"如果我们不能尽快从这里脱身去解救可怜的小埃，天知道他将面临多少可怕的事情啊！"

小划艇像一只被鱼钩钩住的大比目鱼一样在水中上下摇摆。

"那我们该怎么办呢？"碧翠丝神情哀伤地说道。

"I think I have an idea," announced Bartholomew, looking up from the papers. "Felix, the next time that Achoo thing sticks its head out of the water, no matter what it looks like, check the colour of its eyes."

"What? Are you nuts?" said Felix. "What does the colour of its eyes have to do with anything?"

"For once, just once, will you please listen to me. Unless, of course, you have any bright ideas!"

"All right, all right. But this better be good."

With the boat still bobbing madly, Felix eased forward, cautiously watching for the monster's head to re-appear. Within seconds, bubbles began to spew from the white foam and out popped the head of a giant alligator. The head sneezed and uttered "Okay" a few times. Felix immediately shot backward. With a splash, the head was gone.

"Well?" asked Bartholomew excitedly.

"They looked blue to me," said Felix, grumbling as he washed monster boogers off his sleeves.

"Great! Leave the rest to me!"

Bartholomew ripped off his shirt and dove into the water.

"Has he flipped?" Felix exclaimed in horror.

Bartholomew swam up to the surface and placed his finger in his ear. He mumbled a few words and POOF, he disappeared into a cloud of smoke. The group leaned forward, straining their eyes to see what sort of transformation had taken place. There was no sign of anything.

"Bart has transformed himself into thin air. How useful!" said Felix, slapping his head.

The group braced for another series of attacks. Just then, a lizard-like head poked itself out of the water and a dragon-like head sprang up at the stern. Beatrice threw herself backward, landing in the middle of the boat.

"Ahhhhhhhh! We're going to die!" she screamed.

"我倒是有一个主意，"巴塞洛缪放下手中的文件，抬起头来，他宣布道，"菲利克斯，下一次如果再看到阿嚏从水中冒出头来，不论它变幻成哪种生物，记住它眼睛的颜色。"

"什么？你疯了吗？"菲利克斯说道，"它眼睛的颜色跟这些有什么关系啊？"

"就一次，就这一次，你照我说的做就行了，除非，你有更好的主意！"

"好了，好了，你这个办法最好是管用。"

船身还在疯狂地摇摆着，菲利克斯蹑手蹑脚地走到船头，小心翼翼地等待着怪物再次露头。几秒钟后，大量白色的泡沫喷涌而出，水中赫然浮现出一只庞大的鳄鱼。这只鳄鱼打了个喷嚏，然后不停地重复着几次"好吗？""好吗？"，菲利克斯迅速向后退了几步。几秒钟后，怪物在水浪飞溅中消失在了河底！

"怎么样？"巴塞洛缪紧张地问道。

"我觉得它们看起来像蓝色，"菲利克斯一边擦拭着袖子上的黏液，一边低声抱怨着。

"太棒了！剩下的就交给我吧！"

巴塞洛缪扯下身上的衬衫，然后一个猛子扎进了水里。

"他疯了吗？"菲利克斯失声惊叫道。

巴塞洛缪游回水面，只见他将手指插入耳内，口中念念有词，随着**噗**的一声，他就消失在一团烟雾中。船上的众人探出身来，使劲睁大眼睛，想看清楚巴塞洛缪到底变出了什么花样，但是什么都看不到。

"小巴已经变成空气了，这招儿可够绝的！"菲利克斯拍着脑袋说道。

船身再次上下摇晃起来，大家严阵以待，防备着怪物发起新一轮的攻击。但就在一只蜥蜴状的生物浮出水面的同时，一条巨龙从船尾一跃而起。碧翠丝吓得猛地往后一倒，跌坐在船身中央。

"啊啊啊啊啊啊！我们这次死定了！"她惊叫道。

Thomas also had had enough. He went over to Beatrice and the two of them embraced, shaking with fear. Felix thought very seriously about joining his friends when he noticed something different about the dragon monster.

"Hey, look at the dragon's eyes. They're green!" said Felix. "Thomas, hand me the Professor's papers."

Still holding on to Beatrice, Thomas reached under the seat and gave the papers to Felix.

"Hmmm," said Felix. "Just as I thought. Male Achoos have blue eyes and female Achoos have green eyes."

"So?" said Thomas shivering.

"Don't you see, Thomas? That dragon monster is Bart! He has transformed himself into a female Achoo so he can lure away the real Achoo!"

Thomas and Beatrice let go of each other and looked up. The real Achoo looked over at the dragon monster and started to turn a pale shade of red. Its eyes began to bulge and its mouth began to drool. Then it said "Okay." But not the way it had before. No, this was more of an "Okaaaaaaaaaaaay!"

Suddenly, the monster shot out of the water, executed a sort of half flip, then dove headfirst back into the water like a missile.

"Oh, no," said Beatrice. "What now?"

The group looked anxiously toward Bart, still taking the shape of a dragon-like Achoo and hovering close to a sandy embankment that jutted from the shore.

Everything had become eerily quiet. Then, all of sudden, ripples started to show in the water, the type of ripples you usually see when an animal is swimming. The ripples started to move faster and faster. They were heading straight toward Bart.

"Swim, Bart! Swim!" Felix called out. "He's after you!"

托马斯也几乎到了崩溃的边缘。他跌坐在碧翠丝身边，俩人紧抱着对方，害怕得瑟瑟发抖。菲利克斯本想和大家抱成一团，但那只巨龙的异样却引起了他的注意。

"嘿，大家快看第二只怪物的眼睛，它们是绿色的！"菲利克斯说道，"托马斯，快把教授的文件递给我。"

托马斯一只手从座位下方拿出文件递给菲利克斯，另一只手仍死死地抱住碧翠丝不放。

菲利克斯说道："嗯，跟我想的一样，公阿嚏的眼睛是蓝色的，而母阿嚏的眼睛是绿色的。"

"所以呢？"托马斯的声音都在打战。

"你还没想明白吗，托马斯？第二只怪物就是小巴。他想把那只真正的阿嚏引开。"

托马斯和碧翠丝松开了对方，抬起头来。第一只阿嚏一动不动地盯着第二只怪物，然后，它的身体逐渐变成淡淡的红色。接着，它的双眼开始隆起，嘴角不断流出令人作呕的黏液。它大声嘶吼着"好的"，只是与往常不同的是，这一次它似乎故意拖长了声音"好的呃呃呃呃呃呃！"。

突然，这只怪物从水面一跃而起，在空中翻腾了半圈，然后像一枚导弹一样，头朝下直冲水底。

"噢，不会吧，"碧翠丝说道，"现在该怎么办啊？"

众人焦急地注视着巴塞洛缪，只见他摇晃着巨龙般庞大的身体，围着近岸的一处沙堤盘旋游动，河面上的一切都静得出奇。突然间，水中泛起了一圈圈涟漪，预示着水下一定有大型生物游过。涟漪不断激荡扩散，力道越来越强，速度越来越快，掀起的滔天巨浪向巴塞洛缪化身的巨龙奔涌而去。

"快游，小巴！快游！"菲利克斯大声疾呼，"它快追上你了！"

The ripples were really moving along now, occasionally interrupted by a slightly red, lizard-like head that popped itself up to yell, "Okaaaaaaaaaaaaay."

The group looked on with eagerness. It was like watching a horse race. Bart started swimming quickly but the Achoo was gaining speed. Suddenly, Bart made a sharp turn to the left. The Achoo, unable to slow down, crashed into a tree stump. There it collapsed, out of breath and dazed by the collision.

"Not okaaaaaaaaaaaay," it whined, its head spinning from side to side.

Bart swam toward the rowboat where he was greeted by three screaming fans.

"Hurrah!" they all yelled.

A few seconds later, a water-logged Bartholomew climbed back into the boat and collapsed.

"Are you all right?" asked Beatrice.

"Me? I'm okay!" smiled Bartholomew. "I'm okay!"

此时，层层涟漪沿着同一个方向移动，一只浅红色的蜥蜴在水波中时隐时现，不断嘶吼着"好啊啊啊啊啊啊啊啊啊"。

这就像赛马结果揭晓前的那一刻，每一个人都焦急地等待着。小巴在水中奋力游动，但阿嚏的速度也越来越快。突然，小巴猛地向左侧一转，那只阿嚏来不及减速，一头撞到了树桩上。它颓然地倒在水中，上气不接下气，显然已经被巨大的冲击力震得头晕目眩。

"不好啊啊啊啊啊啊啊啊。"它脑袋不停地旋转，发出痛苦的呻吟声。

小巴游回划艇，船上的三个人发出了热烈的欢呼。

"好哇！"他们都开心地大声叫喊。

几秒钟后，全身湿透了的巴塞洛缪终于回到了船上，瘫软在船板上。

"你没事吧？"碧翠丝问道。

"我吗？没事！"巴塞洛缪微笑道，"我没事！"

20

EDWIN IS SPOTTED

The little rowboat continued to zig and zag and bump its way through the Stream of Consciousness. Hour after hour as they rounded each corner, the group expected to see Edwin. But the stream went on and on, echoing the sounds of the creatures living in its midst. Then, without warning, small specs of red and yellow and orange started to appear on the horizon.

"Look! What are THOSE?" asked Thomas, catching sight of the distant colours.

Beatrice and Bartholomew squinted their eyes while Felix peered through his binoculars.

"I don't know, Tom," Felix said eventually. "But whatever they are, they're certainly man-made. This may be the place," he said excitedly. "Come on! Let's row."

With their spirits as high as kites, the group rowed like crazy. At last the bits of colour began to take on shape.

"They're signs," announced Beatrice.

And so they were—about a dozen crudely painted signs nailed to some tree stumps. The group read them and realized they were warnings.

WHY ARE YOU HERE?

GET LOST!

And a ratty looking sign that said, BUZZ OFF!

"How RUDE!" said Beatrice.

"Stop rowing!" ordered Felix.

"What is it, Felix?" asked Bartholomew.

20

发现埃德温

　　小划艇继续在曲折蜿蜒的意识之河道中颠簸前行。一个小时又一个小时的过去了，大家都热烈期盼着埃德温的身影能出现在下一个转角。但他们只看到湍急的河流奔涌向前，只听到河底的未知生物发出瘆人的呼啸。突然，地平线上毫无征兆地出现了红色、黄色和橙色的不明物体。

　　"看！**那**是什么？"托马斯瞥了一眼色彩斑斓的天际线，说道。

　　碧翠丝和巴塞洛缪眯起双眼费劲地看着，菲利克斯也透过双筒望远镜仔细观察着。

　　"我不知道，小汤，"菲利克斯终于开口了，"但是不管那是什么，都不可能是自然现象，那里可能就是我们要找的地方。"他激动地说。

　　"来吧！我们过去看看。"

　　众人士气高昂，拼尽全力继续划桨。终于，众人的视线逐渐清晰。

　　"原来是标志。"碧翠丝断然说道。

　　的确是标志——一丛丛树桩上钉着约十来块粗糙的标志牌。大家仔细看了看，上面的内容大多是些警示性语句，例如：

你为什么会到这里来？

远离此地！

　　一块破破烂烂的标语牌上甚至写着：**滚开**！

　　"真**粗鲁**！"碧翠丝说道。

　　"别划了！"菲利克斯突然命令道。

　　"怎么了，菲利克斯？"巴塞洛缪问道。

But Felix didn't answer. He quickly picked up his binoculars and began scanning the area. Then he focused on one direction.

"Hmmmm," he said, then turned to focus on something else.

"Ooooo," then finally, "Uhhhhh."

"What? What?" cried Beatrice impatiently.

"Gruesome creatures—all over the place," announced Felix. "There's a Rekcus Bird and what looks like hundreds of squirming Yas and . . . "

Felix leaned forward and turned the focus knob to get a better look.

"What?" cried Beatrice. "Not those horrible 'Okay' things?"

"No . . . no, this looks more like a gorilla with a dog's face, a Schnauzer's face, to be exact. Bart, take a look! Then see if you recognize anything in the Professor's papers that resembles this thing."

Bart looked through the binoculars and glanced down at the papers. After flipping some pages and a bit more looking, he turned with a smile on his face.

"BINGO!" he announced. "We're here!"

"Where?" said Beatrice.

"At Drow's! According to the Professor's papers, that ape-looking thing is called Riffraff; he's Drow's sidekick. Wherever Drow goes, Riffraff is usually right behind him."

Beatrice picked up the binoculars to take a look. "Hey! A palace!" she said.

"Did you say a palace?" asked Bartholomew, whirling his head around. "That definitely confirms it. The Professor's papers talk about Drow's famous palace and . . . "

"Wait," yelled Beatrice, fumbling with her binoculars.

"There's a cage beside the palace and . . . THERE'S EDWIN! THERE'S EDWIN!!!" she screamed, jumping up and down. Tom grabbed the binoculars out of her hand and peered through the viewers.

但菲利克斯没有回答，他迅速拿起双筒望远镜，谨慎地扫视着周边的环境，他朝某一个方向看了看。

"嗯……噢。"他沉吟了一下。

然后，他又转过头，看向别的方向。

"噢……唔……"他不停地嘟囔着。

"怎么了？到底怎么了嘛？"碧翠丝不耐烦地问道。

"这里到处都是可怕的生物，"菲利克斯终于开口了，说道，"附近有一只雷克斯鸟，还盘踞着数百条犽和……"

菲利克斯身体前倾，转了转调焦旋钮，以便看得更清楚。

"什么意思啊？"碧翠丝大叫道，"难道又是那些只会说'好吗'、'好吗'的可怕怪物吗？"

"不……不是，这只看起来就像一只大猩猩，只不过头部形似犬类，确切地说，它的脑袋更像是一只雪纳瑞。小巴，你过来瞧瞧！看看教授的文件里有没有提到过类似的生物。"

小巴透过望远镜向远处眺望，然后又低头翻了翻教授的文件。他翻翻又看看了几页，看看又翻翻，最后，终于转过身来，得意地看着其他人。

"宾果！**"**他大声说道，"我们终于到了！"

"到哪儿了？"碧翠丝问道。

"卓尔的老巢！根据教授的文件来看，那只大猩猩叫作混混，是卓尔的左膀右臂，无论卓尔走到哪儿，混混都会常伴左右。"

碧翠丝也拿起望远镜看了一眼："嘿！那边有一座宫殿！"她叫了起来。

"你说什么？宫殿？"巴塞洛缪转头说道，"这足以证明我刚才的推测是对的，教授的文件的宫殿，还有……"

"等等，"碧翠丝一边大叫，一边调节着双筒望远镜。

"宫殿旁还有一个笼子……**埃德温**！**那是埃德温**！！！"她开心得一蹦三丈高，兴奋地尖叫起来。托马斯从她手里一把抢过双筒望远镜，透过目镜向远方看去。

"She's right! She's right!"

"Of course I'm right! I know Edwin when I see him. Oh, thank goodness he's not hurt," she said, quite relieved. "Come on. What are we waiting for? Let's go save him!"

"Not so fast," said Felix. "We can't risk getting caught. Bart, we'll need another transformation."

"Into what?"

"How about a Ya?"

"Ya?"

"Ya!" said Felix.

"Then what?" said Bartholomew.

"Then you get to Edwin as quickly as possible and see if you can free him. If you can't, get as much information as possible about Drow's daily routine—where he goes, when he eats, what he does in the palace—anything that might help us."

"When do you want me to go? Now?" Bartholomew asked.

"No! We'll wait until it gets dark, just to be on the safe side. Then you can make your move!"

"她说得没错！她说得没错！"

"我怎么可能弄错呢！我只要看一眼埃德温就能认出他来。哦，谢天谢地，他没有受伤，"她心里的大石头落下了一半，"来吧！还等什么呢？我们赶紧去救他吧！"

"先别冲动，"菲利克斯说道，"我们可能会被逮个正着，不能冒这个险。小巴，你需要再变一次身。"

"变什么呀？"

"变成犰怎么样？"

"犰？"

"对！"菲利克斯说道。

"然后呢？"巴塞洛缪问道。

"然后你尽快找到埃德温，看能不能把他救出来，如果暂时不能，那么你就要尽量收集与卓尔的日常活动有关的信息——他去什么地方、什么时候吃饭、每天都在宫殿里做些什么——任何可能有帮助的信息都不要放过。"

"你要我什么时候去？现在？"巴塞洛缪问道。

"不！为了安全起见，我们要等到天黑后再行动。到时候，你就可以大显身手了！"

21

BACK AT THE DROWER

"Okay, wordths, hereths your supperths," said Riffraff, taking the key from around his neck and unlocking the gate of the cage. He put a tray containing two large bowls on the floor, then slammed the door shut.

"Enjoy your mealths," he said, bouncing off into the evening darkness.

Large torches surrounded the Drower. They gave off just enough light for everyone in the cage to see.

"Like you know, what's for supper?" asked Edwin.

"Same old stuff," said Tomboy lifting a lid off one of the bowls. "There's C-weed soup and breaded I-balls."

Edwin watched as a few of the words took a sip of the soup but after one mouthful, they began to cough and splutter and grimace at the disgusting concoction. Edwin decided he wasn't hungry anymore.

"Tom, like you know, I'm afraid my friends aren't going to come."

"Edwin, when you told me about your friends, I thought there might be hope. I'm tired of fighting Drow. I always refused to give in to his power. But you're my friend and now you've been converted. I feel left out. Maybe I should just give up and join his side."

"No, Tom! Like you know, you can't. Like you know, don't become Drow just because I have. Like you know, you've got to do what you think is right."

Tom lowered her head in silence and thought of what Edwin had said.

"Come on, Tom. Like you know, cheer up. Maybe we can escape or something, you know?"

21

重回卓尔地牢

混混从脖子上取下钥匙，打开牢房的闸门："好了，单池们，晚馐时间到了。"

它将托着两只大碗的餐盘放到地上，然后又砰的一声关上了铁门。

"慢慢享用你们的晚馐吧。"混混说完，就消失在一片夜色之中。

环绕四壁的巨大火炬将牢房内的每个人都照得真真切切。

"你知道的吧，晚餐吃什么呀？"埃德温问道。

"还不是老样子，"假小子揭开一个碗盖说，"海带汤和酥炸鱼眼珠。"

海带汤看着都让人反胃，埃德温看着其他人一口汤下肚后，不是干咳就是咋舌，表情苦不堪言，他真是一点儿食欲也没有了。

"假小子，你知道的吧，我担心我的朋友们不会来了。"

"埃德温，当我得知你的故事时，我觉得我们还有一线希望。我已经厌倦了反抗卓尔的生活，我一直不愿向他的黑暗势力屈服。现在你是我的朋友，但我却只能眼睁睁地看着自己的朋友被转化，我觉得精疲力竭了。也许我应该放弃挣扎，加入他的军团。"

"千万不要啊，假小子！你知道的吧，你不能这么做。你知道的吧，千万别因为我被转化了就自暴自弃加入卓尔的军团。你知道的吧，你一定要坚持正义。"

假小子低下头陷入了沉默，回味着埃德温的话。

"别这样，假小子，你知道的吧，振作一点。也许我们可以越狱或者想出别的办法呢，对吧？"

"I've thought about that, but the only way to get out of here is to get hold of the key that hangs around Riffraff's neck. And that's next to impossible."

"Yes, but . . . " started Edwin.

"Shhhhh!" said Tomboy. "I hear something."

Tomboy and Edwin stopped moving and listened. Sure enough, there was a rustling sound in front of the cage. Suddenly, Tomboy caught sight of a long hose-like tail.

"It's a Ya!" she screamed. Everyone rushed to the back of the cage. Clouds of smoke started filling the Drower.

"What's going on?" Tom asked.

But Edwin knew what was happening. He had seen smoke like that before. As soon as it lifted, he began searching all around the cage, Finally he found what he was looking for. There, standing in one of the corners, was Bartholomew Book.

Edwin rushed over and threw his arms around his neck. Bartholomew leaned over Edwin and gave him a big hug.

The rest of the words in the cage looked on with great interest as Edwin and Bartholomew talked. Edwin told Bartholomew about the Rekcus Bird and Drow and he introduced him to Tomboy. Bartholomew told Edwin about the Achoo monster and the trip up the Stream of Consciousness.

At last, Bartholomew broached the topic of escape.

"We've got to get our hands on the key that you say hangs around Riffraff's neck," said Bartholomew. "But then we can't simply turn around and leave, Edwin. We've come this far. We still have to confront Drow and put an end to his terrible rule. I need any information about Drow's daily routine that could prove useful."

"But Bart, like you know, isn't it going to be impossible to sneak a sentence that does not have one Drow word in it into Drow's palace?" Edwin asked.

"Wait a minute," said Tomboy. "Tomorrow night Drow is holding his Annual Alphabet Soup Masquerade Party out on the lawn in front of the palace. He invites all his Mumbojumbo friends."

"我早就想过了，但是只有弄到混混脖子上那把钥匙才能离开这里，可是那根本就不可能啊。"

"说得没错，但是……"

"嘘！"假小子说道，"我听到了奇怪的声音。"

假小子和埃德温一动也不动地听着。果然，铁笼前传来一阵沙沙的声音，假小子突然看到了一条长长的尾巴。

"它是一条犴！"她尖叫起来，大家都忙不迭地往铁笼后退。突然间烟雾升腾，笼罩了整座卓尔地牢。

"这是怎么回事呀？"假小子问道。

但是埃德温对这样的场景完全并不陌生，他一下子就明白了。烟消雾散后，他环顾四周，终于看见了他满心期待的那个人。果不其然，此刻站在角落里的那位，不正是巴塞洛缪·书嘛。

埃德温立刻冲过去搂住了他的脖子。巴塞洛缪俯下身来，给了埃德温一个大大的拥抱。

铁笼里的其他人饶有兴致地看着他俩叽里呱啦地说个不停。埃德温将雷克斯鸟和卓尔的事一五一十地告诉了巴塞洛缪，然后还向他介绍了假小子。巴塞洛缪则把阿嚏和意识之河沿途的怪事和盘托出。

最后，两人开始讨论逃跑计划。

"我们一定要拿到混混脖子上那把钥匙，"巴塞洛缪说道，"但是，我们不能就这样转身离开，埃德温。我们已经走到这一步了，我们还是要抓到卓尔，推翻他的黑暗统治，我需要一切与卓尔的日常生活有关的信息。"

"但是小巴，你知道的吧，要想把一个不包含卓尔单词的句子偷偷带到他的宫殿里，这几乎是不可能的啊？"埃德温说道。

"等一下，"假小子说道，"明天晚上卓尔会在宫殿前的草坪上举行字母汤年度化装舞会，他还邀请了所有胡言军团参加呢。"

"So?" said Edwin.

"Edwin, if you were invited to a costume party at Drow's, what type of costume do you think he would expect you to wear?"

"Hmmm . . . like, of course! You'd come dressed as a regular word."

"That's right," said Tomboy.

"Does Drow dress up, too?" asked Edwin.

"Drow? No way! The only reason he has the party is so he can look cool in front of a group of regular words. It's his yearly ego booster."

"Now, let me get this straight," said Bartholomew. "You're saying that if we come dressed as ourselves, Drow will simply think we're some of his Mumbojumbos in disguise?"

"That's right," said Tomboy. "But there is one problem."

"Like you know, what, Tom?"

"You, Edwin. You have Unoitis. Your sentence won't work if even one of you has an element of Drow."

"Like, isn't there, you know, an antidote or something?" Edwin asked hopefully.

"Well," said Bartholomew, "if there is, it will be listed in the Professor's papers. I'll have a look when I get back to the boat. Meanwhile, I want all of you to prepare yourselves for an escape."

"But how will you get the key?" Tom asked.

"Leave that to me," said Bartholomew. "What time is this party tomorrow, Tom?"

"I think I heard Drow say 8 pm."

"Good! Then I want all of you to be ready at 8 pm tomorrow. Now, take care, Edwin, and don't worry. Your friends are here," Bartholomew said confidently.

"Like you know, alright Bart. I'll see you tomorrow. Say hello to everyone for me."

"I will, Edwin," Bartholomew said, patting him on the back. "I will."

"所以呢？"埃德温问道。

"埃德温，如果你有机会参加卓尔的化装舞会，你觉得怎样装扮才最合适呢？"

"嗯……像是……当然！乔装成常规单词最适合不过了。"

"说得没错。"假小子说道。

"卓尔也会乔装打扮吗？"埃德温问道。

"卓尔？他才不会呢！他举办化装舞会的唯一原因就是为了在一大帮子常规单词面前显摆。每年一到这个时候，他就自信爆棚。"

"好吧，恕我直言，"巴塞洛缪说道，"你是说，如果我们以真实面目示人，卓尔反而会把我们当成乔装成常规单词的胡言军团，对吗？"

"就是这意思，"假小子说道，"但还有一个问题。"

"你知道的吧，什么问题，假小子？"

"你，埃德温。你现在患了失语症，如果你们的句子中包含了卓尔单词，那么就没法奏效。"

"就像，难道就没有，你知道的吧，解药之类的东西吗？"埃德温满怀希望地问。

"好吧，不管怎样，"巴塞洛缪说道，"如果有的话，那教授的文件里肯定会有记录的，我回船后就去查一下。在此之际，我希望大家都做好逃跑的准备。"

"不过，你打算怎么弄到那把钥匙呢？"假小子问道。

"就交给我好了，"巴塞洛缪说道，"明天什么时候举行化装舞会呢，假小子？"

"我好像听到卓尔说是晚上八点。"

"好的！那么我希望明晚八点大家都能做好准备。此刻，埃德温，你要好好保重。别担心，这儿有我们呢，"巴塞洛缪充满信心地说。

"你知道的吧，好的，小巴，明天见。代我向大家问好。"

"我会的，埃德温，"巴塞洛缪说着，拍拍他的后背，"我会的。"

Smoke filled the cage once again and a rustling noise was heard as Bartholomew made his way back to the boat.

铁笼内又弥散出漫天的烟雾，伴随着一阵渐行渐远的沙沙声，巴塞洛缪照常用他的变法回到了划艇上。

22

THE PLAN

When Bartholomew got back to the boat, he told the rest of the group the good news first—that Edwin was all right and that he and Edwin had devised a great plan to sneak into Drow's masquerade party. Everyone jumped up and down and started hugging each other, almost causing the rowboat to flip over.

Then Bartholomew told them the bad news—Edwin had developed Unoitis! The group stopped their celebrating and became very quiet.

"Well," said Felix finally, "before we get upset, let's go through all the Professor's papers. Maybe there is some type of antidote for Unoitis."

Everyone took equal shares of the Professor's notes and began reading. With nothing but small candles to provide the light, it was very slow-going. Finally, just as the sun started showing its face the following morning, things began to look a bit brighter.

"I . . . I think I have something," said Beatrice sleepily. "It says here that while there are no recommended treatments for Drow's Unoitis, significant improvement has been observed in Drow patients treated by Dr. Dick Shonery. He suggests the following remedy.

Take 1 set of the *Oxford Concise Dictionary* and place in a meat grinder.

Grind the dictionaries until all the words are condensed into a clear and crisp mixture. Avoid lumps or the victim is liable to become verbose.

Add the mixture to 1 cup of Alphabet Soup and digest the full contents before opening your mouth again.

"Where are we going to get a set of dictionaries in the middle of this stream?" said Thomas.

22

逃跑计划

当巴塞洛缪一回到船上，立刻就把好消息告诉了其他人——埃德温现在安然无恙，而且他和埃德温已经制订了巧妙的计划，准备偷偷潜入卓尔的化装舞会。大家伙儿高兴得又蹦又跳，相互拥抱，差点把小船掀了个底朝天。

紧接着，巴塞洛缪又说出了坏消息——埃德温已经患上了失语症！听到这个消息，小船上的气氛不再欢欣鼓舞，大伙儿个个陷入了沉默。

"好了，"菲利克斯终于开了口，"与其我们坐着发愁，不如一起来查一查教授的文件吧，说不定能找到失语症的解药呢。"

每个人都分到了教授的一部分笔记，埋头找了起来。众人借着微弱的烛光，艰难地辨认着文件上的字迹。清晨时分，冉冉升起的旭日带来了一线曙光。

"我……我觉得我找到了有用的信息了，"满脸倦容的碧翠丝说，"这里写着，目前对于卓尔的失语症并无有效的治疗方案，但相关患者经迪克·萧纳瑞医生治疗后，病情均有显著改善。他推荐了下列治疗方案：将一本《简明牛津词典》放入绞肉机内。反复研磨词典直至所有单词混合成清脆爽口的汁液，应将所有结块搅拌成泥，以免患者服用后发展成啰唆症。随后将混合物加入一杯字母汤中，服食后，请再次闭上你的嘴充分咀嚼。"

"我们现在漂在水面上，上哪儿去找一本词典啊？"托马斯说道。

"They don't call me Bartholomew Book for nothing, Tom." Bartholomew reached behind his back and pulled out a set of the Oxford Concise Dictionary from his knapsack.

"Great!" said Felix. "And I made sure to take a few cans of Alphabet soup from the F.L.A.B."

"Excuse me," said Beatrice. "I don't wish to be a party pooper, but, like you know, there is still the small matter of a meat grinder!"

"I've already thought of that," said Thomas. "Bartholomew can transform himself into a meat grinder, can't you Bart?"

"Yes, but . . ."

Suddenly, Thomas, Felix, and Bartholomew stared in horror at Beatrice.

"But, like you know, what?" asked Beatrice. "Why are you looking at me like that? You guys are making me nervous."

Finally, Felix cleared his throat and spoke.

"Beatrice, I'm afraid . . . I mean I'm sorry to tell you . . . but . . ."

"You're ugly," shouted Thomas with a smirk.

"Oh, be quiet, Thomas. Like you know, I'm serious. What's wrong?"

"What Thomas is trying to say," said Bartholomew, "is that your appearance has . . . how should I put this delicately? . . . It has become . . ."

"Disgusting!" said Thomas, laughing uncontrollably.

"Thomas, please! Show some sensitivity here. It's not Beatrice's fault," said Felix.

Beatrice stared at the others.

"Like you know, what's not my fault? Will somebody please tell me what's going on? You're making me angry!"

"Beatrice, remember when you were attacked by the Ya and you had those red pockmarks on your arms?"

"Yes! Yes! What?" said Beatrice, very agitated.

"Well, you must have developed Unoitis," said Bartholomew. "Your body is already being transformed into something else . . ."

"别人管我叫巴塞洛缪·书，这名号可不是白来的，小汤。"

巴塞洛缪伸手从身后的背包内掏出好几本《简明牛津词典》。

"太好了！"菲利克斯说道，"我负责回热气球拿几罐字母汤来。"

"不好意思，"碧翠丝说道，"我不想扫大家的兴，但是，你知道的吧，绞肉机可不好弄啊！"

"我早就想到了，"托马斯说道，"巴塞洛缪可以变成一台绞肉机，对吧，小巴？"

"说得没错，但是……"

突然，托马斯、菲利克斯和巴塞洛缪都怔住了。他们一言不发地注视着碧翠丝，一脸惊慌失措的表情。

"但是，你知道的吧，什么啊？"碧翠丝问道，"你们干吗这样看着我？你们的表情让我心里直发毛。"

菲利克斯清了清嗓子，终于开了口。

"碧翠丝，恐怕……我的意思是说，抱歉我不得不告诉你……但是……"

"你变得难看死了。"托马斯得意地笑了起来。

"噢，你给我闭嘴，托马斯。你知道的吧，正经点好吗，到底怎么了？"

"其实托马斯是想说，"巴塞洛缪说道，"是你现在的样子……怎么说才好呢？……你现在的样子变得……"

"让人恶心！"托马斯忍不住失声大笑起来。

"托马斯，拜托！有点同情心好吗，这又不是碧翠丝的错。"菲利克斯说道。

碧翠丝看着其他人，仍然没明白他们的意思。

"你知道的吧，不是我的错？你们把话说清楚好吧，真要被你们气死了！"

"碧翠丝，还记得那条狰狞攻击你时，在你手臂留下的红色瘢痕吗？"

"记得！记得！怎么啦？"此刻碧翠丝的情绪变得异常激动。

"好吧，你肯定是那个时候被传染了失语症，"巴塞洛缪说道，"现在你的样貌已经完全变了……"

"That's right. The Loch Ness Monster!" interrupted Thomas in hysterics.

Beatrice quickly peered over the side of the boat and looked into the placid water, straining to catch her reflection. At first, she could see nothing. Then, the moon above eased its way through the clouds and began projecting glimmers of light on the stream.

She saw what looked like fragmented pieces of glass. As the last remaining clouds passed and the full force of the moon's beam lit up the sky, an ear-piercing scream filled the air.

Beatrice could see her new image. She had become hairy and her face was contorted and large. Her skin was lumpy and her eyes looked sunken and distant. Her crooked nose protruded like a hook on a wall and her gapped teeth stared back at her like keys on a piano. She was no longer beautiful. Beatrice Beautiful had become Beatrice Beastly.

"Like you know, what am I going to do?" shrieked Beatrice. "I look simply horrible!"

Thomas felt like making another smart remark but realized Beatrice was totally upset.

"It's alright, Beatrice," said Felix. "Remember, we have the recipe for an antidote. Let's not panic."

Beatrice remained quiet for a few minutes as the group looked on nervously. At last she looked up.

"Fine. Let's do it," she said halfheartedly.

Everyone set about grinding up Bartholomew's dictionaries and stirring the little bits into a bailing can full of alphabet soup. While they ground and stirred, Felix outlined his plan to Thomas and Beatrice.

"Now, the way I see it, Bartholomew will be responsible for freeing Edwin. He seems to think he can do that. We, on the other hand, are going to mingle with Drow's guests. Then, at exactly 9 pm, all of us will walk up to Drow, arrange ourselves in our sentence, then blow Drow away!"

"没错，就像一头尼斯湖水怪！"乐不可支的托马斯插了一句。

碧翠丝迅速从船舷一侧探出身去，在平静的水面上照了照，她费力地在水面上找寻着自己的倩影。起初，她什么也看不见。这时，月亮从云彩中慢慢探出头来，河面上闪烁着淡淡的月光。

碧翠丝静静地凝视着，水中的倒影看起来就像破碎的玉片漂浮在水面。云开月出，皎洁的月光照亮了幽暗的星空。紧接着，一阵刺耳的尖叫响彻整个河面。

此刻，碧翠丝的样貌被映照得一清二楚。她面容肿大，满脸茸毛，表情狰狞。她的皮肤粗糙不堪，双目凹陷，眼神涣散。她的鹰钩鼻滑稽得就像墙上的挂衣钩，而嘴中龇出的獠牙就像凹凸不平的琴键。碧翠丝·美丽已经美丽不再，变成了碧翠丝·野兽。

"你知道的吧，我该怎么办啊？"碧翠丝哭喊着，"我这副模样简直太可怕了。"

托马斯本想再戏谑她一番，但他看得出来碧翠丝的确非常伤心。

"没事的，碧翠丝，"菲利克斯说道，"别忘了，我们还有解药呢，我们先别慌。"

碧翠丝沉默了好几分钟，其他人都紧张兮兮地看着她。终于，她抬起头来。

"好吧，那咱们就试试吧。"她半心半意地说。

大家伙儿开始忙不迭地搅拌巴塞洛缪的词典，然后将磨碎的单词汁倒入装满字母汤的罐子里。与此同时，菲利克斯向托马斯和碧翠丝简要地描述了自己的计划。

"此刻，我觉得，应该由巴塞洛缪负责解救埃德温，他对做这种事自信满满呢。而我们呢，就混在卓尔的宾客里潜入舞会。然后，我们在晚上九点整碰头，以句子的形式出现在卓尔面前，一举将他拿下！"

"Let's just hope the antidote works or Drow may just blow *us* away," said Thomas.

"Well, we have no choice. It's all or nothing!" said Felix.

"Like you know, what about Edwin?" asked Beatrice, still quite sullen.

"He's got the most important job of all. As soon as Drow has been blown away, Edwin must stand up and tell everyone who he is and why our book has been neglected for so long."

"Wow, Felix! Are you sure Edwin can handle such a big responsibility?" Thomas asked.

"Don't be silly, Thomas. Edwin can do anything! Just you watch!"

"我们还是先祈求这个解药奏效吧，不然的话，恐怕一举被拿下的就是我们自己了。"托马斯说道。

"好吧，我们也别无选择了。要么胜利而归，要么全军覆没！"菲利克斯说道。

"你知道的吧，那埃德温怎么办呢？"碧翠丝还是满脸不悦的表情。

"他还有最重要的工作呢。我们打败卓尔后，埃德温就可以站出来公布他的身份，并告诉大家我们的书长期被人类忽视的真正原因。"

"哇，菲利克斯！你觉得埃德温能承担那么大的责任吗？"托马斯问道。

"别傻了，托马斯。埃德温可以做好任何事！大家就等着瞧吧！"

23

THE PARTY

Early that evening, the group began to prepare themselves for the most dangerous part of their mission. They quietly rowed their boat to shore and hid it behind some dead trees.

"This is it," Bartholomew said rather dramatically. "I had better be off!"

"Let's just hope this antidote is ready," said Thomas, giving it one last stir. He handed the small bailing can containing the antidote to Bartholomew and the rope he had requested.

"Wait," said Beatrice, pulling Bartholomew's shirt from behind. "Like you know, what about me, for goodness sake?"

"Oh, right," said Felix. "Bartholomew, give Beatrice the can of antidote for a minute."

Bartholomew handed Beatrice the bailing can. She raised the can to her lips and allowed some of the gooey mixture to roll down her throat. Her hands were trembling. "This stuff is revolting!" said Beatrice.

The rest of the group watched in anticipation, waiting for a reaction. But nothing happened.

"Maybe it doesn't work!" said Beatrice, beginning to panic.

"The Professor's papers say you have to wait for your body to digest the solution before it will work," said Bartholomew. "Be patient."

"Be patient! Be patient! How would you feel if you looked like a Halloween costume?"

"Please, Beatrice. You must remain completely quiet. You cannot open your mouth until the antidote has had a chance to take effect," said Bartholomew.

23

化装舞会

那天傍晚，众人开始为本次任务中最危险的一环做准备。他们悄悄地把划艇划到岸边，然后将它藏到了枯萎的树丛后面。

"就这样吧，"巴塞洛缪正色说道，"我得出发了！"

"希望这个解药能奏效。"托马斯说着，最后再搅拌了一次。然后，他将装满解药的小罐子和巴塞洛缪需要的绳索一齐递了过去。

"等一下，"碧翠丝从身后拉住了巴塞洛缪的衬衫问道，"你知道的吧，老天爷啊，那我怎么办？"

"哦，对了，"菲利克斯说道，"巴塞洛缪，把解药先给碧翠丝。"

巴塞洛缪把解药递给她，她把罐子举到唇边，吞下了几口黏糊糊的单词汁，她的双手止不住地发抖，罐子在手中摇来摆去。"这个味儿真恶心。"碧翠丝说道。

其他人焦急地注视着她的进一步反应。但是，什么都没有发生。

"也许这药压根就不管用！"碧翠丝开始惊慌起来。

"根据教授的文件，解药只有被身体彻底消化后才能产生效果，"巴塞洛缪说道，"再耐心等等吧。"

"耐心等等！耐心等等！如果让你长得跟万圣节装扮的怪物似的，你乐意吗？"

"拜托，碧翠丝，你必须把嘴巴封严实了。在解药生效前，你不能张嘴说话。"巴塞洛缪说道。

The group waited and watched. For 15 minutes they sat consoling poor Beatrice, wondering themselves if the antidote really would work. Then, gradually, smoke started to rise from Beatrice's ears and nose and her body started going into convulsions.

"What's going on?" asked Thomas, looking worried.

"It's okay," said Bartholomew. "It's all part of the process of reverse-transformation."

At last the smoke started to clear and the group could make out the image of a beautiful lady.

"It works!" screamed Felix.

"I don't know. I think you looked better before," said Thomas, chuckling to himself.

"Oh, be quiet, Thomas!" said Beatrice.

Beatrice quickly leaned over the boat and stared into the water; the rest of the group anxiously awaited for her reaction.

She let out a huge sigh of relief.

"I forgot just how beautiful I really was," she said, flicking her hair back over her head.

"Oh, brother," said Thomas. "Here we go again."

"Enough, you two!" said Felix. "Bart's got to head off. We have an important mission to worry about."

Bart grabbed the bailing can and turned to leave.

"Good luck, Bart," said Felix.

Bartholomew looked back at Felix in surprise.

"I mean it," said Felix.

Bartholomew smiled, raised his thumb into the air to signal everything was going to go well, then headed into the woods.

大家伙儿等待着啊，看着啊。随后的十五分钟，他们坐在一起，一边安慰着可怜的碧翠丝，一边暗自怀疑着解药是否真能管用。这时，碧翠丝的耳朵和鼻子内慢慢冒出缕缕烟雾，接着，她开始不停地抽搐。

"这是怎么了？"托马斯露出了担忧的神情问道。

"没关系，"巴塞洛缪说道，"这是反转化的迹象。"

烟雾最终散去，众人再次看到了碧翠丝美丽的面容。

"真的奏效了！"菲利克斯高声道。

"谁知道呢，我觉得刚才你的样子比现在好看多了。"托马斯笑着说。

"噢，你给我闭嘴，托马斯！"碧翠丝说道。

碧翠丝急着从船舷探出身去，在平静的水面上照了又照，其他人焦急地注视她的反应。最后，她终于如释重负地叹了口气。

"我差点儿都忘了自己有多美了。"她把一缕头发轻拂到脑后。

"哦，兄弟啊，"托马斯说道，"又来了。"

"够了，你们俩！"菲利克斯说道，"小巴要出发了，我们还有重要的任务没完成呢。"

巴塞洛缪抓起解药罐子，转身准备离开。

"祝你好运，小巴。"菲利克斯说道。

巴塞洛缪回过头，满脸诧异地看着菲利克斯。

"我说的是真心话。"菲利克斯说道。

巴塞洛缪笑着伸出大拇指，示意他别担心，一切都会顺利的，然后朝树林深处走去。

When at last he reached the outskirts of the palace wall, he placed the antidote behind a bush and stuck his finger in his ear. A few seconds later, he was slithering toward the Drower.

Meanwhile, Edwin Bellamy's body was tingling with excitement. He waited and listened, checking the time every few minutes. At last, just as the hands on his watch moved within 5 minutes of 8 o'clock, a rustling noise came from outside the cage.

"Like you know, that's Bart, Tom—I know it is," said Edwin.

The two of them peered into the darkness. The noise stopped. All they could hear were the sounds of crickets and night flies. Then the noise started up again, only it was a different noise. It was the sound of a large animal bounding through the grass. Suddenly there was a big yelp and a crash.

"What's going on?" asked Tomboy, turning to Edwin.

Edwin and Tomboy held their breath and waited.

"Hi there!" cried a voice.

Edwin and Tom shot up in the air like a pair of Jack-in-the-boxes.

"Hey! It's just me—Bart!"

There was Bartholomew on the roof of the cage and he was carrying a great big golden key!

"Like, how did you get the key?" asked Edwin excitedly.

"No time for questions, Edwin. We have a party to go to."

Bartholomew quickly outlined Felix's plan, then unlocked the cage door. Everyone scrambled out.

"Come on, Edwin," Bartholomew said anxiously, "we've found an antidote! But you must hurry if you want it to take effect in time."

"Like you know, can Tomboy come?"

"Sure, sure. Just hurry."

The three walked carefully along the side of the palace wall, checking over their shoulders to see if they were being followed. They darted across the lawn

终于到达宫墙外后，巴塞洛缪把解药罐藏到灌木丛中，然后把手指插入耳内，几秒钟后，化身犽形的巴塞洛缪就顺利进入了卓尔地牢。

与此同时，埃德温·贝拉米的身体也刺痛得激动异常。他凝神静听，耐心等待，每隔几分钟就迫不及待地看看手表。就在手表指向七点五十五分时，他终于听到铁笼外传来期盼已久的沙沙声。

"你知道的吧，那是小巴，假小子——我就知道肯定是他。"埃德温说道。

两人在一团黑暗中费力地寻找。突然，沙沙声戛然而止，他们现在只能听到蟋蟀和夜蝇的叫声。但是几秒钟后，又传来了异样的声音，不过这次与之前似乎略有不同。只听得一阵从草地疾驰而过的脚步声，然后传来刺耳的狗吠声，随后是剧烈的撞击声。

"发生什么事了？"假小子转头问埃德温。

两人屏住呼吸，继续等待着，可是仍然是一片死寂。

"嗨，你好！"一个声音突然响起。

埃德温和假小子就像玩偶匣里的玩偶一样惊得一下子跳了起来。

"嘿！是我，小巴！"

埃德温和假小子抬头看着牢房的天花板，的的确确是巴塞洛缪，更妙的是，他还衔着一把大大的金钥匙！

"呃，你怎么弄到钥匙的呀？"埃德温兴奋地问道。

"没时间回答你的问题了，埃德温，我们还得去参加舞会呢。"

巴塞洛缪简单地介绍了菲利克斯的计划，然后打开了牢房的铁门，铁笼内的人争先恐后地涌了出来。

"快来，埃德温，"巴塞洛缪焦急地说，"我们已经找到解药了！但是，它需要一段时间才能生效，所以要抓紧时间。"

"你知道的吧，我们能带上假小子吗？"

"当然了，当然可以，快来吧。"

三人蹑手蹑脚地沿着宫墙往前走，不时回头看看，以免被人盯梢。他们

to a clump of trees. There they found Riffraff lying on the ground with his front paws tied to his back paws.

"Waths happenings?" he cried, looking up at them in a frightened manner. "Hey, waith a minute. Gets back in your caydths. Stops! I'm going to tells Drowths. I want my mommies!"

Edwin felt a little sorry for the old mutt.

"Come on, Edwin! There's no time to spare! He'll be all right," assured Bartholomew.

They continued a little further into the woods until finally Bartholomew stopped and uncovered the bailing can full of antidote.

"Here, Edwin! Drink all of this."

Edwin took a sip.

"YUK! Like you know, this tastes awful!"

"You've got to drink it, Edwin. Just guzzle it down!" urged Bartholomew.

Edwin closed his eyes, tilted back his head, and raised the can to his mouth, letting the antidote ease slowly down his throat.

"Like you know, nothing's happened," Edwin said sadly.

"Oh, I almost forgot. You've got to digest it before opening your mouth. Don't say anything right now," ordered Bartholomew.

The group made their way out of the bushes and walked toward the front of the palace. On the front lawn were big torches and hundreds of guests talking and laughing. A rock band was making its way to a large outdoor stage.

"Edwin, it's too dangerous for you to walk in there right now," said Bartholomew. "Drow already knows what you look like. You must hide somewhere until just before 9 o'clock. Then head for Drow. We all will be there waiting for you."

Edwin watched as Bartholomew walked into the gathering. He looked like any of the other guests, except he didn't have a tail peeking out from

穿过草坪，飞奔到一排树丛边。混混正躺在地上，前爪和后爪被紧紧地绑在一起。

"发森甚么四啦？"它惊恐万状地抬头看着他们，"嘿，懂一下。你们都给我赞住！赞住！我要把你们的四都告诉卓尔先森。哎呀，我的妈妈呀！"

埃德温停下脚步，看着可怜兮兮的混混，他又替它难过起来。

"快来呀，埃德温！我们没有多少时间了！它不会有事的！"巴塞洛缪安慰他。

他们继续往树林深处跑去，最后巴塞洛缪终于停了下来，拿出满满一罐解药。

"来，埃德温！把这个喝光了。"

埃德温小尝了一口。

"**啊呀**！你知道的吧，这个味道太恶心了！"

"那也要喝，埃德温。只要一口倒进嘴里就行了！"巴塞洛缪催促着。

埃德温张开嘴巴，闭上眼睛，把罐子往嘴里一倒，解药顺着喉咙流进了肚里。

"你知道的吧，什么效果也没有啊。"埃德温伤心地说。

"哦，我差点忘了，在解药完全消化前，你还不能张开嘴，现在闭上你的嘴巴！"巴塞洛缪命令道。

三个人走出灌木丛，朝着宫殿走去。巨大的火炬将宫殿前的草坪照得通明透亮，成百上千的宾客正聚在一起谈笑风生。一支摇滚乐队正要登上户外的大型舞台。

"埃德温，你现在去参加舞会实在是太危险了，"巴塞洛缪说道，"卓尔已经见过你了，你一定要先找个地方好好藏起来，等到九点再去找卓尔，到时候我们自会跟你碰头。"

埃德温看着巴塞洛缪走进舞会。舞会上众生百相，巴塞洛缪看起来跟其他宾客相差无几，唯一不同的是，他没有在外套下露出一截尾巴，或是在帽

under his coat or large horns under his hat or furry arms under his long sleeves.

"Well, Edwin, where shall we hide?" asked Tomboy.

Edwin shrugged his shoulders, remembering he wasn't supposed to talk.

"How about just inside the palace entrance?" said Tomboy. "Everyone seems to be outside. That way we can watch what's going on through the open door."

Edwin nodded in agreement.

The two eased their way to the front of the palace and carefully pulled open the door. With a quick glance over their shoulders, they slipped inside. No sooner were they inside the palace, smoke started pouring from Edwin's ears and nose.

"You're changing back! You're changing back!" cried Tomboy.

The smoke gradually disappeared and Edwin slowly opened his mouth.

He took a deep breath and spoke.

"Isn't . . . isn't the weather nice today, Tomboy?"

For a moment, he wasn't sure. He looked over at Tomboy who raised her thumb to signal it had worked.

"Yippee!" he cried. "Look at me, Tomboy! I'm Edwin again."

"That's fantastic, Edwin. Now you can help your friends. Come on, let's see what's going on."

Edwin and Tomboy could watch the party through the partially open door. After a while, Edwin started to get bored. He looked at his watch. There were still 15 minutes to go. He turned around to get a better look at the inside of the palace and realized something was very, very wrong. He opened the front door a little more to allow light from the party to filter in.

It was then that he made an incredible discovery.

子旁拱出两只角，还有的袖子外露出毛茸茸的胳膊。

"好吧，埃德温，我们躲哪儿好呢？"假小子问道。

埃德温想起巴塞洛缪叮嘱他不要说话，所以只是耸了耸肩。

"咱们躲在宫殿大门里面，如何？"假小子提议道，"所有人都在大门外呢，这样，我们就可以透过门缝看到外面的情况了。"

埃德温点了点头表示同意。

两人蹑手蹑脚地走到宫殿前，小心翼翼地推开了门。他们飞快地回头看了一眼，然后悄悄溜了进去。他们刚进得门来，埃德温的耳朵和鼻子里就开始冒出缕缕烟雾。

"你正在变回来了！你正在变回来了！"假小子开心地叫道。

烟雾渐渐散开了，埃德温慢慢张开了嘴，他一动不动地站了一会儿。最后，他深吸了一口气，终于开口了。

"今天的天气真好啊，是吧……是吧，假小子？"

有那么一瞬间，他并不确定解药是否奏效了。然后，他看了看假小子。假小子伸出大拇指，示意他一切都很顺利。

"好耶！"他叫了起来，"你看我，假小子！我变回自己原来的样子了。"

"太棒了，埃德温。现在，你可以去帮助你的朋友们了。走吧，我们去瞧瞧外面的情况。"

宫殿内灯光幽暗，但是透过半开的门缝，更便于埃德温和假小子将舞会上的情况看得一清二楚。不过，只过了一会儿，埃德温就开始觉得无聊了，他看了看手表，还有十五分钟呢。他转过身来仔细地看着宫殿内部，但这时，他却发现了极为蹊跷的事。他轻轻推开前门多一点空隙，好让更明亮的光线透照进入宫殿内，他就可以看清楚一些。

随后，他发现了一个令人难以置信的秘密。

"Tom, look!"

Tom turned around.

The two stared with looks of complete disbelief on their faces. Instead of a fabulous staircase or some lovely rooms with huge soft couches and high-back chairs and instead of marble floors and huge richly panelled walls with impressive oil paintings, there were trees and bushes and blades of grass and bugs. In fact, all the things that grew outside the palace were also inside the palace. This great palace with its tall golden walls and huge towers was a fake. It was nothing more than a cheap imitation-Hollywood set.

"This is unbelievable!" exclaimed Tomboy.

"It's crazy!" said Edwin.

"Don't you see, Edwin? That little stinker is nothing but a cheat. And it's time we showed everyone in this book what sort of rotter he really is."

Edwin glanced at his watch. It was 5 minutes to 9. He looked out the opened door. The band started playing. Everyone had turned to get a good look at the musicians. Edwin knew he had to make his move.

"Tom, it's time for me to go."

"Well, good luck, Edwin. I'll stay here and watch to make sure you don't get into trouble," said Tomboy.

Edwin took a quick look out the door, then dashed into the group of guests clapping to the beat of the band. He tried to peer over their heads but he was just too small. Looking through a guest's furry legs, he caught sight of a calculator hanging from a belt.

"Bartholomew!" he thought.

He pushed himself through the guests and came within a few metres of the calculator. As he moved his head upward, he realized it was not Bartholomew at all.

Edwin turned away. Time was becoming a factor and he was starting to feel anxious. He shoved his way through a wall of bodies, frantically searching in all directions for his friends. Just as he was about to give up, he noticed

"假小子，你看！"

假小子也转过身来。

俩人一时间面面相觑。宫殿内既没有富丽堂皇的旋转楼梯，也没有宽大舒适的沙发、高背椅和温馨的房间；既没有奢华的大理石地板，也没有华丽的护墙板和精美的油画。这里只有树木、灌木和蚊虫出没的草丛。实际上，宫殿内部倒像是宫殿外所有场景的倒影。金色的宫墙、巨型塔楼和宏伟的宫殿都不过是一场海市蜃楼，只是一个虚假的幻象和一座好莱坞电影布景。

"真是难以置信！"假小子惊呼道。

"这太疯狂了！"埃德温也附和道。

"你还没想明白吗，埃德温？那个坏蛋是一个彻头彻尾的骗子，现在我们应该当着这本书所有单词的面揭发他的丑恶嘴脸。"

埃德温看了看表，正是八点五十五分，他透过门缝再次向外张望，乐队刚刚开始演奏。每个人都转过身来，准备好好欣赏几位艺术家的精彩表演。他知道轮到自己出招了。

"假小子，现在该我上场了。"

"嗯，祝你好运，埃德温。我会待在这儿，帮你解除后顾之忧。"假小子说道。

埃德温飞快地看了一眼门外，然后向着那群伴着乐队的节奏鼓掌的宾客冲了过去。他努力地想挤过人群看个究竟，但他的个子实在太小了。正当他隔着一位宾客毛茸茸的腿向外张望时，竟瞥到了一个挂在皮带上的计算器。

"是巴塞洛缪！"他念头一闪。

他费力地挤过周围的人群，隔计算器仅有几米之遥。但是，他抬头一看，却发现并不是巴塞洛缪。

他转身就走。时间越来越紧迫，他也越来越着急。他在拥挤的人墙中推搡挪步，疯狂地四处搜寻着几位朋友的身影。就在他快要放弃的时候，眼角

Drow out of the corner of his eye.

Edwin cautiously turned his head, then snapped it back. Drow had seen him. He tried to look away, but Drow moved his body into Edwin's view. He could see Drow's eyebrow twitching. His deep black eyes stared at him with a penetrating look. Edwin couldn't move. Drow's eyes were holding him like a magnet.

"STOP! STOP! STOP!" cried Drow. "EVERYONE STOP!"

The band looked over at Drow and stopped playing. Everyone stopped talking. Drow got up onto the stage and grabbed one of the band's microphones.

"We have a REGULAR word with us tonight!" cried Drow.

Edwin tried to make a run for it.

Drow looked out at the crowd.

"Stop him!" he ordered.

Two guests looked down at Edwin and grabbed him by the arms. They lifted him in the air and everyone started to boo and yell insults.

"Bring the little sneak up here!" demanded Drow.

Edwin was dragged to the front of the crowd and heaved onto the stage beside Drow.

"Now," said Drow. "What do you have to say for yourself, you wretch?"

"Ya!!!" cried the crowd. "You traitor!"

Edwin stood before the crowd. Everything looked blurry and he was getting butterflies in his stomach.

"Well?" said Drow.

Edwin remembered what he had seen in the palace. He shut out the noise of the crowd and walked up to a microphone.

"Drow's a big phony!" he yelled.

A hush fell over the guests.

"What are you talkin' about, you little slime bucket?" said Drow with fear

却瞟到了卓尔的身影。

他小心翼翼地转过头来，又忍不住回头偷偷看了一眼。

而此时，卓尔也认出了他。他试图把目光移开，但卓尔却一步步向他逼近。埃德温看到卓尔的眉毛在抽动，他深黑色的双眼死死地盯着他，目光如炬。不知怎的，在卓尔的注视下，埃德温好像被磁铁吸住了一样，完全无法动弹。

"停下！停下！停下！" 卓尔大声说道，**"所有人都不准动！"**

乐队看了看卓尔，停止了表演，所有人都噤若寒蝉。卓尔走上舞台，拿起乐队的麦克风。

"我们有幸请到了一个**常规**单词参加今晚的舞会！"卓尔大声宣布。

埃德温努力向外挣脱。

卓尔看了人群一眼。

"拦住他！"他命令道。

两位宾客低头看见了埃德温，立刻抓住了他的胳膊。他们把埃德温高举到半空中，其他宾客有的喝倒彩，有的高声叫骂。

"把那个小东西给我带过来！"卓尔说道。

他们把埃德温拖到人群前，然后一把丢到舞台上卓尔的脚下。

"现在，"卓尔继续逼问，"你有什么要说的吗，你个小坏蛋？"

"没错！"宾客们齐声高呼，"你个叛徒！"

埃德温站起身来，低头看着台下的人群，眼前的一切开始模糊起来。此外，他的胃开始不停地翻涌。

"嗯好了？"卓尔说道。

这时，埃德温想起了刚才在宫殿内看到的景象，他不再理会台下人声鼎沸的宾客，不假思索地走到了麦克风旁。

"卓尔是一个大骗子！"他大喊道。

现场顿时一片寂静。

"你在说什么呢，你个臭小子？"卓尔神色慌张地看着埃德温。他立刻

on his face. He immediately pulled out his cell phone and hit the speed-dial button. "Ya . . . it's me. Get me security. Fast!"

At that moment, a tremendous squeaking sound came from behind the crowd. The walls of the palace were starting to buckle and shake. Then, with a swoosh and a flop, all the walls toppled forward to the ground.

As the dust began to clear, "oooohs" and "ahhhhs" began echoing through the crowd. Edwin could see Tomboy standing with a big crowbar behind the fallen walls. Everyone turned toward Drow.

"Oh, that," said Drow dropping his cell phone and laughing nervously. "I . . . I never got around to decorating the inside."

More sounds were heard in the distance. Edwin looked up. There was Riffraff running at about a hundred and twenty kilometres an hour. Strands of string were hanging from his body and he was yelling something. As he got closer, it appeared he wasn't going to be able to stop.

"I want my mommies! I want my mommies!" he shouted, charging toward the stage.

"Slow down, Riffraff!" cried Drow. "Watch out, you silly mutt!"

But it was too late. Riffraff dove onto the stage and lunged at Drow.

"Drowy! Drowy! Help me. I waths tho scareds," he sobbed, clawing onto Drow's outfit.

"Get off me, you idiot hound," cried Drow.

But Riffraff continued to cling to Drow, shivering away like a little baby. Drow pulled and tugged at Riffraff.

Then the most amazing thing happened. As Drow tried to remove Riffraff from his body, one of Riffraff's claws got caught in Drow's chain suspenders.

Clink! The first link of the chain started to unravel, followed by a series of clinks until finally Drow's pants began to droop. But with Riffraff still clinging to his body, Drow couldn't reach down to stop what was happening. His pants dropped to the ground. Riffraff also fell down, taking Drow's shirt and bow tie with him. Drow was left standing with nothing but his baby-blue underwear and white cowboy boots.

掏出手机，按下了快速拨号键："对……是我。叫保安过来，赶快！"

就在这一刻，人群后面传来一声尖厉耳的噪音，所有人都转头看过去。宫殿的墙壁开始剧烈地震动，伴随着轰的一声巨响，整面外墙向前轰然倒塌，直接坠到了地面上。

飞扬的尘土逐渐消散，人群中不断传来此起彼伏的"噢噢噢噢噢噢"和"啊啊啊啊啊啊"的叫声。埃德温看到，倒塌的宫墙后站着的不是别人，正是手拿一根大撬棍的假小子。在场的所有人都愤怒地看着卓尔。

"哦，这个嘛，"卓尔放下手机，紧张地笑了笑说道，"我……我一直没腾出工夫做内部装修。"

远处传来更大的响动。埃德温抬头看了看，只见混混正以每小时约120公里的速度飞奔而来。它身上挂着绳索，还发疯似的大喊大叫。眼看着它离舞台越来越近，看起来好像刹不住车了。

"我滴妈妈呀！我滴妈妈呀！"它一边大叫着，一边朝着舞台狂奔而来。

"快停下来，混混！"卓尔大声叫道，"给我小心点，你个蠢家伙！"

但为时已晚。混混径直冲上舞台，一头撞上了卓尔。

"卓老大！卓老大！救命呀！吓石我啦！"它哭泣着一把抓住了卓尔的衣服。

"快从我身上下来，你个白痴！"卓尔大叫道。

但是瑟瑟发抖的混混像个孩子似的死抓着卓尔不放，卓尔又是拉又是拽着混混。

这一刻，最令人咋舌的事发生了。就在卓尔试图挣脱时，混混的爪子不小心钩住了他的背带链环。

啪嗒一声！一条背带从裤头上掉落下来。随后，传来一片啪嗒啪嗒的声音，卓尔的裤子开始晃晃悠悠往下掉。仍被混混死缠着不放的卓尔只能眼睁睁看着悲剧发生。最后，他的裤子整个儿掉到了地上。混混也跟着趴倒在地，手里还紧抓着卓尔的衬衫和领结。只穿着淡蓝色内衣和白色牛仔靴的卓尔在原地傻呆呆地站着。

Then everyone saw something far more startling. You see, without his outrageous outfit, Drow somehow didn't look the same. In fact, on closer examination, it was clear that the Drow was really nothing but a little boy.

Edwin stared down at this pitiful sight. Felix Fix, Thomas The, Beatrice Beautiful, and Bartholomew Book walked up on stage and positioned themselves beside him to form this sentence.

FIX THE BEAUTIFUL BOOK, EDWIN!

Within seconds, the ground began to shake and this little boy, once feared and revered, began to get smaller and smaller. A gust of wind swept past the crowd and picked him up off the ground. As the wind carried Drow into the distance, a series of small dots started to emerge on the horizon. Drow had turned into an et cet er a!

A few minutes later, the grass started to get greener and the trees sprouted leaves. Then the crowd of party guests started to shed their costumes. As they did, they revealed not Drow words but regular words.

Nouns and Verbs.

Adjectives and Articles.

Pronouns and Adverbs.

Present Participles and Past Participles.

Edwin's friends grabbed him and hauled him up on their shoulders.

"Come on, Edwin," said Felix. "This is it! You've got to tell everyone who you are. Tell them everything!"

Edwin was lowered back down in front of the microphone and Felix introduced him to the assembled words. Edwin proceeded to tell everyone about his school and his English class and how he had to read books. He explained why their book had not been read for such a long time. He also promised that as soon as he returned to the library, he would free their book and everyone would have lots of work to do once again.

The crowd started cheering. As far as they were concerned, Edwin Bellamy was a hero.

可是，压根没有人在意这乱哄哄的一幕，因为还有比这更瞠目结舌的事——褪去了那一身虚张声势的外套，卓尔仿佛不再是那个卓尔了。实际上，只要瞟上一眼就看得出来：卓尔不过是个小毛头而已。

埃德温低头看着惨兮兮的卓尔。就在这时，菲利克斯·修复、托马斯·这个、碧翠丝·美丽和巴塞洛缪·书齐刷刷地走上舞台，站到了埃德温的身边。他们组成了一个完整的句子：

"修复这本美妙的书，埃德温！"

整个大地都开始晃动起来，这个一度被奉若神明的小毛孩在一瞬间变得越来越小。一阵风掠过人群，卓尔被高高卷起，消失得无影无踪。卓尔销声匿迹后，远方的地平线上开始闪现出星星点点的斑点。

几分钟过后，小草开始焕发出绿意，树木开始抽出了新芽。舞会上的宾客们也纷纷脱掉了身上的舞会装。卸下伪装的他们，都从卓尔单词恢复了常规单词的本来面目：

有的是名词，有的是动词，

有的是形容词，有的是冠词，

有的是代词，有的是副词，

有的是现在分词，还有的是过去分词。

埃德温转身看着他的朋友们，大家兴奋地抬起他，扛在了众人的肩膀上。

"来吧，埃德温，"菲利克斯说道，"现在就是最好的时机！你得告诉大家你的身份，把一切实情都告诉大家！"

大家把埃德温重新送回麦克风旁，菲利克斯把他介绍给了在场的所有组装单词。然后，埃德温把与学校、英语课和阅读有关的事情一一告诉了所有人。他也解释了这本书长期无人问津的真实原因，并且保证回去后一定会把这本书送回图书馆，让大家伙儿再次都有大量的工作可做。

人群中爆发出热烈的欢呼声。在大家的眼里，埃德温·贝拉米无疑是一位英雄。

And so he was!

The boisterous words started hugging and kissing each other as they rushed back into their sentences. Edwin noticed that even Tomboy was full of excitement as she discovered her old sentence. She noticed Edwin staring at her. With her fingers pressed to her lips, she secretly blew him a kiss. Edwin turned a little red and waved back. He then felt something rubbing up against his leg. It was a small dog—a Schnauzer, to be exact—with horn-rimmed glasses in his mouth. Edwin stroked its head, then it dashed off to its sentence where it was warmly greeted by its fellow words.

　　他也的的确确是一位英雄！

　　单词们纷纷赶回自己的句子与亲友团聚时，兴高采烈地开始互相拥抱和亲吻。埃德温注意到，连假小子也因为找到了句子老朋友而异常兴奋。她发现埃德温正盯着她，她把手指放在嘴唇上，偷偷地给了他一个飞吻。埃德温的脸羞得通红，挥了挥手算是回应。突然，他觉得有什么东西在蹭着他的腿，原来是一条小狗——确切地说，是一只雪纳瑞——它的嘴里还叼着一副角质框眼镜。埃德温轻轻抚摸了它的头，然后它转身冲向了自己的句子，和句子朋友们欢聚在一起。

24

THE END

As the F.L.A.B. slowly floated down through the open ceiling of the Contents Room, Edwin could see Peter Preface and the Professor dancing around, holding each other's hands and singing. Word had spread quickly about the famous Edwin Bellamy.

Soon Peter was helping the group off the balloon's ladder.

"Welcome! Welcome!" cried Peter. "Oh, Edwin, you clever boy! You must come and celebrate with us."

But in the balloon, Edwin had already discussed the matter of celebrating with his friends. Edwin's idea of a celebration was having the chance to go home. And he decided to do it right away.

It was a very emotional scene. Beatrice in particular had trouble letting go of Edwin as she gave him one last hug. But Edwin was ready. He knew he would miss his new friends very much but he knew he needed to get home before Cedric discovered he was missing.

"Bye, Edwin," said Beatrice, holding her trusty mirror. "I'll miss you very much. Think of me whenever you read a book," she said, kissing him on the cheek.

"I will. I promise, Beatrice," said Edwin.

"So long, Ed," said Felix, locking up his tool kit. "You're a brave boy. We couldn't have saved this book without you."

"Thank you, Felix," said Edwin.

"Yes, we'll certainly miss you, Edwin," said Bartholomew, looking up from his calculator. "Good luck and never forget our story."

24

结局

热气球穿过天花板上的大门，缓缓降落到目录室的地面上。埃德温一眼就看到了彼得·前言和教授，两人正欢呼雀跃地搂着对方，嘴里还哼唱着愉快的小调。鼎鼎大名的埃德温·贝拉米凯旋的消息不胫而走。几分钟后，彼得领着大家走下了舷梯。

"欢迎！欢迎！"彼得大声说道，"哦，埃德温，你真是个聪明的孩子！你一定要来参加我们的庆祝活动。"

其实，埃德温已经在热气球上与朋友们讨论过如何庆祝了。此刻，庆祝对于埃德温而言，只是想能有回家的机会。于是，他决定马上离开。

分别的时刻总是无限伤感，碧翠丝最后一次抱了抱埃德温。对于埃德温的离开，她显得尤为不舍。但是，埃德温已经准备好要回家了。他知道，自己一定会非常想念这些新朋友。但他更清楚，必须在塞德里克发现自己失踪之前快点赶回去。

"再见，埃德温，"碧翠丝挥了挥拿着镜子的手，"我会非常想念你的。你读书的时候，一定要记得我。"她一边说着，一边亲吻着他的脸颊。

"我会的，我保证，碧翠丝。"埃德温说道。

"再见了，小埃，"菲利克斯扣上了他的工具包，"你是个勇敢的孩子。没有你的帮助，我们肯定无法拯救这本书。"

"谢谢你，菲利克斯。"埃德温说道。

"是的，我们一定会想念你的，埃德温，"巴塞洛缪从计算器的一大堆数据中抬起头来，"祝你好运，永远不要忘记我们的故事。"

"I won't, Bart," said Edwin.

"Now, Edwin," said Thomas, patting him on the shoulder. "To get out of this book, you must hold your breath, stick your finger in your ear, and say 'The End.' "

Edwin glanced over at his friends one more time. He tried hard but he couldn't hold back the tears any longer.

"Bye, everyone. Bye," he said sadly. Without waiting for a reply, he shut his eyes and followed Thomas's instructions. There was a big swish and a sound like the turning of pages, then a big boom.

"我不会的，小巴。"埃德温说道。

"好了，埃德温，"托马斯拍着他的肩膀，说道，"要离开这本书回到人类世界，你必须屏住呼吸，把手指插到耳朵里，然后大声说'落幕'。"

埃德温朝他的朋友们再次瞟了一眼，他拼命压抑内心的情感，但泪珠却止不住地往下掉。

"再见，大家，再见了。"埃德温伤感地说道。埃德温不忍心再听到朋友们难过的声音，于是，他闭上了眼睛，按照托马斯的要求念起了咒语。只听得嗖的一声，紧接着是一阵窸窸窣窣的翻书声，最后是一声震耳欲聋的轰隆声。

25

THE TRUTH ABOUT EDWIN'S FATHER

As Edwin opened his eyes, he could see the familiar cobalt-blue light. He was back in the library. He struggled to stand, but felt a bit dizzy. Then all of a sudden, a full set of lights flickered on.

"You little sneak," screamed a voice from out of nowhere. Edwin whipped around to see Dr. Phonic hovering over him. "How did you get in here? Answer me, boy!" he demanded.

"I just pressed the button for the sixth floor and . . ."

"Don't lie to me, boy. I programmed your swipe card so it would access only the observatory."

"Then perhaps you gave him the wrong card," said another voice.

Edwin looked up to see Cedric, now beside Dr. Phonic.

"Cedric, this boy has breached our security. I told you it was not a good idea to show him the elevator," said Dr. Phonic angrily.

"Preston, would you mind leaving Edwin and me alone for a while?"

"Bbbbut . . . " said Dr. Phonic stammering.

"Please, Preston. I need to handle this myself."

By now, Edwin was beginning to shiver. He looked up at Cedric, straining to find the faintest hint of a smile. But Cedric's expression was stoic. Edwin couldn't figure out what he was thinking.

Then Cedric picked up the copy of *A Student's Guide to the Great Adventure Story* and Edwin thought he saw him gasp for a second as he studied it.

25

关于父亲的真相

当埃德温睁开双眼，马上就看到了那道熟悉的蓝光，他又回到了图书馆里。他挣扎着站起身来，只觉得一阵头晕目眩。然后，整个房间的灯光突然大亮。

"你这个小鬼头，"不知从哪儿冒出一个尖厉的声音。埃德温转身一看，发现弗尼克博士正虎视眈眈地看着他："你到底怎么进来的？快老实回答，小子！"他命令道。

"我只是按下了六楼的按钮，然后……"

"你休想糊弄我，小子。你的卡我已经重新编程了，只有可到观景台的访问权限。"

"那或许就是你给错卡了。"另一个声音说道。

埃德温抬头看到了塞德里克，此刻他正并肩站在弗尼克博士的身旁。

"塞德里克，这个孩子违反了安保规定。我早就告诉过你，让他搭电梯本身就是个错误的决定！"弗尼克博士愤愤地说。

"普雷斯顿，我能和埃德温单独待一会吗？"

"但但但是……"弗尼克博士结结巴巴地说。

"拜托了，普雷斯顿。有些事我需要亲自处理。"

此时此刻，埃德温已经紧张得发抖了，他抬头看着塞德里克，希望能看到一丝笑容。但是塞德里克的表情却异常严肃，埃德温猜不透他脑子里到底在想些什么。

然后，埃德温看着塞德里克拿起《〈伟大的探险〉学生导读本》翻阅了起来，有那么一瞬，他看见塞德里克屏住了呼吸。

When Dr. Phonic finally stormed from the room, Cedric looked back down at Edwin, this time with a smile on his face.

"Come and sit down, my lad," he said, ushering Edwin to one of the long tables with the green reading lamps.

Edwin sunk into a leather chair beside the table, his two legs squeezed tightly together and his back upright.

"Relax, my boy. I'm not here to punish you. But I do need to know exactly what happened. Tell me everything."

Edwin fell back into his chair and spent the next hour recounting all that had happened. But as fantastical as Edwin thought his story was, it did not seem to faze Cedric. When Edwin finally finished, there was an awkward silence while he waited for a reaction.

Cedric turned to him and said, "What do you see over there, Edwin?" pointing to a shelf above the table.

Edwin saw six leather-bound volumes, each with the title *The Great Adventure Story*.

"Oh, those must be the books discussed in *A Student's Guide to the Great Adventure Story*, the book I entered."

"Edwin," continued Cedric. "Who wrote the books in front of you?"

Edwin read the author's name on each book.

"Dorian Bellamy."

"Is that my great-great-grandfather?" asked Edwin excitedly.

"That it is," said Cedric. "That it is. But here's the interesting part," he continued. "Yer great-great-grandfather could neither read nor write."

"What?" said Edwin, now totally confused.

"Edwin, I would now like you to look at the author of the book you entered today."

Edwin picked up *A Student's Guide to the Great Adventure Story* and read the author's name aloud.

"Edwin Bellamy."

弗尼克博士怒气冲冲地走出了房间，塞德里克再次看向埃德温，这时，笑容又回到了他的脸上。

"过来坐下吧，孩子。"他领着埃德温在一张放有绿色台灯的长方形书桌旁坐定。

埃德温沉坐在桌子旁的皮椅上，两条腿紧紧地夹在一起，背挺得笔直。

"放松点儿，孩子，我不是来责罚你的。但是你得把事情的来龙去脉一五一十地告诉我。"

埃德温靠在椅背上，花了一个小时详详细细地讲述了他的经历。虽然连埃德温自己都觉得这个故事有点不可思议，但塞德里克似乎并没有被吓到。当埃德温全部讲完后，两人陷入了尴尬的沉默之中，埃德温静待着塞德里克的反应。

突然，塞德里克转身对他说："你在那边看到了什么，埃德温？"他一边说，一边指着书桌后的一个书架。

埃德温看见了六册皮面书，每一册的封面上都写着：《伟大的探险》。

"哦，这些肯定就是我今天去过的《〈伟大的探险〉学生导读本》里提到的那些书。"

"埃德温，"塞德里克继续问道，"你看看面前的这些书是谁写的？"

埃德温大声读出了每一本书封面上的作者名："道林·贝拉米"。

"那不是我的高祖父嘛？"埃德温兴奋地问道。

"没错，"塞德里克说道，"就是他。但有趣的是，你的高祖父既不识字，也不会写作。"

"什么？"埃德温说道，他完全被搞糊涂了。

"埃德温，我现在要请你再看看，今天你去探险的那本书的作者是谁。"

埃德温拿起《〈伟大的探险〉学生导读本》，大声地念出了作者的名字：

"埃德温·贝拉米。"

Edwin stared at his name and tried to register what it all meant.

"I don't understand," he said finally.

"Edwin, what I am about to tell you will be hard to comprehend at first but you need to understand your unique ability."

"My unique ability?" asked Edwin quizzically.

"Since the history of language began, we have always known the power of words. Authors, poets, and musicians all know how important it is to find the right choice of words. But we have always assumed *we* are the ones who find the words when, in reality, it is often the words themselves that find us. Great writers, for example, have a special ability to communicate with words, even if they don't realize it. And then there are a select few—a very select few—who have the ability to interact with words. For generations, the Bellamys have had that unique ability. That is why, even though yer great-great-grandfather could neither read nor write, his name is attached to so many books. He could enter books, interact with words, and experience a story firsthand. He could even affect the outcome of a story through his persuasiveness. You have that same ability, Edwin. It's called Etymological Transfiguration. And because you helped to re-shape *A Student's Guide to the Great Adventure Story*, that book is now yours. You are its real author."

"But what will the original author say if he sees my name on his book?" Edwin asked.

"He won't, because the words in that book will prevent him from seeing your name."

That was a lot for Edwin to digest. He pondered what Cedric was saying.

"So, you have that ability, too?" asked Edwin.

"Alas, my boy. I do not. While I love language, I did not seem to inherit yer unique ability."

"What about my father?"

埃德温盯着自己的名字，想弄清楚到底是怎么回事。

"这我就不懂了。"埃德温说道。

"埃德温，我现在要告诉你的事可能很难理解，但是你应该要明白，你是个天赋异禀的孩子。"

"天赋异禀？"埃德温满腹狐疑地重复着这句话。

"自从语言诞生以来，我们就知道文字具有强大的力量。作家、诗人和音乐家都了解遣词造句、推敲揣摩的重要性。我们总认为，是人类发现了文字的魅力，但事实上，恰恰相反。比方说吧，伟大的作家都有一种特殊的文字表达能力，有时候甚至他们自己都没有意识到这一点。还有一部分人，确切地说，是极少数的人，拥有与文字互动的能力。而贝拉米家族的历代成员，就是其中的一分子。这就是你那既不能读也不会写的高祖父，他的名字却能被附加到这么多著作的原因。他可以进入书籍的内部世界，与文字交友谈心，然后将他的亲身经历记录下来。能言善道的他甚至可以扭转整个故事的结局，你具有同样的能力，埃德温。这就是所谓的词源变形，因为你改写了《〈伟大的探险〉学生导读本》这本书的命运，所以你现在成了它的主人和真正的作者。"

"那要是原作者看到我的名字在上面，他会怎么说呢？"埃德温问道。

"他不会有任何意见，因为那本书里所有的单词有法子不让他看到你的名字。"

埃德温思索着塞德里克的每一句话，他需要一点时间慢慢消化如此大量的信息。

"所以，您也有这种能力吗？"埃德温问道。

"唉，孩子，我不行。虽然我热爱语言学，但我却没办法继承你们家族独有的能力。"

"那我的父亲呢？"

"Yer father definitely had the ability. And that's why he and I worked so closely together. He would help Dr. Phonic and me by going in and out of books and discovering hidden meanings, confirming translations, and helping us understand cultural differences," said Cedric.

"What book was he working on before he died?"

"Before he what?" said Cedric.

"Before he died," repeated Edwin.

"Edwin, who told you yer father is dead?"

"My mother. She said it was the gas that caused it. Why, is he . . . is he alive?"

"Edwin, I can now tell you that your mother was trying to protect you. Mary loves you a lot and she doesn't want to see you get hurt. But in answer to your question, she and I don't know if your father is alive. We are hoping for the best but expecting the worst."

Edwin felt numb. His head began to spin inside as this whole situation became more and more surreal.

"What do you mean you don't know?" Edwin asked, realizing the tone of his voice was becoming a bit curt. "And what was the gas thing about anyway? Was there an explosion somewhere?"

Cedric smiled. "Laddy, G.A.S. is an acronym, an abbreviation for **G**reat **A**dventure **S**tory. Early in May, your father entered Volume Six of *The Great Adventure Story* and we have not seen him since. He passed through the story but never came out."

"So that's what my mother meant when she said my father had passed."

Cedric looked directly at Edwin and held his hands.

"Listen, Edwin, it was no accident that your mother sent you here. It was important for us to discover whether you had inherited the same abilities as your father. I was going to use my own tests to determine it but you have clearly confirmed your ability yourself."

"Why was it so important to find out if I had this ability?"

"你父亲同样拥有这种能力，这就是我们能紧密配合的原因。他可以进入书籍内部的世界，帮助弗尼克博士和我寻找隐藏的含义，确认翻译的准确性，还有消除文化差异。"塞德里克说道。

"他去世前与您合作的是哪一本书呢？"埃德温问道。

"他什么前？"塞德里克满脸惊诧地问道。

"他去世前。"埃德温重复道。

"埃德温，谁告诉你你的父亲去世了？"

"我的母亲。她说，我的父亲死于瓦斯爆炸事故。怎么了，难道他……他还活着吗？"埃德温心里生出一丝希望。

"埃德温，我可以告诉你，你母亲这么做是为了保护你。玛丽非常爱你，她不希望你受到伤害。至于你的问题嘛，我和你母亲都认为，你父亲目前生死未卜。我们都抱着最好的希望，但也做了最坏的打算。"

埃德温感到头皮发麻，他只觉得天旋地转，整个事件变得越来越离奇。

"您说生死未卜是什么意思？"埃德温意识到自己的语气有点生硬，"还有这些跟瓦斯爆炸又有什么关系呢？真的有瓦斯爆炸吗？"

塞德里克冲他笑了笑："孩子，G.A.S.就是《伟大的探险》的缩写啊。自从你父亲在五月初进入了《伟大的探险》第六册，我们就再也没有看到他了，他自此一去不复返。"

"所以，虽然母亲说他过世了，但其实这才是真相。"

塞德里克握住埃德温的双手，直视着他的眼睛。

"听着，埃德温，你母亲把你送到这里来，自然有她的一番苦心。我们需要确定你是否也继承了跟你父亲同样的能力，这一点很重要。我本来打算让你参加测试，但现在你已经很清楚地证明了自己的能力。"

"证明我有没有这种能力为什么如此重要呢？"埃德温问道。

"Edwin, Dr. Phonic and I don't have the ability to enter books. Your mother doesn't have the ability, either. Only you do, Edwin. And only you can try to find your father."

"Find my father?" said Edwin. "But how?"

"You will need to enter *The Great Adventure Story*, starting with Volume One, and try to trace your father's steps," said Cedric.

"Why can't I just enter Volume Six—where my father disappeared?"

"You cannot simply jump into the middle of a book and expect to understand what is going on. You always need to start at the very beginning," said Cedric with a smile. "We need to understand what was motivating your father, who he worked with, and whether he created any enemies. If you just jump right into Volume Six, you could put yourself in grave danger."

Edwin thought about what Cedric was saying and his own experience with Drow and the possible dangers his father could be facing.

"Sir Cedric, my mother said she needed to travel to get my father's affairs in order. What did she mean by that?" asked Edwin.

Cedric's expression became serious. He stood up, put on a pair of white gloves, and reached for Volume Six of *The Great Adventure Story*.

"Edwin, take a look at this book," he said, handing Edwin a pair of white gloves to wear.

Edwin studied the volume, then realized a whole section in the middle of the book was missing.

"There are pages missing," said Edwin.

"Right you are, young lad," said Cedric. "That poses a rather tricky problem and it may be the reason your father has not returned. With the book divided, there is a risk yer father could be stuck in a section of the book and have no way of moving forward. We need to find those missing pages. But this book has been out of print for years. Your mother is travelling throughout Europe, visiting antique booksellers, trying to find another copy of Volume Six of *The Great Adventure Story*."

"埃德温，弗尼克博士和我都不具备这种能力，你的母亲也没有。只有你可以，埃德温，也只有你可以找到你的父亲。"

"找到我的父亲？"埃德温问道，"可是，怎么找呀？"

"您需要从《伟大的探险》第一册开始追踪你父亲的踪迹。"塞德里克说道。

"为什么我不直接从父亲消失的——第六册开始呢？"埃德温问道。

"你得明白，埃德温，没头没脑地扎进其中一本书，是不可能把整个系列都理解透彻的，万事都得从头开始。"塞德里克微笑着说，"我们需要打探清楚——你父亲的动机是什么，他曾与谁一起合作，还有他是否曾树敌。如果你盲目地扎进第六卷，可能会面临极大的危险。"

埃德温思索着塞德里克的话，又想到了自己与卓尔斗智斗勇的经历和父亲可能面临的危险。

"塞德里克爵士，母亲说她需要出远门处理父亲的事务，她这句话是什么意思呢？"他问道。

塞德里克的表情立刻变得严肃起来。他站起身来，戴上一双白色手套，拿起了《伟大的探险》第六册。

"埃德温，你来看看这本书。"塞德里克递给埃德温一双白手套。

埃德温仔细读了读该册，然后发现这本书中间的一整节内容已经不翼而飞。

"有几页不见了。"埃德温说道。

"你说得对，小伙子，"塞德里克说道，"这个问题相当棘手，很可能这也是你父亲无法回到现实世界的原因。如果内容不连贯，那么你的父亲很可能会被卡在某一个章节内无法前进。我们需要找到那些丢失的书页。但是，多年前这本书就已经绝版了。你母亲正在整个欧洲搜寻古董书店，希望能找到另一本《伟大的探险》第六册。"

"I see," said Edwin. "So when . . . when can I enter Volume One and start searching for my father?"

"All in good time, young Edwin. That is for another day. Dr. Phonic and I need to prepare you first. But always remember, it will not be you who finds the words. The words must find you first before you are allowed to enter any book. Tomorrow, we'll get started. You've had enough adventure for today!"

"我明白了，"埃德温说道，"那么，我……我什么时候能进入第一册，开始寻找我的父亲呢？"

"在适当的时候，小埃德温，不过那是以后的事了。弗尼克博士和我需要提前为你做好准备。但是千万要记住，不是由你去找那些单词。在你被允许进入任何一本书之前，那些单词必须主动先来找你。明天，我们就将开始第一课。今天你的探险已经够刺激了！"